The Child of Dust

The Child of Dust

ISBN: 978-1-7391736-0-9

Published by **A J Warner**

Instagram: @ajwarnerauthor

Instagram: @thechildofdust

Cover Image Copyright: Adobe Stock #345046361

Prologue

Dust was falling like blackened snow from the rust ridden beams of the dimly lit shack. It drifted peacefully downwards, floating like wafer thin slithers of ash that had managed to escape a once great and tumultuous fire.

Thick ancient bolts that held the structure together creaked and groaned as they desperately tried to cling on to their hexagonal partners, having been married up and intertwined with them countless years ago.

Below, an uneven floor strewn with shattered tiles began to shake erratically, sending the newly acquired dirt dancing across their once glossy surfaces and into the many intricate cracks that spidered out from their centres.

The squat metal lined walls that ran the circumference of the building bowed back and forth like the sails of a tacking ship as the storm outside swelled against them.

Rust had managed to burrow small holes into the thick steel plating which, accompanied by the wind's howls, created an eerie ensemble of wails and shrieks within the room.

From outside, the screams emanating from within could have been mistaken for causing this dilapidated building to move and shake. As if it were a metal cage holding back some fearsome beast - a beast fighting to break free from its enclosure and wreak havoc on anything and everything it found. However, if whatever was inside did manage to get out, be it beast or breath, it was doubtful that anything more could be done to what remained of this city.

The buildings had crumbled; they were derelict and unliveable.

With each passing second, distant crashes signalled further collapses as sweeping torrents of grey clouds slammed against the ancient cityscape.

Great tall metal titans that once stretched high into the sky were now stripped back to their bones and leaned with seemingly murderous intent over the small shuddering building in the centre of the square. After countless years of high winds and subsidence, however, their intimidating stature had had the opposite effect. Their frameworks had become twisted, warped and intertwined, weaving themselves together until they formed an intricate lattice of steel that shielded the fragile building below. Now, if any pieces of debris came hurtling over the landscape, they were caught amongst the strong metal beams like insects trapped helplessly in a spider's web.

Dense black clouds above brought lashes of lightning that whipped across the sky in large white tendrils; every few seconds, a bolt would cast itself down to connect with one of the tallest skyscrapers and send a spray of sparks arcing high into the sky.

The cowering metal structures hummed as their steel skeletons reverberated, further adding to the symphony of sounds that bounced around the street.

However, cutting through all of this, through the clashes, cracks, wails and booms, were the gut-wrenching screams coming from inside this little building.

Underneath the falling dust, surrounded by a few dim lights arranged in an almost ritualistic manner, lay not some ferocious animal but a woman; sprawled out on the floor atop a thin white blanket, which was quickly becoming more of a dirty mix of greys and pale reds between her legs.

She let out another piercing cry that seemed to rip at her vocal cords.

The drawn out, shrill noise broke in places like the tuning of a radio as her face grew paler and her eyes disappeared backwards into the confines of her skull.

Like most other mothers, she had imagined that when the time had come she would have been lying down in a comfortable infirmary bed as nurses administered a colourful concoction of drugs to make this bearable - pharmaceutically carried away to a place where below her waist didn't feel like some otherworldly creature was clawing to get out.

Most women also tended to have their partners by their side, clenching their hands in an attempt to syphon off some of the pain as they whispered kind words of encouragement. But this was not the case for her.

There was nobody to mop her brow, no words of love or reassurance, just the falling dust and earthquakes that were shaking apart the building around her.

"Be safe my love. Protect them both!"

Her husband's parting words echoed in her mind, before a feeling of guilt overwhelmed her - she had failed, even if only in part to accomplish this request. During the chaos of the last few hours, the containment module had ruptured and the particle - the culmination of ten-years' work - had been lost.

She clamped her eyes shut as tears swelled and fell from their corners. The dewy droplets cut thin shimmering channels through the dust that had settled on her reddening cheeks before being quickly soaked up by her dirtied collar.

She tried to imagine that the vibrations were her husband patting her on the back, congratulating her for fulfilling, arguably, as a parent, the most important half of his request. But it was foolish to believe that this could be turned into something comforting, especially when instead of just a gentle pat on her back, the ground was violently shaking her whole body along with the rest of the building.

Just as she was managing to rid her eyes of their sorrow, the muscles deep within her abdomen had other ideas and quickly began to constrict again, causing her to well up once more.

The pain was becoming too hard to bear. But still, with every contraction, she wished for the baby to stay inside.

Most mothers usually wanted to push, to get past this moment and hold their new-born in happiness. But how could she feel that way? She wanted nothing more than to keep her baby locked away from all that was around her; a run-down shack on a dead and desolate world.

However, regardless of her wishes or hopes, she knew that she could not fight biology. The baby was coming and simply lying there moaning through gritted teeth, allowing her own body and mind to torture her, now just seemed pointless.

This realisation stirred something inside her.

She had survived this long. The attack, the escape, the landing and now... she had to survive for her baby.

The woman turned her head to the side and, after biting down on a generous fold in the blanket, began to push.

Letting out a loud muffled groan, she felt the fabric clenched between her teeth begin to dampen and squeak. A bit of her lip must have got caught between her incisors, as the taste of blood hit the back of her throat and joined the musty scent of the room flooding her nostrils.

With her arms locked straight, she wrestled with handfuls of the fabric, feeling it tighten and stretch around her fingertips as she kneaded the heels of her hands against the ground.

The baby was coming now; she could feel it leaving her body bit by bit.

Minutes passed as she bore down on the ground at her waist as if trying to helplessly pull herself out of quicksand.

Through laboured breaths, the sodden bundle of cloth in her mouth fell out as she flung her head back and howled into the air.

All of a sudden, a wonderful warm feeling began to fall over her, almost as if she was being draped in a blanket of pure relief. Beginning at her toes, the numbing sensation slowly began moving up her legs, snaking its way past her hips and around to the small of her back.

Then she heard it, as if far off in the distance - a baby crying.

Her baby crying.

She had done it. All had not been lost.

The comforting sensation had almost enveloped her whole body now; It felt like she was floating upon the surface of a hot soothing bath and her face was the only thing left cresting above the water. She let out one last sigh that seemed to smother her ears, and as her head fell back, she was submerged.

Unfazed and unperturbed, the falling dust continued to spiral its way down from the ceiling, now coming to rest on both the bloodied child and its mother's lifeless body.

CHAPTER 1 - The Climb

Small slithers of light flashed through the tiny gaps in the steel plating that comprised the front wall of the squat dwelling.

The beams ricocheted off the countless glass ornaments that hung from the ceiling, sending an array of different colours spiralling around the room.

This bright and brief illumination was followed by a deep, rumble of thunder which caused the contents of every box and container that lined the walls to rattle ferociously. Like a thousand tap dancers had materialised all at once within the dark stone space, one by one they began their own complex routines across every solid surface available to them.

Coupled with the sound of the vibrating objects within the room, was the deafening noise of the various bits of debris being pelted against the front wall by the storm's high winds. Vicious and eager to join the fun, the gatling-gun clatter of noise took their dancing partner's hand and joined in the swell of invisible footfall bouncing around the room.

In the centre, huddled over a workbench and seemingly unfazed by the storms attempts to pierce its way into both his home and eardrums, was Hadwin - A six-foot-tall, burly man wrapped from head to toe in a multitude of thick layers of clothing that managed to give the impression that he was almost as wide as he was tall.

If someone were to come across this scene, as impossible as that would be in this barren world, they probably wouldn't have noticed that Hadwin was standing there at all. The dark, uneven colour of his clothes and the small visible portion of his grime coated face mimicked the surrounding walls, making this boulder of a man look as if he had been hewn from the rock face itself.

Hadwin, whose blackened exterior seemingly sucked all light from the room, actually welcomed the brief flashes that the storm brought. The small remnants of homemade candles that were dotted about his home had all but burned out and the few light bulbs that hung from the ceiling swung powerless and unlit.

Hadwin rubbed hastily at his unfocused eyes, acutely aware that fixing his armour was a difficult process at the best of times, let alone now in near complete darkness. But regardless of the conditions, repairing it was of the utmost importance to him. Hadwin knew that if he decided to step outside, however unlikely that choice would be given the current conditions, it would be just his luck that one of those seemingly innocent pieces of debris, that were currently chiming a tune against the thick metal wall, would set its sights upon this small exposed patch in his armour and rip a hole right through him.

After a warming blow of breath into his cupped hands, Hadwin quickly worked his fingers back and forth in front of him as if pumping them around a pair of invisible hearts. This futile action barely sent any of the slightly warmer blood that was swilling around his torso down to their cold icy tips.

Unperturbed, he reached blindly, yet cautiously, across the table as his numb fingers knocked unknowingly against the various rusted tools and implements strewn across the uneven metal surface.

Finally, his index finger connected with a heavy, cylindrical object, which Hadwin took quickly in his hands and began pulling at a sharp offshoot that scratched at his palm.

Another flash of lightning thankfully gave him a brief glimpse of the spool of dark metal wire that now stretched between his outstretched arms.

He continued to unwind the coiled cable as the silhouetted image of his hands imprinted on the back of his eyeballs slowly faded back to black.

With a sufficient length in hand, Hadwin lifted the armour up and brought it closer to his rapidly ageing eyes, then he waited...

After an oddly long time, with only the drumming of debris and the rattle of his breath to fill the emptiness of his home, another flicker of light danced around the room followed by an angry crack like the end of a bullwhip.

Hastily using the freeze-framed image of his workshop and the weather-beaten armour within his grasp, Hadwin began to stab the sharp end of the wire into one of the small metal eyelets that lined the rough edge of the replacement armoured plate.

After several minutes of squinting and countless grunts of frustration, Hadwin used a pair of pliers to bend and cut the last of the wire links into place.

He stood back triumphantly and waited patiently to inspect his handy work.

"Not bad, Hadwin!" he said to himself in his low grumble as the lightning flashed once more.

Hadwin found that he was speaking to himself more and more these days. A habit that he chalked up to his ever-progressing years.

If he had to guess, he would have put his age in the region of forty-years, however, due to the thick black clouds on this planet that rolled days into nights for weeks at a time, it was tough to keep track.

Hadwin let out a sigh that bounced around his throat like a stone down an empty well before bending down to pick up the now repaired armour and draping it over a small bracket that stuck out of the wall by his front door.

Creeping blindly yet expertly back across the room, he instinctively stooped under the bulge that hung down from the solid stone ceiling and lowered himself into the soft embrace of the sofa that was positioned against the back wall - this wasn't actually a sofa, but the front three seats from a truck cab that he had managed to salvage a few years back.

In the barren landscape that stretched beyond his home, it was proving more and more difficult to find anything that wasn't composed of metal or stone. It had been well over a century since any new fabrics had been woven and to find even a scrap that hadn't perished in the long, harsh years since was a blessing. Even a few layers of Hadwin's thread bare garb had belonged to his great grandfather - passed down from parent to childlike heirlooms; the garments were now covered in countless roughly sewn patches of cloth in an attempt to repair the growing number of holes and rips that marked it's time-worn surface.

So it wasn't hard to imagine the wonder and joy that Hadwin had felt when he had cracked the door open on a half-submerged truck, wedged awkwardly in the side of a newly formed hill, to find this stretch of seating perfectly preserved and untouched by the harsh environment that encircled it.

As Hadwin sat there running his heavily calloused hands over the soft weaves of the fabric, allowing each of the stitches to creep across his fingertips, he wondered how long this particular storm was going to continue. The last had been only a meagre few days and not nearly enough to meet his requirements.

Suddenly, just as his mind had begun to run the numbers for what had to be the millionth time, a very strange noise reached his ears; it was a long, sustained scraping sound of metal on rock that grew louder and louder over the storm's continued drumming.

As the noise steadily crescendoed, Hadwin jumped to his feet allowing the springs of the relieved sofa to creak beneath him as they stretched back out to their original shape.

In a lightning's flash, he bounded across the room, threw on his heavy armour and fastened the thick leather straps securely across his chest.

Now resembling a six-foot-tall armadillo, Hadwin fumbled through the dark to his helmet which sat on a nearby shelf and quickly crammed it down upon his head.

The heavy, bucketed thing also consisted of thick metal plates that covered almost the entirety of his head. Except of course for the half inch-wide slit across the front that allowed him to see. Even then, this opening was covered with a strip of toughened glass and a mesh of tightly crisscrossed metal to stop any unwanted debris from blinding him.

The smell of his stale breath immediately filled the cavity in front of his face and the anxious back and forth sound of air striking the visor almost masked the fast approaching noise from beyond his front door.

After quickly pulling on his gloves, Hadwin turned and wrestled with the door's thick steel locking bar with both his hands. Thanks to the frantic beating of his heart, his fingers no longer felt like ice picks and they quickly got a good grip on the solid steel handle before sliding it loudly out of its reinforced frame.

The door's hinges whined like banshees as the billowing wind swept through the narrow opening and threw knife-like shards of metal into Hadwin's home.

Standing there - a windbreaker against the howling storm front - the debris simply glanced off of Hadwin's thick armour and fell inaudibly at his feet. Unfortunately, however, some of the more mischievous and determined fragments still managed to find the gaps in his bulky form and defiantly began peppering the wall behind him.

The sound of shattering glass met Hadwin's ears as various jars of what he called "useful salvage" - mainly odd sized bolts and replacement parts for long destroyed machines - were sent crashing to the ground.

Hadwin didn't turn around to check but was sure he heard the dull thud and tearing of fabric amongst the shards chiming against the stone floor. The prized and pristine sofa, it seemed, had finally joined the rest of the other beaten relics that filled his home.

In that moment, as Hadwin poked his head out and the scraping sound reached a peak, the cause of the noise materialised with a loud crash - a mass of twisted metal and cabling fell at the foot of the door.

After one identifying glance downwards at the mangled pile of rivets and frayed wire, Hadwin speedily backed into his home and allowed the door to slam shut with a booming clang.

Just as the sound of the door reverberated through his body, so too did the ramifications of what had just dropped onto his doorstep.

Whilst he appreciated the lightning providing him with small glimmers of light whilst he worked, the main reason that Hadwin welcomed a storm was because of the power that it generated.

A number of years ago and after months of salvaging, he had managed to cobble together enough materials to make a lightning rod. By securing this high above his home and running cables down the cliff face to an array of jerry-rigged batteries, Hadwin was able to power the few machines that kept him fed, watered and able to see around his home.

These machines were his lifeline and were the only thing that separated him from the life of relative comfort in which he now lived and the one of desperation that he thought he had left behind years ago.

Dotted around the large darkened room, the machines now lay inert and without power. All save for one that twinkled dimly in the back corner like a distant lighthouse in a cold and cloudy sea of black.

It had been at least a month since the three-day storm and Hadwin's power reserves - over a hundred reconditioned batteries stacked neatly in rows up against the side wall - were all but depleted. He had diverted what little power remained within them to keeping that lonely heat lamp at the rear of his home alight over his little vegetable garden, but even now that was beginning to flicker as it desperately attempted to draw what morsels of power had been secured since the lightning had begun a couple of hours ago.

Hadwin knew that time was of the essence, so hurriedly he turned and began moving around the now dishevelled room.

Whether by the grace of the adrenaline now coursing through his veins, or the moon's successful attempt to peek through the clouds above, Hadwin was beginning to see the outline of his home partially emerging from the darkness.

Not one to look a gift horse in the mouth, Hadwin darted amongst his stores and grabbed feverishly at the various tools and supplies that he might need for the repair job.

With any luck, he hoped that the lightning rod itself was still intact and the winds had simply worked the cabling loose. If, however, luck was not on his side and this too had been carried away by the storm, then judging by his dwindling supply of food and clean water he doubted very much that he would live to see his fifties.

Hadwin gathered himself up and with a final deep breath forced the door open once more.

He squeezed his large frame awkwardly through the thin opening and winced slightly at the sound of more of his possessions being smashed by the shards sneaking in behind him. After stepping sideways out, the door slammed shut and the gonging sound disappeared immediately amongst the swirling clatter of the wind's bluster.

Lowering himself onto one knee, Hadwin clasped his metal bound fingers around the mass of tangled cabling and fastened it tightly to a thick metal hook attached to his belt. Once secure, he shot an upwards glance at the towering cliff face that rose imposingly up above his home.

The small stretch of the cliff wall that was visible beneath the clouds was being hammered repeatedly by small slugs of metal - these whipped up fragments were shattering as they struck the granite material that comprised the lofty rock formation and rained down upon his helmet like shimmering, metallic hail.

This wasn't going to be easy, Hadwin thought to himself - nothing ever was here.

Moving to the left of his front door, he grabbed tightly around the first metal rung of the ladder and pulled himself up. With each rung painstakingly drilled a couple of feet apart into the cliff face, this ladder would take him all the way to the top of the mountain and to where he hoped and prayed that the lightning rod still remained.

After several steps up, the ground beneath him was quickly swallowed up by the swell of grey and black swirling around the courtyard.

This disappearance of solid ground caused Hadwin to gulp slightly as the daunting and life-threatening task that he was undertaking finally hit him.

Perhaps there was another way for him to get the power that he needed?

Of course, he knew that there wasn't, but regardless of this truth, he teetered for a moment on the rounded steel footings as determination and doubt battled for control of his body.

Finally, the courageous victor hauled him upwards as the colossal weight of his armour and that of the two-hundred-foot length of cable swung from his side.

Despite his decision, Hadwin could feel the grit and small rocks crunching beneath his fingers as he grappled with the salvaged steel bars. Each new rung felt like it was taunting him as he climbed higher and higher.

"Go on, slip and fall. It will be easier that way." said the disembodied, mocking voice that his mind gave them.

He knew, not even that deep down, that they were right. A brief fall and an even quicker death would be a very easy way out for him.

The life that Hadwin led on this barren and toxic world, was not without its fair share of hardship, and to just survive was a constant battle in this place. It was a struggle that had consumed everyone he had ever known, one by one until only he was left.

Holed up in his little nook on the side of this mountain, the recurrent storms that crossed the area threatened to throw any number of objects that they picked up along their path into his direction. These were not always small, like the stone granules that were scraping beneath Hadwin's hand or the shards of metal striking his back, but sometimes far larger and far more destructive ones.

On one such occasion several years back, Hadwin had woken during a particularly vicious storm to find a battered frame of an old automobile had careered through one of the perimeter walls of his home. How he had managed to sleep through it, Hadwin would never know, but if it had landed ten metres closer then he may very well have never woken again.

This recurrent and statistically high threat was enough to make anyone anxious. But to Hadwin, the fear had become a dull ache which he had pushed to the back of his mind at a young age and he now blamed it for the spreading grey patch in his hair.

Staring up at the next rung with a coagulated mix of both annoyance and longing, Hadwin couldn't deny that he was beginning to tire of the life that he had been living these past thirty or so years. It had been a solitary and joyless existence since the passing of his mother.

As he hung there, beads of sweat were already beginning to drip down the sides of his forehead, he thought of her last words to him.

"Do not let this world break you!"

Over the deafening noise, echoing from every inch of his metal lined body, his mother's voice cut through and her words strengthened him.

"No, I won't!" Hadwin growled through gritted teeth as he hoisted himself further up the ladder and away from the goading rungs.

Defiant, he continued to climb, panting hot exhausted breaths against the inside of his helmet. The humid air pressed against his face like a damp mist that drew and receded in waves.

It couldn't be that much further, he told himself. But even before the words formed in his head, Hadwin knew that once again he was lying to himself.

Optimistically however, praying that the true quantity of steps had somehow become lost amongst his rattled mind, Hadwin raised his head in an attempt to see through the grey mass of clouds crashing against the rock face; this was an act that he instantly regretted as suddenly he felt his right hand give in to the lower rungs taunts and lose its grip.

Helpless to act, Hadwin watched as his arm swung out in slow motion and drew a large arc through the sky behind him. The rest of his body acted like a sail against the winds and swept him around until his right leg flew out in unison. With his left hand now clamping on for dear life and his foot pirouetting on the lower rung beneath him, Hadwin was sent crashing painfully backwards into the cliff face.

The force whipped his head back and he struck the wall with a deafening bang that rattled his brain and sent a blinding white flash in front of his eyes. With his vision obscured, Hadwin's senses focused on the hot patch that was quickly beginning to spread downwards from the back of his head. The blunt trauma had obviously been too much for his helmet to contend with, he thought, as the coppery smell of his blood was whisked around and into his nostrils.

Shaking his head in a feigned attempt to banish the stars now sparkling about in his returning peripherals, Hadwin waited a moment for a slight break in the wind before placing his foot flat against the wall and pushing off.

As his body swung back around, he felt his left wrist painfully crunch and loosen - like his armour it would seem that his body couldn't contend with such trauma either - but despite this, his fingers continued to grip, vice-like, around the metal rung as if knowing full well the consequences if they didn't.

Through fear that his injured hand could give way at any second, Hadwin snatched frantically at the approaching ladder and felt his body begin to solidify.

Every one of his muscles and joints seemed to be going on the defensive. They constricted and curled up so tightly that much of his body was now pressed against the cold cliff face, making him look like a disfigured barnacle clinging to the hull of a tall stone ship.

"Come on! Get a hold of yourself!" growled Hadwin at his seized limbs.

After a few moments of rest, they seemed to accept the encouragement and allowed him to wrap his injured arm around the handle just above his head.

Reaching over, Hadwin tightened the strapping around his now throbbing wrist and a shooting pain pulsed down towards his shoulder, causing his chest and back to twitch uncontrollably.

If the rest of the climb wasn't already daunting enough, it would now have to be at a much slower, one handed pace.

Hadwin's fingers felt numb once more and the climb - just as expected - slipped to a snail's pace.

His body ached and the inside of his armour felt like a furnace as his muscles radiated from exertion.

Coupled with his injured arm, the further that Hadwin ascended up the ladder, the more of the thick metal cable he had to drag up behind him. This ever-increasing weight, swinging wildly in the wind, threatened to yank him away with each subsequent gust.

Finally, however, Hadwin received a sign that his journey was reaching its end - a whistle above his head, over what he could only surmise was the mountain's peak.

He could almost hear his body crying out in joy as he pulled himself one handed up onto the plateau and fell with a clash on to the uneven stone floor.

Exhausted, Hadwin lay there for a minute as his heart beat a chorus of thumps against his ear drums and rib cage.

With his eyes tightly closed, he pleaded silently to all the luck and chance in the world that the climb had been worth it, and when he finally plucked up enough courage to open his eyes and look skyward, Hadwin saw the thick metal frame of his lightning rod pointing proudly into the blackened sky like the mast of a ship; unbroken and unmoving against the relentless sea of stones and metal shards.

Hadwin let out a sigh of relief. Despite his injured head, wrist and fatigued body, the climb had been worth it.

After letting his muscles relax and loosen for a further gracious minute, Hadwin turned himself over and pushed himself up into a kneeling position.

The towering rod stood poignantly in front of him, held upright by large reinforced struts that splayed out at forty-five-degree angles.

With a look of adoration, Hadwin silently thanked the thick bolts which still secured these struts to the rock surface for not breaking from the immense strain that they were undoubtedly being put under. The very top of the pole swayed peacefully in the storm, as if unaware of blustery and vociferous elements that were swirling angrily around it.

Hadwin smirked, almost envious of how unaffected his creation was, then reached to his side and began uncoupling the end of the cable.

Not wanting to leave it to chance, he kept a solid grip on the thick reinforced length with both hands; knowing that if the storm managed to wrestle it from him, that there wasn't a hope in hell that he could repeat this arduous journey again.

Hadwin moved towards the spire's base and pinned the cable tightly beneath his foot as he slid a multi-tool out of one of the numerous concealed pockets that covered his armour.

His heart skipped a beat as the storm let out an almighty gust and he felt the cable move slightly, however, by shifting his mass, Hadwin bore down on it with his thick weighted boots and the metal ground to a halt - that cable was going nowhere.

Unexpectedly, for the second time today, just as Hadwin reached down ready to begin repairing the junction that the cable needed to be attached to, a peculiar sound met his ears. Unlike the high-pitched screech of metal on rock that the falling parts of the lightning rod had made, this sound was deep and penetrated in such a way that it rattled at Hadwin's bones and shook his belly like hunger.

Quickly scanning around for the source, Hadwin was surprised to see it originating from a small white light high up in the sky which shone inexplicably brighter than both the sun and moon combined.

Transfixed, Hadwin watched as it widened across the dark stormy sky and the swelling noise that was rolling around his insides like a carousel, rose to a deafening roar.

Beneath his feet, the entire mountain top began to tremble, and the tip of his lightning rod arched back upon itself as if cowering away from this new arrival.

At the last second, the same fear finally gripped Hadwin and he was instantly stripped of all other worries except for the one now careering towards him.

Instinctively and not a moment too soon, he threw himself forward onto the floor giving no further concern to the cable as it whipped out from beneath his foot and clattered away across the summit floor.

Hadwin let out a deep pained howl as his weight dropped on to his injured wrist, but the cry was lost as whatever it was flew overhead with a loud whoosh.

Beneath him, the solid stone shuddered and shook against his chest as the sound of wrenching metal ripped through the air behind him.

Hadwin continued to lay there, face down with one arm huddled over the top of his helmet in a feigned attempt to protect himself from further harm.

The injury on the back of his head must be worse than he thought; a possible concussion causing him to hallucinate and imagine something that couldn't possibly be real.

As the noise continued to diminish, Hadwin rolled himself over and his eyes moved to the now bare, scratched rock face beneath his feet. The lightning rod was seemingly gone, snatched away in the same manner as the cable that he had worked so very hard to carry back up.

He had to give it to his brain; it was working overtime in coming up with this hallucination.

Hadwin scrambled to his hands and knees before crawling slowly towards the scored stone, shaking his head in disbelief as he went.

"No no no no no..."

The word spun around his helmet like a siren - alarming him more so than comforting.

Finally, Hadwin's hands reached the spot and begun fumbling through the deep gouges cut into the ground. All that was left of the rod was a few long shards of warped metal and the remains of those once dependable struts. Still firmly secured to the ground by those immovable bolts, the brackets stretched out like jagged fingers still attempting to grab at what had just been stolen from them.

There was no denying it now, this was no hallucination. The evidence was as real as the adrenaline now flooding through him.

Continuing to crawl, Hadwin made his way along what he believed to be the trajectory of the flying object - judging by the bent metal supports and rough cuts scratched into the plateau - until his fingertips reached the precipice and a fleeting feeling of vertigo washed over him.

The sight of the barren valley far below was momentarily visible through the monstrous dust swells as strips of faint moonlight shone like spotlights through the failing clouds.

Hadwin squinted, focusing his eyes as best he could through the narrow slit in his helmet, and in the distance saw a white light shining faintly, casting large halos of light around several twisted structures that littered the landscape's floor. After a few more seconds, the light finally flickered then succumbed, like everything else, to the barrage of the storm.

Hadwin had seen meteors before; streaking across the sky. The deafening boom as they hit with fire being spewed in all directions. But this, whatever it was, was different. Its light was bright enough to shine through a couple of miles of storm clouds and if he was mistaken, other than the crash he had heard as it had careered through his lightning rod, it had not made a sound as it had landed.

"Landed"

He muttered to himself as the salty taste of the sweat that covered his face managed to edge its way through his open lips.

After a further few seconds of contemplation at the word, he felt the blood rush from his face and a tingle of excitement tearing throughout his body - whatever this thing was, it had landed!

With a surge of adrenalin, Hadwin jumped to his feet, rushed over to the ladder, and, without another thought to the loss of the lightning rod, began to descend.

Rung after rung sped past him.

He was entranced and elsewhere.

His fatigued limbs reminders and the whispering fears of height and haste were silenced by the thoughts of the unknown object that had just landed on this planet.

The minutes passed by in a haze as he shot down the ladder - his mind flitting frantically from one explanation to another, with each as crazy and as unbelievable as the next. But as he hurriedly lowered himself, Hadwin wished he had given more of his attention to what his hands were doing.

Suddenly, and not quite unexpectedly, his injured wrist suddenly twanged with pain, causing his hand to seize up before he had the chance to get a handle on the lower rung.

As if in slow motion, Hadwin fell.

Feebly, he stretched his unburdened arm out in a last bid attempt to grab the ladder and save himself, but it was too late. Whatever that light was, its origins, it's purpose here, none of it would ever be known to him.

His drawn-out final cry was stolen away by the high winds as he plummeted downwards and disappeared into the swirling dust...

CHAPTER 2 -The Light

"Am I dead?"

Hadwin asked quietly through gritted yellowed teeth.

There was no response.

He took this as a good sign and inched open his eyes to see a thin layer of dust piling up on the toughened glass surface of his visor. Just visible beyond this was the flat stone cliff face stretching up above him.

Somehow, Hadwin's mind had been so absent on the climb down that he was totally unaware of how far he had actually managed to descend before slipping. Fortunately, having only fallen for a couple of seconds, the impact of crashing into the ground at the base of the ladder had obviously not been enough to kill him.

Still the fifteen-foot drop was enough to make his back groan.

Like the cold night's chill, the deep-seated pain quickly began to stretch up over his shoulders. It penetrated deep into his bones and crept down his arms and legs until his limbs felt like rigid blocks of ice.

Lying there frozen to the floor, the last several unused rungs looked down at Hadwin teasingly from the stone wall - if only he had taken more care, then they would have saved him all this added pain - he knew it and so did they.

As Hadwin tried to regain control of his aching extremities, he realised that the stone floor felt oddly uneven and squashy beneath him. It was only when he wrenched his head sideways that he saw that he wasn't lying on the floor at all, but the coiled-up metal cabling that had fled the plateau and retreated back down to the stone courtyard below.

Hadwin silently thanked the inanimate object as he turned himself over, sure that his injuries would have been far worse if not for its soft and cushioned assistance.

If not for the continuing clatter of rocks and metal striking every solid surface around him, Hadwin was sure that he would be able to hear his joints exclaiming with loud crunches and creaks as he got himself awkwardly to his feet.

Again, as he had done with his throbbing wrist, which at the moment was calling to him from a distant corner of his mind, Hadwin brushed the creeping pain from his back to one side. This tactic could only last for so long and he knew that if and when he found a moment's rest, these injuries were going to hit him hard.

"Come on." he grunted angrily to himself and after a few moments, his weakened body jumped reluctantly back into action.

In a renewed, barrelling frenzy, Hadwin rushed into his home, hardly giving an ounce of thought to the shards of debris that followed him in, as a quick scan told him that the damage enacted by their predecessors was already done.

Looking over at him from the back wall was the once proud row of seating. It lay there like a defeated soldier, ambushed unexpectedly by a hail of gunfire with its foam innards spilling out from beneath torn cotton coverings.

Hadwin wanted to take a moment, just a moment of respect, but his attention was whisked away once more by the images of that thing flying past him on the mountain top.

He pulled his eyes from his fallen comrade and began darting feverishly around looking for any equipment that he might need to help traverse some of the inevitable obstacles between him and that object's landing site.

During such weather, the harsh landscape beyond the walls of Hadwin's home became a dumping ground for all manner of objects collected along the storm's vast swathing paths. Every inch of this unending wasteland, with sweeping dunes composed of scorched earth, ash and stone, was plastered with the rusted relics of an all but forgotten time.

His mother, a hardened yet gentle woman, used to tell him stories of sprawling cities that once covered this planet. How her grandparents had even once lived in that seemingly lost paradise.

She described a place where every man, woman and child lived clean and effortless lives. But even as a child, the very idea of that kind of life seemed absurd to him. Like an unattainable dream. A dream not just out of reach, but a thousand miles away from his now blistered and blackened fingertips.

In reality, all that was now left of that world were thousands of half-submerged buildings and the rusted remnants of what had once filled them.

In fact, it was actually a bit of a guessing game for Hadwin on the odd occasions that he left the confines of his small, high-walled home. The landscape beyond was in a perpetual state of flux, constantly rearranging itself with new mountainous piles of debris blown from far and wide. If not for these submerged structures, gripping tightly to their foundations and that once idyllic, glorious past, then the entire place would be unrecognisable from one day to the next.

With those towering buildings in mind, Hadwin grabbed hold of a long reel of rope and secured it tightly across his chest. He snatched up a further few pieces of rusted climbing gear and stowed them amongst the lining of his armour.

The shattered glass strewn across the floor crunched loudly under his feet as it feebly and unsuccessfully attempted to puncture the thick hardened soles of his armoured boots.

As Hadwin made for another shelf, however, his foot connected with something hollow that proceeded to roll loudly across the floor before coming to rest against the leg of his workbench.

Squinting down through the room's darkness, Hadwin saw that it was his canteen. It was this small metal container that held the remainder of his stock of purified water.

The importance of getting that lightning rod operational again had been lost to Hadwin since the arrival of the white light and now staring down at the bottle, a momentary feeling of dread overcame him. Even after he uncovered the mystery of the unknown object, he would still need food and water to survive past this day.

Hadwin bent down, gently picked it up with both hands and

brought it close to his chest like a parent would their new-born child.

Turning it slowly over in his hands, he became more aware of the thirst that was causing the inside of his mouth to tighten and contract. However, as his lips opened excitedly in anticipation, his heart sank deeper than he thought possible as a one-inch hole on the reverse side came into view, undoubtedly blown inwards by one of the shards of metal that had shot into his home.

The bottle now looked up at him, defeated and useless.

In desperation, Hadwin began to twist the lid off whilst raising the chin of his helmet to uncover his cracked and dehydrated lips.

The shard of debris that had punctured the side rattled by the neck of the bottle as the tiny dregs of water fell in solitary drips into Hadwin's eagerly awaiting mouth.

A fleeting feeling of euphoria spread throughout him; perhaps his body's begrudging way of thanking him. Hadwin imagined that it was still a little disgruntled at the injuries and exhaustion that he had inflicted on it, but that it was thankful all the same.

Turning to leave, Hadwin lingered on the threshold as his eyes fell on to the pile of long items leaning up against the wall next to the door. He didn't know whether he would find friend or foe at his destination, so airing on the side of caution, he snatched up a sharpened, spear-like pole and fastened it quickly to his back before making his way out into the blustery courtyard once more.

Hadwin crossed the dark stones towards the metal barricade that stretched the length of the opening between the two large arching walls that circled his home.

Over the top of these barriers, the torrents of dust almost seemed like an upturned ocean, with crashing waves of debris sending sharpened metallic spray up into the air and crashing onto the ground all around him.

Before Hadwin managed to reach the barricade however, a sensation began coursing up his legs, causing him to stop dead in his tracks.

He sighed deeply once more and shook his head from side to side. As if the conditions weren't already bad enough: an earthquake.

These, like the ferocious storms, were commonplace in this region, but Hadwin had at least hoped that he might have been spared this additional inconvenience on today of all days.

He mustered himself up and marched forward determinedly; none of nature's attempts, from either the sky above or the earth below, were going to stop him reaching that light.

Raising a hand, he pulled down on the steel lever that started up the whirring of various cogs and counterweights that kept the doorway shut, but unfortunately, even with the hinges fully unlocked, the door did not swing open as expected.

"Useless!"

He exhaled to himself.

With a loud clang, Hadwin struck his shoulder against the thick metal and his boots scraped backwards across the cobbled ground. He heaved with all his might and slowly but surely, the gate began to inch open.

Finally, with one last push it swung aside, sweeping through the large pile of dirt and debris that had sloped up on the other side.

Hadwin stepped out of the perimeter, paused for a moment to gather his bearings, then pointed himself in the direction of the mysterious flying object. This trajectory, of course, put him face first into the storm's strong headwind.

Hadwin couldn't be certain, but it was beginning to feel like someone, or something, was actively trying to throw as many obstacles in his path as possible.

His mother had once told him all about how her ancestors had believed in a higher powers; omnipotent gods that had blessed them with the planet and all its wonders. But after telling him, she had simply baulked at the idea.

"If this was the best that their gods could give, then they weren't worthy of our worship anymore!"

This was something that Hadwin couldn't help but agree with.

No, this wasn't someone's doing. Nobody was looking down on him with an interest about whether he lived or died. This was misfortune, pure and simple.

Hadwin knew all too well from living alone for the last thirty years, that there wasn't much luck left in this world. Things like his prized sofa and the discovery of a slightly less tainted spring of water were the most he could ever hope for.

Lowering his posture slightly in a feeble attempt to make himself more aerodynamic, Hadwin pushed forward.

In between the colossal storms that ravaged this landscape, the terrain resembled that of a blackened desert. With the half sunken buildings sporadically dotted around like time worn tombstones in a boundless graveyard. This uneven, treacherous terrain forced him to move very slowly with calculated steps - one false move and he might find himself falling into a hidden ravine or slipping and causing an equally dangerous landslide. Coupled with the low visibility, Hadwin wasn't taking any chances.

As his feet crunched through the sand-like material, Hadwin felt a quake returning beneath him and through the spray of dust glancing off his visor, he could just make out wave-like patterns forming across the surface of the debris.

The blustery noise that was swelling all around him suddenly parted like the curtains of a stage to give way to a dramatic bolt of lightning. The glimpse it imparted to him filled Hadwin with horror as he saw that he was nestled in the basin of several high banked dunes.

On any "normal" day, this would not give him cause for alarm, but now, as the ground shuddered and his feet slowly began to be enveloped by the rising earth, his heart almost exploded from his chest.

In between these earthquakes, the high winds were granted the freedom to form the monstrous dunes like the ones that now surrounded Hadwin on all sides. They pulled all the grit and minuscule fragments from all across the planet to create these vast smooth mounds that weaved amongst the remnants of the old structures. When the earthquakes shook these unstable mountains, they were flattened by the shaking motion and the terrain was returned to a smooth and barren plain.

Hadwin stood in a well, cut between several of these, and knew that unless he reached higher ground, the inevitable shifting earth would bury him in seconds.

Sprinting forward, he felt his feet begin to disappear into the soft ground. It was like running in quicksand; the more he struggled to push himself upwards, the deeper his boots sank.

"Argghhhhh!"

Hadwin let out a self-motivating roar as his legs, now half buried in the dirt, screamed from the stress that they were being put under. Thankfully, Hadwin felt one of his boots connect with something solid and unmoving beneath the surface as the earth swallowed his thighs. Quickly, he dragged his other, still sinking foot, to meet it and centred his weight atop the obscured object.

Hadwin watched through the darkness as the ground continued to retreat steadily downwards all around him. From his skewed perspective, it almost looked as if he was the one rising from the ground; flying up and out of the planet's clutches to freedom.

Around him, the dark structures, jagged and spindly, grew like shoots from withered seeds. Their reinforced concrete stems reached out from the earth towards a sunless sky that would and could not help them.

Once the tremors shook their last, Hadwin dropped down the few feet that now separated him from the top of the ancient concrete wall and the now smooth, still ground below.

He turned and gave the concrete blocks a gentle pat of appreciation before continuing on his way.

After what seemed like an age, thanks to his footsteps being even more wary, Hadwin made it to one of the large collections of buildings that he had seen from the cliff top and hurriedly began looking around for any sign of the object hiding amongst the broken pillars and misshapen walls.

What if its light had gone out? What if unlike him, it had been swallowed up by the shifting earth?

These panicked questions were silenced, however, by the sight of a dim light casting long ominous shadows up the side of a crumbled structure some ways in front of him.

Hadwin thundered forward.

His armour clanked loudly like a jammed mechanism as he moved excitedly from the shelter of one wall to another, and his breath became a roaring mixture of anticipation and exacerbation inside the confines of his helmet.

As the light grew brighter and it's shadows longer, Hadwin felt an overwhelming breathlessness rush up and seal the back of his throat once more. Just in the nick of time, he ground his heels downwards and slid to a halt as the pitter-patter sound of loose earth echoed far below him.

He was standing on the edge of a deep gorge - his boots teetering dangerously over the precipice as his body arched awkwardly backwards to stabilise itself.

Another flash of lightning illuminated the tightly arranged cityscape out in front, lying fifty feet or so beneath his feet. With his body now as solid as a statue, Hadwin's eyes darted unperturbed across the wide spanning area taking it all in.

From the looks of it, the once strong foundations that held up this part of the city must have weakened over the years and collapsed all at once; dropping the ground level of the entire area like a sheet of ice and creating the high, prison-like walls that lined the entire perimeter.

Finally, regaining some semblance of control over his movements, Hadwin took a step back and felt his toes press thankfully once more against the solid ground.

After a quick glance at the base of the cliff, he let out a sigh and began to heave the length of rope from his shoulders.

"More climbing!"

He grunted quietly to himself as the cable scratched against the side of his helmet and his muscles whimpered inaudibly beneath his skin.

Thankfully, more moonlight was managing to work its way through the gaps in the dark clouds above, which aided Hadwin in locating a metal beam sticking awkwardly out from the nearest decrepit building. He secured the rope around the rusted, yet strong steel and gave it a quick tug to check that it was taut. Responding to this action, his back released a small twinge of pain that niggled at the base of his skull and crept around to his forehead; a not so subtle reminder of his recent fall. Hadwin took the hint and wrapped the rope around the beam several more times, just to be sure.

After winding his arm around the reinforced cord, Hadwin cautiously lowered himself from the lip and onto the cliff face, feeling his boots slip slightly in the bare earth as he leant back over the edge.

The rope slid slowly and controlled between his tightly gripped gauntlets but scratched against the sharp ridges of each of his fingers which sent a sawing sound traversing up through his plated armour that niggled loudly in his ears.

Thankfully, the wall that lay beneath him was shielded somewhat from the storm's barrage and whilst this meant it would be a safer descent, the sight of the unobscured drop stretching out beneath him sent another twinge of vertigo clutching at his innards.

After taking a deep breath in an attempt to alleviate the bottomless feeling in the pit of his stomach, Hadwin fixed his eyes squarely out in front and tried to focus on the solid earth that continued to crumble away beneath him with each step.

Cracked and ancient pipe work jutted out from the gorge's exposed foundations, creating an awkward criss-cross maze through which Hadwin had to navigate, but finally, after narrowly avoiding the ends of several spear-like pipes, the solid ground at the base crunched beneath Hadwin's feet and the rope went slack between his hands.

As he turned on the spot, a dip in the storm's strength ahead gave him a clearer view of the light amongst the crumpled and collapsed buildings. These mammoth-like structures were huddled around the pulsing light like frigid campers warming by a fireside.

The light shone like a clear morning through the litany of roughly formed holes that had punctured the clustered building's outer shells, as the familiar droning noise sympathetically grew and diminished.

The undulating sound drew Hadwin's mind back to the mountaintop and how this thing had mercilessly ripped his lightning rod asunder. He hurriedly fumbled the improvised spear from his back and held it tightly to his chest as he stepped forward, somehow convinced that this was protection enough.

As Hadwin approached, between the shelter of two tall concrete structures, the winds all but dissipated and only the mild vibrations of the quakes remained. The lightning, however, still cracked loudly above him, flashing at an even more frequent rate than usual.

Hadwin knew that this was due to the numerous metal frameworks reaching high into the sky, as buildings like this had been his inspiration for the lightning rod in the first place. Once again, his loss on the mountain top flashed into his mind, causing a brief feeling of worry to fall over him. However, like his eyes, his mind quickly refocused as he stepped out into the clearing.

His suspicions on the mountain top had been correct - standing in front of him was a spaceship, gleaming like a single star amongst the darkness of the gorge.

Hadwin stood there, unable to hold the weight of his jaw as it hung loosely against the chin strap of his helmet.

Straddling the sleek tear-drop shaped body of the ship, on slightly stunted wings, sat two large engines - one of which was responsible for the deep hum that continued to rumble in his chest. From its rear the brilliant white light was expelled as it gradually powered itself down, whilst the other engine, slightly hidden by the ship's main body, sparked and spewed out vast plumes of dark smoke. The fumes momentarily drifted upwards before being whisked away by the gentle swirling winds to join the rest of the blackened haze that enveloped the night sky.

Hadwin had never seen anything quite as beautiful as this ship in all his life. Aside from the smoking engine, the shining metal plating that lined its hull showed only a few minor imperfections. It looked practically new, almost as if it had just rolled off of an assembly line.

In his rusted world, finding metal in such a condition was unheard of.

As Hadwin moved along the ship, he noticed some scorched gouges that sliced here-and-there across the belly's polished steel. More than likely caused by its entry into the planet's atmosphere, he thought, or perhaps it's untimely high-speed collision with an unfortunate lightning rod.

He dropped his head slightly as he passed by one of the ship's three thick metal legs which dug deep into the cracked earth and spotted a pillar of light emanating from the opposite side. Somehow, the enigma that was this ship had completely driven from his mind that someone would have had to pilot it down.

Hadwin let out an odd sigh of relief as he realised that, be they either friend or foe, he was no longer alone in this place.

Cautiously, keeping his footsteps quieter than that of the engine's splutters and the continuing rattle of the storm against the building's peaks, Hadwin made his way around the ship's nose.

The tip of his spear was the first thing to cross the radiant light's threshold. The end of the sharpened pole now looked like it was aflame and stuck out in front of him like a welder's torch.

As Hadwin rounded on the opening, he felt his irises shrink to the size of pinpricks as they were dazzled by the inside of the ship. Slowly, as they adjusted, he could see colours blooming as an array of brightly lit screens and consoles, which were surrounded by a pair of rounded chairs that emerged from the white.

As he continued to stare, Hadwin suddenly saw something moving inside which created a shifting shadow against the adjacent wall. He felt his armoured fingers tighten around the spear as his heart rate jumped sky high.

Seconds later however, a few sparks and the beginnings of small fire crept across the deck plating and into view. There was no one there, just the rounded shadow of one of the chairs being sent dancing across the bulkhead by the firelight.

Hadwin felt the deep breath he had been holding on to rush free from his mouth.

Where was the crew? What if the ship had in fact been unmanned?

Prising his eyes away from the ship for a second, he angled his head towards a set of strangely wet prints that were trailing down the landing ramp at his feet.

Hadwin dropped down onto one knee to closely inspect the prints and felt his breath catch in his chest. They were human feet; thin and petite like those of a child.

Where had they come from? Where had they been for over a century? More importantly, what was he going to say to the first person he had seen in over thirty years?

Hadwin knelt there, frozen; the multitude of questions racing through his mind as his eyes stared, unblinking, at the thin slender marks pressed into the ground.

Then all of a sudden, a sound shook him from his trance; a distant scream carried to his ears upon the light wind.

A selfish notion floated to the forefront of Hadwin's mind as the shrill noise echoed away amongst the concrete; if the owner was in trouble and didn't return, then he would be able to help himself to their ship.

Hadwin stared back at the glistening silver thing and thought of how their unexpected encounter on the mountain top brought its untold wonders within his grasp. It all could be his, even an outside chance to leave this world if he could get it repaired.

But as the cry rang out again, it seemed to snap him back to reality, along with an overwhelming sense of guilt.

Hadwin was not, and had never been, the kind of person who could stand idly by whilst someone else was in danger. It seemed, however, even for just a moment, that living in total isolation for thirty years and only thinking of the wellbeing of oneself, was enough to make even the most decent person a little selfish.

With a renewed sense of self, Hadwin turned his back to the ship, slid the long spear away behind him and stepped forward into the darkness. There was someone else on this planet and they needed his help.

Unfortunately, due to rising winds and the loss of the ship's aura, Hadwin was quickly back to stumbling through the darkness.

Nevertheless, he pressed on, pausing every few moments to listen again for the cry in the night.

Overhead, a massive bolt of lightning was cast which connected loudly with a nearby rooftop causing the ground to tremble in fear beneath his feet and sent a clatter of disturbed masonry to crash down all around him. A scream followed the clap and fortunately, this time, it sounded much closer to where he stood.

A small light twinkled at him from amongst the darkness. Unlike the ship's engines, this was a warm, yellow light that flickered through the plating of a small shack about twenty metres away.

After a brief pause, where Hadwin looked nervously at the mangled steel that formed a canopy high above him, he heard the cry again. It could have been his proximity, but somehow it sounded different this time; higher pitched and repeating much faster in frequency.

Hesitantly, Hadwin approached as the hue of yellow light leaked from the outline of the steel door.

What was he going to say?

Should he call out before entering so as to not startle whoever it was?

As if pressing Hadwin to make a decision, the wind blew a powerful gust against his back and pushed him forward. He was now standing but a few feet from the door, his body shaking slightly in nervous apprehension.

Hadwin took a deep breath to calm his nerves, reached out his metal bound hand and grabbed hold of the handle. As he swung the door open, his dark metal body was doused in light.

Hadwin stood frozen in the doorway, surveying the scene as torrents of dust and dirt swept around him into the dimly lit room. He didn't know what he had expected to find but quickly realised that the screams should have prepared him for the worst.

Lit by only two small roundish devices at the edge of the shack was a woman. Lying in the centre, her body was pale and glistened with a sheen of sweat from the faint yellow light.

A sodden white dress was pulled up to her waist which, like

litmus paper, was sucking at the deep red of the quickly expanding pool of blood that surrounded her.

He was too late.

Transfixed, Hadwin bent his knees and lowered his head so that his spear dropped below the door frame as he slowly moved inside.

The eager wind, that had so readily shoved him into this place, seemed disinterested in being party to this meeting and so promptly slammed the metal door shut behind him. The doorframe let out a sound like a gunshot that seemed to traverse along every connected panel and magnify the noise tenfold. Suddenly, the woman's high-pitched crying resumed.

Like an electrical current had been passed through his boots, Hadwin felt his body tense beneath his armour as the noise shuddered through his ears - the last thing he had expected after seeing the dead woman was to hear any more sound from her. But as he stepped closer, Hadwin saw that it wasn't her making the noise after all, but the baby boy settled between her legs, camouflaged from head to toe in his mother's blood.

He stared down at the new-born with as much disbelief as he had shown it's mothers ship. Both seemed so unnatural in this place - life among lifelessness.

Hadwin crept forward slowly with gentle, smooth motions, as if worried the child were a bomb just waiting to go off. He lowered himself into a squat and reached towards the boy with one of his grubby, gauntleted hands.

The child's screaming immediately intensified and Hadwin instinctively retorted his hand as if he had been burnt. Looking down at his fingers, however, he quickly realised how his current attire must look to the poor thing. His harsh and intimidating appearance, with sharp angled armour plating covering almost every inch of his body, must have seemed quite monstrous compared to the smooth and slender legs that surrounded him.

Raising his hands up, Hadwin pulled back his helmet, disturbing an inch-thick layer of dust that had built up on the top during the journey, and pointed his grizzled yet kind face towards the boy.

Weathered skin hung loosely around Hadwin's eyes, but they gave off a warmness that was quite unlike his cold, rugged metal exterior.

Perhaps he could sense that Hadwin was not a threat, or perhaps it was that their eyes were now able to connect, but for whatever reason, the boy finally began to stifle its cries.

One by one, Hadwin pulled at the fingers of his claw like gloves, pausing for a moment to show the child each of his flesh coloured, albeit heavily calloused, hands and finally its cries ceased all together.

Hadwin slowly slipped one hand under the blood-stained boy's head and the other in the small of its back before hoisting him off of the ground. As he did so, his eyes flashed guiltily up at the boy's mother, lying there pale and lifeless, as if half expecting her to stop him.

Hadwin pulled the boy close to his chest and with his now unused hand, reached around the back of his armour. His fingers inched slowly up his jacket and lingered over the handle of a small serrated blade, before removing it from its sheath and rounding it silently towards the child.

Never, Hadwin thought, did he think that his little knife would be used for such an act.

With a quick slice, the floor was sprayed with a fresh coating of blood and Hadwin breathed a sigh of relief - the cord that connected this boy to his mother had now been broken and Hadwin quickly realised in a strange way that this signified that the responsibility of looking after this boy now fell on his shoulders.

This was a lot to take in.

This morning, Hadwin had awoken as, what he believed to be, the lone survivor on this barren planet. Barely scraping by on his small patch of vegetables and rationed supply of water, a solitary voice amongst the twisted steel and stone. But now, his singular life was anything but that. Now, his survival was no longer the only thing that he had to fight for.

Nature's moment of respectful silence for the woman's passing seemed to come to an end as Hadwin felt the earthquakes rapidly returning up through his legs.

The entire building began to shake all around them as a couple of the metal beams that held up the ceiling began to audibly strain and groan.

Seconds later, as Hadwin looked confusedly down at the child, one support snapped violently out of place and the returning winds howled angrily through the newly exposed hole in the shack's roof.

Hadwin had no time to lose. He had to get them out of there or risk suffering the same fate as the boy's mother.

Hurriedly, he looked around for something to wrap the child in, however, it looked as if every blanket or piece of clothing was drenched in blood.

Just as he was going to admit defeat and hope that the naked child could bare the chill, Hadwin spotted out of the corner of his eye what looked like a folded-up leather bundle nestled in the small of the woman's back.

Hastily, he tugged it out from behind her, sending her body slumping down on to one side. Her face now rested ungracefully on the filthy floor as her limbs lolled at her side.

This undignified position was no way for anyone to be left, but the pressing need to get them out of this collapsing building was far more important than some dead person's dignity.

After wrapping the boy in the soft yet tough material, Hadwin hesitated on the spot for a moment as the yellow lights twinkled in his eyes.

The scavenger inside him couldn't bear to leave empty handed, so he took a moment to snatch up the two metal orbs that lay next to the woman with his unburdened hand.

As his fingertips gripped around the last one, the light that they were emitting was abruptly extinguished and the room was plunged into darkness. Quickly, Hadwin squirrelled them inside his pockets and blindly made for the door as he heard more of the ceiling beginning to crash around him.

Hadwin threw open his jacket as he bounded across the room and nestled the now wailing child against his chest. Carefully, he fastened the armoured coat shut and took the boy's weight in the crook of his arm. His hastened and heavy footfall across the tiled floor joined the cracking sound of more bolts becoming dislodged from the fragile, failing structure above.

Ahead, the door which was now distinguishable by the soft moonlight bleeding around the edge rushed to meet him. But before Hadwin could take the final few steps, a plume of dust filled his vision and a large girder fell diagonally in front of him with a deafening crash.

Hadwin quickly stooped low, forcing his boulder-like frame through the newly formed triangular space and the only exit now available to him. Almost instantly however, his forward motion ground to a halt as if a giant hand had swooped in and grabbed him firmly around the middle.

Snapping his head around, Hadwin saw the tip of his spear was lodged above the quickly shrinking crawl space. It chimed and sang as he frantically fought back and forth against the girder's grip, all the while trying to keep a hold of the child.

Feeling the panic rising throughout his body, Hadwin reached awkwardly up his back and pulled at the small loop of metal that acted as a scabbard for the weapon.

In the last moment, as the heavy beam bore down and began to buckle his shoulder plates, Hadwin felt the small catch slide aside and the spear fall with a clatter behind him.

Hadwin wasted no time in getting to his feet and kicking the door with the sole of his boot. The rusted hinges, aged and weak like Hadwin's joints, were clearly unable to contend with such a force and sheared off completely.

Wind flew in once more and a few bits of grit sliced small cuts into the tiny piece of exposed flesh between Hadwin's helmet and the collar of his armour. He reached up and shifted it so that the protection was once again seamless as debris continued to glance off of him.

After one last look back at the boy's bloodied mother, who was now almost completely shrouded in the collapsing building's darkness, Hadwin rushed out into the roaring tempest clutching tightly to a child that was now his responsibility to bear.

CHAPTER 3 - The Chase

No sooner had Hadwin stepped across the threshold, the once safe refuge began to collapse behind him.

The steel frame buckled and wined helplessly into the night as the roof caved in triumphantly on itself. Its metal cladded walls quickly followed suit and folded like a tower of cards as plumes of dust swelled up and sent debris rattling against Hadwin's back.

Unperturbed by the noise and recent change in its surroundings, the boy now breathed calmly against Hadwin's rapidly beating chest. It seemed that being born inside a maelstrom of thunder and earthquakes had already begun to harden the child. This was good, Hadwin thought - it wasn't going to get any easier for him.

For a moment, Hadwin stood there looking down at the bulge by his belly, feeling quite lost. Not by bearings or destination, but by how he was going to keep this child safe. Now, every object and surface that peeked at him from amongst the darkness seemed threatening to the small life clutched beneath his armour.

Just as the building behind him had fallen, so too had the veil that shrouded Hadwin to every danger of this place. To him, a fall or a cut was just the way of life here, but to this pale and innocent, thin skinned child, it would be a death sentence.

Tightening his grip, Hadwin willed his legs forward and set a course back to the mother's ship. The ship had survived atmospheric entry, not to mention a high-speed collision with solid metal and stone, so Hadwin was sure it could withstand this storm for a few hours at least. If the small fire could be put out, it was his hope that he could take that time to rest within its hull and plan what he was going to do next.

Hadwin stepped purposely through the darkness, keeping his head angled to the floor in an attempt to locate his deeply pressed footprints. He stretched one hand out in front of him, reaching for a direction, whilst the other endeavoured to keep a secure yet gentle grip on the boy. However, in all the commotion of the collapsing shack, he had managed to get himself completely turned around and unfortunately the gales that were now whipping between the arching buildings made it impossible for him to find his tracks.

Hadwin stopped for a moment and began rotating his head slowly from side to side in an effort to spot the spaceship's light. But it would seem that the bright white engines had finally finished powering themselves down, as he could see nothing but darkness all around him.

A few distant bolts of lightning traced their way through the clouds, causing the sky above the gorge to glow a deep shade of purple. Just as the magenta sky faded through a mix of deep blues, Hadwin spotted something familiar a short way down the road, towering above the other concrete high-rises - the criss-crossing structures that he had found the spaceship nestled beneath.

Hadwin cracked a smile and sped forward; he was drawn blindly to the ship's location like a sailor to a siren's song.

As he stomped ahead, Hadwin was pleased to feel the intensity of the storm's winds lessening against his chest. This thankfully made his hurried steps quicker and less strenuous on his aching knees.

Finally, as the gusts diminished and the debris began to settle, Hadwin turned the last corner to find the ship waiting for him.

The seconds seemed to stretch into hours as he stood there gazing down the road. His eyes stretched wider and wider until they risked popping out altogether.

He had expected to find feelings of solace and safety at the sight of this miraculous ship, but now all it brought was a fear that froze him to the spot and crushed his windpipe in on itself.

Thankfully sanity, like a separate entity pulling his strings, finally managed to wrench his legs free from their paralysis and tighten his grip around the boy. He was driven backwards and thrown behind the safety of a nearby wall.

After a few seconds, fear finally relinquished control of him, but Hadwin still gave his body a few seconds to pump some much-needed blood back up to his brain, before slowly peeking his head back around the edge of the rough concrete.

His eyes flitted over the ship in disbelief.

The story, the one that Hadwin thought his mother had dreamt up as some sort of life lesson, was true. Circling and climbing over the ship were numerous machines, not rusted or ancient, but gleaming, vicious looking machines.

His memories carried him backwards, like a piece of elastic tied invisibly to those days.

"This world was once very different from Hadwin" His mother had whispered years ago as the light from their dwindling fire danced in her eyes.

"It was full of life and endless blue skies. No one scavenged for scraps of food or dug within the blackened ground for water. It was a paradise!"

She grabbed at the loose earth beneath her feet and let it trickle poignantly through her fingertips.

"But our ancestors became too arrogant, too lazy and so they constructed machines to tend to their every need. They made them smarter and smarter until one day, their creations decided that they no longer wanted to serve."

Her voice used to turn bitter and angry at this point, which had always scared his younger self.

"They killed everyone and for good measure, turned their creator's world into ash!" she said, issuing a hand at their surroundings.

"But, where did they go? Where are they now?" Hadwin had asked every time, waiting eagerly on tenterhooks for an answer.

This was the part of the story that he had liked the most, partly perhaps because he could tell that his mother truly didn't know. Every time, she would give a different answer like, "they blasted off into space" or "buried themselves deep underground."

But it was also this unknown that, as Hadwin grew older, made him begin to question the validity of her story. If she knew the beginning, how could she not know the end?

But here he was thirty or so years later, staring at the very machines that she had described.

They were more horrifying than childhood imagination could ever have thought up. Four-legged, monstrous forms with harsh angular bodies that moved in swift regimented motions as they clambered, spider-like, across the hull of the ship.

Like Hadwin, every inch of their bodies was wrapped in a carapace of thick scaled armour, but unlike his, the polished plating, which was reminiscent of the metal that comprised the ship itself, seemed to be constantly altering itself. It morphed and shifted its placement to fit around their complex bodies as their arms bent back on themselves and rotated to get new footings across the ship's hull.

As if their construction wasn't intimidating enough, long blades protruded from the end of each of their limbs and dug audibly into the debris-covered ground, as they circled like hyenas around their weakened and wounded prey.

Where you would expect a face to be, situated between two of their bladed arms, there was an arrangement of devices which sent focused red lasers over the ship's surface; scanning the contours from bow to stern then across the pockmarked, fire-blasted underbelly.

Hadwin, his heart racing like a hummingbird, continued to watch the swarming creatures with a mix of bewilderment, fear and intrigue.

He wondered how he hadn't seen even a hint or glint from one of their bodies in his few decades of scavenging through this wasteland. They, just like the spaceship, were other worldly to him - so out of place and therefore, easy to spot in his rusted world.

As one of the creatures placed a bladed claw on to the boarding ramp, a loud shriek suddenly cut through the night causing Hadwin to wince. His shoulders tightened and his boots shifted uneasily in the grit laden floor as the ear-splitting sound bounced away down the broken streets.

Fear told him to run, but it also rooted him immovably to the spot.

A conflicted Hadwin teetered as the origin of the noise emerged slowly from the darkness, cutting into the blood red clearing like a knife.

It was a machine quite unlike the others.

Standing upright at least twelve feet tall, it's form closely resembling that of a human - a towering monolith of a man, powerful and commanding in comparison to it's spindly counterparts.

It stepped into the swarm and crossed unapologetically to the ship's side as it's thundering, titanic footsteps cut a path through the four-legged machines. Their bodies shuddered slightly before cowering away to let the colossal thing pass.

Slowly, the thing surveyed the hull, not with lasers, but with mechanical eyes, before stooping low and entering the ship through the now flame engulfed doorway. The fire whipped around it's body, licking up through the layers of armour and then, like a pair of bright orange curtains, closed quickly behind it. Seconds later, the fiery light inside started to flicker and diminish.

Instantaneously, as the flames were finally snuffed out, the amber light was replaced by a pulsing red that shone out of the bridge's glass window and projected a large square onto the collapsed building on the opposite side of the street.

Another piercing cry cut through the air and the wounded ship trembled in response.

With loud clashes, as their bodies became a mass of intertwined limbs and torsos, the crowd of smaller machines suddenly turned their backs to the ship in unison. They continued to sidestep and shift, as if their bodies were carrying them upon buried tracks, until they had formed a perfect circle around the perimeter of the craft.

For a brief second they all looked like guards, equally spaced and defensive, then all at once, with terrifyingly similar motions, they began to use their razor-sharp arms to swipe and slash through the surrounding debris.

Effortlessly, they sliced apart the solid metal and stone, all the while keeping their laser beams pointed at the ground. Hadwin could have been wrong, but it almost looked as if they were searching for something.

"What could it be?" he murmured softly to himself.

Then, as his eyes continued to dart from machine to machine looking for any pattern to their search, the small round bulge fidgeted in the crook of his arm and he immediately understood.

Of course. They were looking for the ship's pilot.

Almost involuntarily, Hadwin could feel a newfound paternal instinct rotating his body so that the child was further shielded from the mechanised creatures by his shoulder and back.

If every detail of his mother's stories was now to be taken as fact, then his role as the child's new guardian had just gotten a lot tougher - these things had killed every human on this planet and from what he had seen, he had no reason to believe that their ethos had changed over the last one hundred years.

The approaching clatter bouncing off a nearby wall told Hadwin that the robots were already beginning to widen their search into the adjacent structures.

He let his eyes rise once more above the cover and watched them relentlessly clawing closer - ripping and overturning pieces of the ancient buildings in a ruthless yet calculated manner. If these things could effortlessly tear through solid metal and stone, Hadwin could only imagine the ease with which they would go through him and the child.

With that harrowing thought at the forefront of his mind, Hadwin realised that they needed to escape from this place as quickly and as quietly as humanly possible - his body, once again, would have to wait for it's respite.

Their only chance of survival was for Hadwin to somehow make his way around the perimeter of this wide gorge, back to the rope that he hoped still waited idly for him and retreat to the safety of his high walled home. But the odds of making it, without these mechanical search parties detecting their presence, was growing slimmer with each passing second as their quickly expanding search pattern was starting to close in on the pair's hiding spot.

Thankfully though, a particularly violent shake of the ground gave Hadwin exactly the window of opportunity that he needed - if ever there was a reason for him to consider the existence of a higher power, as his long dead ancestors once did, Hadwin knew that what happened next was one of them.

A towering building, directly between them and the searching machines began to groan like a wounded animal. It's peak writhed against the winds as broken concrete started to shed downwards from it's belly and a metre-wide crack spread along the crumbling wall. With a final snap of wrought metal and broken stone, the top half of the building suddenly sheared off, falling dramatically sideways and bringing hundreds-of-tonnes of twisted metal and concrete cascading down in front of Hadwin. This mass of crumbled stone, which now lay like a sleeping giant between the two rows of buildings, conveniently blocked the robots from view and for good measure, threw up a thick shroud of disturbed dust all around them.

So, quickly, gathering himself up and taking a deep mustering breath, Hadwin darted across to the adjacent street trying to make as little noise as possible as he went.

The unsteady piles of broken concrete at his feet that had fanned out from the fallen building did not make this task any easier. With every footstep, the debris tilted and wobbled beneath him, but with energy he didn't know his body still possessed, his movements remained silent and purposeful as he sprung, cat-like, behind cover.

Continuing on from building to building, Hadwin resisted the urge to glance sideways at the lit-up area of the ship that now shone through the various gaps in the skeletal remains of the other structures. He knew that it was better to stay calm and focus on his destination to avoid any unnecessary panic - fear only led to mistakes, and mistakes on this planet, whether being hunted by robots or not, always ended badly.

After several minutes of sneaking, Hadwin thankfully reached the foot of the cliff face where the reinforced metal rope still hung. The tip of the cord swung gently from side to side, giving Hadwin a playful wave as if it was greeting an old friend.

Hadwin slid his hand into another one of his pockets and pulled out a small device which he hastily began to fasten around the dependable rope. This tiny apparatus was a rappel, a simple yet useful piece of equipment that would enable him to climb the rope one handed whilst still holding on to the child with the other.

As he fastened the hoop of metal into place, Hadwin felt his other senses prick up and the thumping of blood that had been filling his ears fall away to make way for a another new arrival - the boy, nestled in the folds of his jacket, who had thankfully been silent up until now, had begun to cry.

The long, ear-splitting bawls, that could have easily competed with the shrieks of that giant machine, wailed around the gorge like an air raid siren. Almost instantaneously, Hadwin saw large red outlines of the surrounding buildings cast against the cliff face - the umpteen machines and their scanners, which had only moments ago been obsessively directed at the ship and the surrounding ground, were now focused on a new target.

Hadwin could feel the overflowing mix of fear and adrenaline surging through his body - there was no time to find somewhere to hide and no time for hesitation either.

Feverishly, he grabbed at the rope and began to climb.

With muscles screaming, Hadwin heaved himself up as the metal rappel dug unforgivingly deeply into each of his fingers.

Frantically, he slashed his feet against the crumbling dirt wall in a vague attempt to climb faster as all notions of minimising his noise were well and truly gone.

Hadwin could hear them below now; the shrill mechanical noises were echoing nearer and nearer as they approached the high-pitched call emanating from beneath his grasp.

For a fraction of a second, Hadwin twisted his head to the side to see if his efforts were for naught, but like his optimism on the cliff face above his home, he regretted the movement instantly. Taking advantage of Hadwin's distraction, one of the numerous pipes that protruded spear-like from the cliff wall caught his arm and pierced through the metal plating as he pulled himself upwards.

Feeling the downward tug, Hadwin snapped his head back around and frantically tried to wrench the pipe from the jagged hole that had been punctured into his armour just above his elbow.

The boy's howls grew louder and louder as Hadwin shook himself and the child wildly in all directions.

"Come on! Come on!" grunted Hadwin through gritted teeth as his eyes involuntarily began to weep and his cheeks burned a fiery red.

Finally, as he heaved himself up the rope with an almighty tug, Hadwin felt the pipe release his arm. But it, like the scavenger it had attacked, did not want to leave empty handed and so unburdened him of a few sections of toughened plating.

Like water flowing through a burst dam, the cold air rushed quickly through the torn opening and Hadwin could feel goosebumps rippling up his exposed arm.

Breathless and weak, he clambered to his feet at the top of the wall and awkwardly smuggled the boy across to the embrace of his undamaged side - a welcome silence fell as the child adjusted to the movement.

Hadwin's eyes flashed to the ground below just in time to see several of the machines converging from different alleyways and bursting effortlessly through solid rock walls. They stopped at the base of the muddy cliff and began to sweep their sensors over the swinging rope that still hung there. Searing strips of lasers continued to rise up the cliff face and hovered every few feet as they no doubt took in the contours of the scrappy footprints that he had left on the surface.

As the red beams glinted up and over the cliff top, Hadwin turned and began to run; his heavy boots slipping wildly on the dirt floor spraying fragments of earth over the precipice in his wake.

A choral cry rang through every atom of air and earth - it was a call to action, like a hunter's horn, to any of the machines that had not left the ship.

As he ran, the buildings that scattered the gorge's perimeter sped past him and Hadwin instantly felt the close, almost oppressive nature of the tightly knitted buildings disappearing behind him. The sun seemed to be coming up behind the dense storm clouds as a few rays of sunlight were able to peek their way through and illuminate the open landscape.

It was like stepping out from a dense wood into a clear glade. The now flattened terrain that stretched out in front of him - like an oxidised graveyard of ash and stone - was a pleasing sight.

He knew this place. The stillness of it.

Breaking this small semblance of comfort, however, was the return of the boy's cries that were undoubtedly renewed by the jarring motion of Hadwin's legs as he meandered his way through the litany of obstacles that lay at his feet.

Far ahead, a distant column of light shone through the swathes of debris that were still being carried through the air like flocks of birds in the wind. This majestic, almost biblical looking beam cast itself down to the landscape below and revealed the peak of Hadwin's home towering above the horizon.

Was something guiding him home and to safety?

Could he have been wrong? Did someone up there want him and the boy to survive?

Behind him however, Hadwin heard several loud crashing noises and this notion of divine intervention was instantly dashed. Their robotic pursuers were hot on their trail and closing the gap with each passing second.

Hadwin summoned up every ounce of energy left to him and coaxed it into his burning legs, but even with this, he could already feel that his pace was beginning to slow.

As Hadwin bounded up a small incline, he raised up a swollen knee but felt the toe cap of his left boot clip the edge of a metal beam protruding slightly out of the ground. Unable to will his aching body into righting itself, he tumbled forward and instinctively fell onto his right shoulder to protect the boy from the blow.

Hadwin was not sure how much further he could go on.

He rolled himself over onto his back and saw the distant red aura of the searching robots approaching. Their bladed limbs could be heard even at this distance, slicing angrily at the ground beneath them.

"Get up! It's not much further!" he shouted furiously to himself over the child's continued caterwauling.

Somehow, whether from fear of his own voice, or the thought of the machine's bladed arms, it worked.

Hadwin rose unsteadily to his feet and continued onwards as his feet dragged awkwardly behind his forward leaning body.

Finally, he staggered to the foot of his home's large steel door which still stood conveniently ajar. After darting clumsily inside - his shoulders knocking on each side of the frame in turn - Hadwin placed the still screaming boy on the courtyard floor before rushing back towards the door. He threw all his weight into his shoulder and slammed it against the steel which began to whine as it inched shut.

In the split second before the door was finally sealed, the whispering remnants of the storm gave out one final desperate gust and sent numerous shards of metal rattling through the tiny opening. One particularly determined fragment managed to find its mark and shot straight into the damaged section of Hadwin's armour. The devious piece of metal plunged deep into the exposed layers of clothing which slowed its momentum somewhat, but not nearly enough to stop the tip from puncturing his skin.

Hadwin let out a booming howl and used the surge of adrenaline to help him grind the door firmly shut. With a loud thud, the counterweights dropped the heavy locking pins into place.

Hadwin backed away in silence, clutching at his now limp arm as blood seeped from the wound leaving a deep red trail of droplets on the uneven floor.

Coupled with the injury to his wrist and upper arm, this limb was almost completely useless now. So, after leaving it to swing at his side, throbbing and maimed, Hadwin scooped up the child with his uninjured hand and continued to step back slowly across the courtyard - his ears poised for any sounds of their mechanical followers.

The boy's cries became broken, like the spluttering of a faulty engine, before ceasing altogether.

The silence that now blanketed his home was no longer comforting. It felt to Hadwin like he was standing in the eye of a storm - gentle and still - being lulled unwillingly into a false sense of security before an angry and tumultuous gale rushed to meet him.

After a further few agonising seconds, there was a bolt of lightning overhead and Hadwin felt his entire body tighten. Coupled with exhaustion and the threat of those vicious robotic claws, his nerves were in tatters.

Then he heard it, as if the lightning had been a starting pistol; the screeching sound of blades scraping against the metal walls.

They were here.

Sparks bounced across the courtyard floor as a pair of bladed claws suddenly sliced parallel gouges into the steel door. The solid metal tore and warped to the blades intent as red light shone like fire through the newly formed openings.

Hadwin couldn't help but fall backwards in terror.

He cowered away, sliding the heels of his boots against the grey stone as he moved desperately towards the front door of his home.

As other pairs of deep slashes began to slice one after the other through the rest of the wall, Hadwin summoned up enough courage to scramble to his feet and retreat inside.

Hurriedly, he slid the locking bar into place with a nudge of his upper arm, backing away until he fell onto his now tattered sofa.

After a few moments of clashing and slashing from outside, the courtyard once again fell silent.

Hadwin sat looking down at the gently cooing boy, before removing his helmet and placing it to one side.

It was useless, wherever they went, wherever they tried to hide, nothing was going to stop those things from reaching them.

The child slowly opened his eyes and looked up at him. His irises, a vivid shade of green, almost seemed to glow in the faint light of the room. Hadwin's dark, aged eyes were dull in comparison and seemed to swallow the light like a pair of deep bottomless pits.

The boy reached forward a little podgy arm and curiously touched Hadwin's nose. A small grin pulled at the child's mouth as his eyes screwed up into small eye-lashed folds.

Hadwin was stunned by the overwhelming rush of feelings he suddenly felt towards the boy. A child who he hadn't even known to exist when he had woken this morning.

"Do not let this world break you".

Hadwin raised his head and his brow became focused.

His eyes scanned about his home before falling on the smooth black stone floor. A square of metal, roughly half a metre wide, was sunken into the surface. .

It was his only option.

After placing the boy on the sofa, Hadwin dropped to one knee and scratched his claw-like fingertips into the snug groove that ran around the edge of the dark metal. Finally, he got a hold of the steel sheet and lifted one side as hidden hinges squeaked on the other.

When Hadwin had first begun refitting this place into a home, he had constructed a narrow escape tunnel, just in case the front became blocked by debris falling from the cliff above. The now uncovered shaft led deep into the earth before going fifty foot through solid rock and out the other side of the perimeter wall.

The problem with this plan and Hadwin's main reason for not considering this escape route earlier, was that the robots were clearly not deterred by metal or solid rock. This hatch wasn't going to hold up any better against the machines' blades than the perimeter wall had.

Looking around the room, Hadwin suddenly spotted the mass of jerry-rigged batteries stacked along one wall and an idea began to spark in his mind.

Years ago, a bad soldering job had accidentally caused a short circuit during a previous lightning storm and underneath his layers of clothing and armour, Hadwin wore a painful reminder to never repeat this mistake again. At that time, only a singular battery had overheated, exploded and doused him in acid - burning straight through the thick metal plating of his armour before luckily neutralising onto his skin. Now, as Hadwin rubbed a hand over his heavily scarred and bloody arm, he tried to imagine what kind of damage an entire wall of batteries could do.

As he hurriedly tried to piece together the beginnings of a plan, the bright red searching lasers began to sweep over the front of his home. They slipped through the various small gaps and holes in its construction and created a criss-cross of red lines in the dust that hung in the air.

Hadwin just needed to figure out a way to get the batteries hot enough so that they would explode; the lightning rod, that had preluded this unfortunate night, was gone, so the conditions could not be recreated that way.

He scanned his eyes around the room and settled on a jerry can under a table in front of him. Hastily, Hadwin crawled over and gave the can a shake. To his relief, the gasoline it contained, syphoned from one of the many automobiles that were dotted around, swashed around inside signalling that it was almost half full.

Without a second thought, Hadwin began to empty it out on top of the batteries before trailing the last few drops towards the door. He could hear the clatter of the machines' metal limbs against the stone floor just outside as he threw the empty can loudly across the room.

After picking up the boy, Hadwin lowered himself down into the tunnel and wedged himself against the roughly cut walls to stop them from dropping downwards. His injured arm shot a stabbing pain across his chest as he reached up and grabbed the hatch door, then he waited.

The red light that was penetrating into his home continued to pass back and forth, skewing into almost beautiful spirals as it bent through the fumes rising up off of the ground.

Finally, as Hadwin's nerves reached breaking point and his breath became a rapid pant, the lights went out.

There was no more shifting of bladed bodies. No more mechanised whirring coming from beyond the doorway, only silence.

Try as he might, Hadwin could not bring his frantic panting lungs under control. His fear and anticipation filled the empty home just like the smell of fuel.

As a momentary suggestion of either hope or ignorance sparked amongst the silence, deafening screeches ripped through the air and numerous pairs of claws dug their way through the metal door and walls.

Sparks suddenly flew in all directions as the torn metal was peeled back and the terrifying machines slid themselves inside.

"Come on..." whispered Hadwin to himself through gritted teeth as focused beams dazzled his eyes and red dots emblazoned his chest.

The front runner of the machines spotted Hadwin and began towards him with a single arm pulled back like a scythe.

His eyes were wide with horror, then all of a sudden, glistening with firelight as one of the white-hot embers finally ignited the pool.

In an instant, a whoosh ripped through the home as all the oxygen was sucked from the air. Hadwin clenched the boy tightly to his chest as he slammed the hatch shut and plummeted down the dark hole to the rock floor below.

Less than a second passed before an almighty boom beat Hadwin's ears and shook the roughly cut stone on which he lay. Above him, fire and smoke rippled around the edges of the bowed hatch as further explosions punched at his already deadened ears.

Wasting no time, Hadwin threw on the emergency backpack that he kept at the bottom of this escape hatch and began to crawl awkwardly through the pitch-black tunnel.

Struggling to keep the child off the ground with his good arm, Hadwin was forced to shuffle forward by propping himself up with his elbow as the agonising wound on his lower arm screamed silently in pain.

The length of this tunnel was not far, but time seemed to pass at a snail's pace as Hadwin's ears rang and his punctured arm threatened to collapse under him at any second.

He could feel the shaking motion of the boy's cries travelling through the fabric of his jacket, but the deafness caused by the explosion meant he could no longer hear the bawls.

Finally, Hadwin's head knocked into something solid and with his bloodied, gauntleted hand, he reached up and punched forward, dislodging the sheet of metal that covered the exit.

Strips of daylight shone onto his dirt covered face as remnants of the thick clouds sped away towards the horizon.

As he stood, his body shaking from exhaustion, Hadwin could see the vast plumes of fire and smoke billowing over the high walls of his home beside them.

As secondary explosions continued to batter his ears, a gentle breeze whisked past his face and tickled at his scraggly beard.

Hadwin rolled his eyes at his own stupidity for leaving his helmet behind, then opened his jacket and raised the small boy up so that they were eye to eye.

"Well, looks like we are in this together then." said Hadwin cheerfully looking at the boy, who was still wrapped in the soft leather garment taken from his mother.

The boy's rosy, vulnerable face stretched, and his eyes screwed up as he let out a miniature yawn. Hadwin gave the boy a small, slightly jealous, smile before turning to scour the horizon.

Without another look behind him, whether through fear of being pursued or the sadness that he felt at abandoning the place that had been his home for all those years, Hadwin gathered the boy tightly back underneath his arm and hobbled forward into the barren world in search of a new home for them both.

CHAPTER 4 - The Cave

*

A candle flickered in the centre of the small room, illuminating the various pictures drawn onto the stone walls and ceiling.

The gentle light seemed to breathe life into the different scenes; the dark cladded man holding a pickaxe that was chipping away at the side of a mountain, to a cluster of plants swaying towards a beam of sunlight above a bluish white pool. In the small cave-like room, each coloured line and shaded face danced to the candle's tune - thankful for this chance to move and re-enact the various events that they depicted.

Beneath the scenes, upon the threadbare covers of a dull metal bed that was nestled into the back corner of the room, lay an animal with rich cotton-like fur. It sat there quite still, soaking in the candlelight's warmth as it's coat swayed along with every flick and crackle of the small flame.

With auburn eyes that glowed like gemstones, it gazed unblinkingly towards the light as if hypnotised by its beauty.

Silently and without the creature noticing, two small green orbs rose into view at the end of the bed. They hovered above the slightly rusted, dark steel frame and studied the creature with the same unbroken concentration that it showed the candle.

The vivid green circles narrowed before blinking shut.

Their owner, a scruffy haired boy with washed out grey clothing, pulled himself effortlessly onto the foot of the bed without making a sound.

He balanced gracefully, positioning one hand down between his feet for support, whilst the other wrapped around the leather handle of a serrated edged blade that was sheathed at his side.

The boy crouched deeper, poised to attack, his breathing barely audible in the dome shaped room. The polished surface of the knife glistened in the dim light as its bearer drew it slowly up to his chest.

As the animal continued to stare in the opposite direction, completely unaware of what was about to befall it, the child pounced high and the blade became a silver blur.

It was over in an instant.

The oblivious animal fell to the floor without so much as a grunt and over one hundred round beads began to fall out of the one-inch gash cut into it's back.

The stones bounced across the floor, disappearing under the few bits of dented furniture that lined the walls and knocked into the toecaps of a thick pair of armoured boots that stood rigidly on the opposite side of the room.

"Gavril, must you always do that?"

Standing high in the doorway, his form blocking almost all the light that was trying to edge its way in from the chamber beyond, was Hadwin.

He let out a long, frustrated sigh - it had taken him days to gather those stones and many more to sand them down into smooth uniform beads to fill that toy animal.

But part of Hadwin couldn't help but marvel at the boy's spirit. It was a feeling that materialised as a hint of a smile in the corner of his mouth as he stared down at him.

"It is practice!" the boy exclaimed.

A gleeful smile spread across his face as he looked down at the mess he had made.

Before the boy could catch a glimpse of the smirk, Hadwin forced his face back into its usual serious scowl.

In truth, there was no need for such practice. Animals, like the one Hadwin had modelled the soft toy on, were only seen in the pages of musty old books.

"Yes, but your practice Gavril, always leads to me having to practise my stitching!"

His voice was now layered with a hint of annoyance, which did not go unnoticed by the small boy and smile fell instantaneously.

He quickly hung his head to avoid Hadwin's judgmental gaze, knowing full well that a lesson was coming.

"You know that this thread doesn't grow on trees!" he said loudly, as expected.

This was a strange phrase that Hadwin had learnt years ago from his mother. She, just like him, had never even seen a tree in real life, but sayings like this came from her great grandparents who had actually been lucky enough to own a garden full of the leafy things.

Unbeknownst to Hadwin, this thread had actually grown on a tree, but this truth did not matter. He had taught Gavril the meaning of the phrase, just as his mother had taught him, because whilst a tree had not graced this planet's soil for well over a hundred years, the saying could not have been more fitting for life here.

Hadwin knew that it was essential to remind the boy frequently of the respect that he should show all the items in their home as some of the most simple and trivial objects that were littered around it were irreplaceable, and the boy should understand that if he was to survive.

With his head still angled towards the ground, Gavril's long fringe hung in front of his face and shielded him from Hadwin's gaze.

"Sorry, Father," he murmured.

Gavril tried his hardest to give his voice a sense of sincerity, but his father knew him better than that.

Hadwin crossed the entirety of the room in two large steps, placed his hand on the boy's head and ruffled his hair into an even more messy mass. It also revealed the boy's grinning face now looking up at him.

It was an infectious expression.

Hadwin chuckled and the small smile returned to the corners of his mouth.

It was hard to stay mad at him. Their years together, since that night in the collapsing shack, had been the happiest in Hadwin's now forty-something years.

"Come on, boy, we have work to do!" said Hadwin, as he strolled through the doorway and out of view.

However, as Gavril rose from the bed to follow, Hadwin's voice echoed sternly from around the door frame.

"Not before you find each and every one of those beads, mind you!"

The boy froze mid step at the words, causing his balance to shift sending him toppling onto his outstretched foot. He stomped it down in a mock tantrum before smiling and scrabbling around on the floor to gather the small stones that were strewn across the surface.

Once each one had been accounted for, one-hundred and forty-two to be exact, Gavril piled them up together with the stuffed toy's remains on top of his bed covers and sprinted after his father.

Hadwin was waiting for him, standing in the centre of the large cavern which acted as the main hub of their underground home.

High above Hadwin's head, surrounded by short stalactites of milky white stone was a naturally formed two-foot wide hole cut into the ceiling. Through this, a column of daylight shone downwards and glistened upon the surface of a small pool of water directly behind him. It was this tiny reservoir, coupled with the skylight, that had convinced Hadwin to turn this subterranean oasis into their new home a little over ten years ago.

In the days that had followed since their escape, Hadwin had constantly kept them moving. Driven by the fear of their mechanical hunters, he never stayed in one place long enough to call it home.

How could he? Nothing even came close to the safe haven that lay burnt out tens-of-miles behind him. Every crumbled building. Every collapsed metal shell. They all paled in comparison to what that place had been.

Unfortunately, not staying still for longer than a few hours also meant that Hadwin was unable to get any real rest. This was not only compounded by the baby boy's cries, but mostly by the distant search lights that he saw every few days, telling him that the robots, despite the melting of their comrades, had not abandoned the hunt.

Whilst the cut on Hadwin's arm had finally healed, the rest of his body had become weak, and whilst he couldn't see himself in a mirror, Hadwin knew that he was looking frail. His stomach ached and he could feel his body eating carnivorously away at his once thick muscles as the days crept by.

Hadwin had done what he could to ration the few scraps of supplies, but the emergency backpack, as its name suggested, was for emergencies. It wasn't supposed to support him, let alone the added belly of a child, for more than a week at most.

Water had been the last to go.

For every drop of the purified stock that he drank, Hadwin gave at least two to the boy. But as this too dwindled, Hadwin was forced to seek out different sources for himself.

Whether it was pooled in some rusted wreck, or in the bowels of some half-destroyed building, the yellowish tinged water had an all too familiar tang to it. Hadwin had to keep reminding himself that the foul taste and a few years shaved off his already limited life span was far better than dying from dehydration.

Barely, he thought to himself. Barely.

It had been three arduous weeks since their journey began and nearly two full days since the clean water had run out, when Hadwin was forced to take shelter at the foot of a shallow mountain.

The weather, which had been kind to them for the most part of their journey, decided that it was high time to remind the weakened guardian of what it was capable of.

Without access to any of his equipment, Hadwin had been unable to repair his torn armour, plus his helmet, which had spent its last moments sat atop the squashy sofa watching machines clawing amongst flames towards it, had not been replaced.

So, weak from malnourishment and dehydration, clutching at his face as grit and stones slashed painfully at his cheeks, Hadwin had pushed deeper and deeper into a mountainside.

He squeezed himself between boulders and fissures of cracked stone until all the light and sound of the approaching storm had disappeared entirely.

His half delusional mind assured him that the deeper they went, the safer they would be, and whilst this was likely to have been true, it didn't remind him that any hope of finding a fresh supply of food and water probably wouldn't be on the inside of some dark and cramped cave. However, against the assumptions of the rational part of his brain, this was exactly what he found.

Crawling on his hands and knees as the wailing boy swayed in the rucksack secured across his chest, Hadwin had pulled himself into the large cavern where his present-day self and Gavril now stood.

The sight would have made him weep if his parched body had any spare moisture to give.

Not only was there a source of clear and untainted water in the centre of the circular cave, but surrounding it, covering the floor and creeping up the walls to the now failing light, was vegetation. Yes, it had only been some form of moss back then, but it had been enough to sustain them both for a short while at least.

After securing the access tunnels and planting a few seeds he had safely stored in the lining of the backpack, Hadwin was able to convert this hidden oasis in the bowels of this mountain into a refuge from both the elements and their unrelenting mechanised stalkers. It was a place that he and his adopted son could finally call home and had done so ever since.

"Right Gavril, hop to it!" Hadwin commanded, pointing a gnarled and scarred finger across the room.

Like any home, this place too required maintenance and ever since he had grown big enough to hold a wrench, with some guidance from his father, this had become Gavril's job. From routinely checking the stability of the several access tunnels that led to the surface, to tending their small vegetable garden.

Hadwin was becoming increasingly aware that he wouldn't always be around to care for the boy and just like his mother had done for him, he had decided it was necessary to teach him how to maintain this place on his own. Not that he told the boy the true reasoning for doing so - drawing on his own experience, Hadwin didn't want to go springing the weight of that impending loneliness on him too soon.

Instead he watched as Gavril, in childish and blissful ignorance, lazily trundled towards the entrance of the nearest tunnel that splintered off from the central hub of their home and led to the first access point.

Gavril squinted down the passageway and the pitch-black interior stared back at him.

He let out a weak sigh, then, without looking, raised a hand to the edge of the misshapen opening and began to rotate a small metal crank that stuck out from the surface.

As the spindle turned, ancient bearings wined, and a taut metal wire wound it's way around the rotating pulley wheel. Like a coiling snake, it slid over the spiralled helix of metal, getting tighter and tighter with each turn.

Stretching high into the cave's ceiling, the wire tugged on a rusted metal contraption located near the skylight, which slowly began to move sideways under Gavril's influence. Coiled springs that connected to various complex joints began to lengthen as a large sheet of polished metal was released and pulled into the path of the column of light. The diffused glow that had lit the domed room fell as the beam's trajectory was bent towards the darkened tunnel where Gavril still stood. After securing the crank arm with the purposely placed loop of wire, he stood aside and allowed the light to cascade, unobstructed, through the passage opening.

Suddenly, the stone tunnel was bursting with colour as similar reflective surfaces that lined the walls split the beam into hundreds of thin refracted streams that ricocheted their way around the twists and bends, before disappearing out of sight.

Gavril turned and ushered his father in first with a wave of his hand. Hadwin, however, remained quite still.

With his arms crossed and a serious expression pushing at his brow, he tapped his foot impatiently on the ground.

The boy let out an exasperated sigh and climbed into the illuminated tunnel, whilst Hadwin brought up the rear.

Always the same thought Gavril to himself.

Like clockwork, as they snaked their way down the passage, Gavril began his usual line of questioning.

"Father, when can I come outside with you?" he said in the usual practised and innocent tone.

Now it was Hadwin's turn to sigh deeply.

"You already know the answer to that Gavril and asking me every day isn't going to change it" stated Hadwin plainly.

The boy was trying to wear him down, he thought, like blown sand polishing a rough stone.

But it wouldn't work.

Unfortunately, ever since Gavril had started forming sentences, he had become obsessed with finding out as much as he could about the outside world.

He was fascinated by the treasures that Hadwin brought back from his long ventures above ground; every one as unique and as mystifying as the next.

However, as Gavril grew older, every rusted trinket had become a carrot of sorts, constantly being dangled in front of his face like that of a mule. It drove him to want to know more; to know the place they came from.

"I just want to help!" Gavril retorted.

"You are helping Gavril, never forget that." he said before reaching out a hand and patting the disheartened boy on the back.

Unfortunately, over-stretching in this manner caused one of Hadwin's feet to slip slightly on a small incline rising from the tunnel floor.

As his boot scratched against the smooth stone and pain flooded his side, he had no choice but to shuffle sideways to prop himself up on the curved wall.

Hadwin's involuntary gasp and pained expression did not go unnoticed by Gavril, who in a flash was at his side and helping to steady him.

"Are you okay?" Gavril asked, his high-pitched voice full of concern.

Hadwin hurriedly stifled the pain before righting himself and brushing Gavril's helpful hands aside.

"Of course I am, just lost my footing, that's all!" he said jovially, with only a hint of the continuing discomfort pulling at the features of his face.

After a deep breath, Hadwin impatiently waved an arm in front of him which told Gavril two things - one, to continue onwards and two, to not ask any more questions about what had just happened.

For a moment, it looked like the boy wasn't going to comply with either, but as Hadwin's brow tightened further, Gavril relaxed and he sped off, understanding that this wasn't open for discussion.

When Hadwin reached the first irregularly shaped metal wall a few minutes later, he found Gavril there, already getting to work.

With a small ratchet, the boy skirted around the edge of panelling that stretched from one side of the tunnel to the other and tightened each of the fixing bolts that dug deep into the stone circumference.

Beyond this plating were mounds of dirt and large rocks, which Hadwin had placed to completely hide the metal barrier from prying eyes.

Of course, he had given a very different explanation to the boy, telling him instead that the frequent storms above would blow through these tunnels if they were ever to become uncovered or loosened and could inevitably destroy their home.

It was a half-truth that Hadwin had hoped would reinforce the importance of routinely checking the barriers. However, as the months passed and his incessant questions about the outside world became more frequent, Hadwin could sense that this sole purpose was beginning to become somewhat monotonous to Gavril.

In silence and under the watchful eye of his father, Gavril repeated this process down the numerous other passages until they reached the final, largest tunnel. This one, unlike the others, was not blocked by a solid plate of metal but by a thick, iron hatch.

Gavril paused as he approached.

He could feel his father's eyes burrowing into the back of his head, just as his own were burrowing through the metal plating to the unknown world that lay beyond.

"Look, son…" Hadwin said, placing his hand on the boy's shoulder again and swivelling him round so that their eyes met.

"…you are safe here."

He wrapped his free knuckles against the hatch which let out a weak, gonging sound.

"Beyond this door are dangers that not even your brilliant little mind could outthink!"

Hadwin had hoped to distract the boy momentarily with the compliment, but he could see only moments later that it was going to take more than this brief explanation and an ego boost to quell Gavril's determination.

The boy shook off his father's hand, and with one last twist of the ratchet, pushed past him and stomped away down the passage.

"Give me strength" Hadwin muttered as he cast his eyes upwards.

Another one of his grandparents' strange phrases.

Gavril could not shake his frustration as he stomped angrily back to the atrium, some twenty feet in front of his father.

It was okay for him, he thought, as he was able to leave the confines of their home, to walk where there wasn't just rock above his head but vast open grey skies.

For years now, that was all Gavril wanted. He dreamt every night of a world without walls and repetitive safety checks.

He was constantly reminded by Hadwin of the dangers that the outside world posed; harsh landscapes and frequent ferocious storms. But all of these warnings had begun to fall on deaf ears. He was quick on his feet and strong enough to deal with everything his father had described. Gavril just couldn't shake the feeling that his father simply didn't trust him.

Dropping to his knees and rather heavy handed, Gavril began to check the leaves of the plants growing in their little floating pots that drifted across the surface of the pool. The vegetables reached deep into the water with their thin tendrils and sucked up all the minerals that they needed.

From the few seeds squirrelled into Hadwin's backpack all those years ago, they had flourished in this space, which acted as a natural greenhouse. It gave them access to all the light that the two-foot patch of grey skies had to offer, whilst simultaneously shielding them from the harsh winds above.

The idea to grow the plants in such a fashion had actually been suggested by Gavril when he was just five years old, when he had seen that his father had been struggling to keep the source of their food from overgrowing into the surrounding soil.

Hadwin had not been surprised by this ingenious idea as almost every little device in their home had, in one way or another, come from the small boy's mind.

Even the mirror lighting system had only come to him after seeing Gavril playing by the pool with a small piece of polished metal. The boy had waded into the water and used it to reflect the light from the ceiling playfully into Hadwin's eyes before settling it on one of the nearest tunnels.

Hadwin, slightly hobbling now on his left leg, entered the high walled room and knelt down next to Gavril at the water's edge.

Time to dangle another carrot, he thought.

"In a few years you..." Hadwin began calmly before being abruptly cut off.

"In a few years?! I cannot wait that long!" shouted the small boy, his face becoming instantly as red as one of the fruits of the small tomato plant he was tending to.

For a second, it looked like Hadwin was deciding which way to go with this argument, settling finally on responding in kind.

"You will wait that long!" Hadwin boomed.

"Because I have said you will wait that long!"

The boy fell silent and in the instant before his long, wavy hair covered his face again, Hadwin could see tears forming in Gavril's eyes.

Silence hung between them for what had to be a minute, as the pair continued to check the crops.

After a couple of sniffs, Gavril turned to his father, grabbed hold of his arm and nestled his face into his shoulder.

"I'm sorry father, I just don't want to see you injured anymore."

Hadwin was taken aback.

How did the boy know - he had taken care to shield his injuries from view upon his return to their home and tended to the wounds in the confines of his own room at night.

"Injuries, what injuries?" he said with mock innocence.

He raised the boy's chin with a single finger so that they were now eye to eye.

"Father, how could I not know" gesturing a hand around their small home.

For a moment, Hadwin was lost for words.

"I am fine, there is nothing for you to worry about" Hadwin said dismissively, before raising his voice and speaking again.

"And... and never you mind! I do what I do to keep us safe!"

Gavril opened his mouth to respond, but, seeing the furious look swelling in his father's eyes, decided against it.

As Hadwin stood up, his leg shot a twang of pain up his side and he walked over to his room, trying his hardest not to limp, slamming the door angrily behind him.

Gavril knelt there as the tears began to dry on his cheeks.

Why had he pushed the point, he knew his father only had his best interests at heart. But Gavril could not shake the confusion as to why his father was hiding the injuries from him in the first place. Was it the severity or the cause? He thought to himself. What was he keeping them safe from?

Behind the closed door, Hadwin lowered himself onto his bed and pulled down the leg of his trousers to reveal a deep cut. The wound had obviously opened up again when he had slipped in the passageway as fresh bright blood was beginning to ooze.

The truth was that Hadwin ventured out not solely for the purpose of gathering supplies. Sure, this was an added bonus that also gave him a valid excuse to tell Gavril that these excursions were necessary, but the real reason was for him to undertake reconnaissance.

Hadwin conducted these excursions above ground to try and find out what the machines were doing. To try and figure out their patterns and to ultimately determine whether or not they had given up their search. Thus far, after the long years since their last interaction and numerous sightings, they did not show any sign of doing so. Relentlessly, they continued to comb the area in search patterns for any sign of Hadwin and the boy.

And whilst the robot's strength and determination was seemingly unaffected by the passage of time, the same couldn't be said for Hadwin, who was beginning to struggle more and more with daily life and could not shake off the reality that his body was beginning to fail him.

Hadwin had already reached and passed the age that his mother had been before she had died, which was a milestone that he contributed to the abundance of food and water that their new home provided. But like the dilapidated buildings that covered the landscape, it seemed that he too was becoming more weathered and weaker as the years rolled by. Hadwin had not suffered the injury on his leg from being attacked, but through sheer arrogance, thinking that he could still do the things his younger body could.

After climbing a particularly difficult structure to gain a vantage point of the valley, he had overstretched himself and an injury that he had sustained many years ago, caused his hand to seize and once more miss its footing. Sliding from his position, his arms and legs unable to right him in time, his thigh got caught on a jagged piece of steel which then ripped through his armour and slashed deep into his flesh.

Unable to scream in agony, for fear of attracting the attention of the searching robots, defeated he had limped for over an hour back to the hidden entrance of their home.

Now, sitting there, reflecting on his own decreasing ability to look after them and feeling guilty for lying to his son once more, Hadwin picked up a needle and reel of thread from a small metal tin that lay on a table beside his bed. The very same reel of fine cotton that he intended to use to fix Gavril's toy later.

After wetting the tip of the cotton in his mouth and following several failed attempts, he finally managed to poke the end through the eye of a needle and began to re-stitch the wound shut.

"This thread doesn't grow on trees, Hadwin." he quietly reminded himself as his face grimaced.

On the other side of the door, with his ear pressed firmly against it, Gavril listened to Hadwin's muffled mutterings then his groans and grunts of pain.

After a few minutes, he heard a sigh of relief, his father bustling around the room a bit and then a steady snore signalling that he had turned in for the night.

Now, making sure to tread lightly, Gavril made his way across to his own room. Not that making any sound really mattered. In more recent years, once his father fell asleep, it would take the power of several thunderstorms to wake him unexpectedly before morning.

Gavril knew that this gave him at least a six-hour window before he needed to be back in bed, ready to be "awoken" by his father to begin the following morning's safety checks.

With childish excitement, he crossed the room before dropping to his knees and reaching one arm blindly to the very back of the dark space beneath his bed. After a moment, his fingertips connected with the metal box that lay there and he slid it out hurriedly.

This was where Gavril kept all of his private possessions, culminating in a small pile of various objects that Hadwin had brought back from the world beyond the outer hatch. He picked them out one by one, placing them softly upon the covers of his bed. Each of them rattled against the stone beads that still sat there, until all that remained was his most prized item, lying flat across the bottom of the box: a thick book called "Astrology Through the Ages".

The most useful ability that Hadwin had ever taught Gavril was that of reading. Of course, he wasn't an expert - the knowledge had been passed down by Hadwin's ancestors, who in most part used it to aid them when scavenging, so most of the words within this book were still quite alien to him, but Gavril knew enough to ascertain their general meaning. Besides, it was the colourful swirling gases and bright white dots amongst the pitch-black emptiness which adorned the pages that had always fascinated him.

On a night when the sky had been clear enough through the round hole in the ceiling of the central cavern, Hadwin had explained to him that the dots in the black sky were distant stars, even managing to match a few of the constellations to ones pictured in the book.

Gavril's amazement that night was not only reserved for the stars in the sky, but also for his father. He couldn't help but marvel at his understanding of the world above.

Gavril gazed down at the faded front cover as he had done many a night and thought back to that starry night, where he was full of admiration towards Hadwin. The memory derailed his nerves like a speeding train and he suddenly began to have reservations about whether what he was about to do was the best decision.

Maybe his father was right, maybe the dangers above would be too much for him. Then the words that Hadwin had spoken to him earlier began to echo repeatedly in his ears - A few more years…

Gavril shook his head, as if trying to shake the doubt from his mind.

No, he couldn't wait that long.

He reached into the box and lifted the book out, revealing a bundle of black metallic clothing lying hidden underneath.

His father wasn't the only one keeping secrets...

CHAPTER 5 - The Son

The dark garments chinked together as Gavril pulled them out of the box and draped them over the edge of his bed.

For a moment he stared at them, thinking back to the countless days and sleepless nights that it had taken him to fabricate them without his father knowing. An off cut of metal here. A dismantled bit of machinery there. Every square inch carefully stockpiled in secret until there was enough to finally construct his own full set of armour.

Gavril didn't like keeping things from Hadwin, but like everything else that he had learnt in his short lifetime, he had been taught deception by his father.

At barely ten years old, Gavril already had a certain degree of self-awareness. He knew that he was smart, or at least smarter than Hadwin had been at his age judging by the way that he treated his ideas.

As well as being a quick study of everything that Hadwin instructed him in, this seemingly heightened intellect also allowed him to notice certain patterns and changes in all manner of things - from predicting the coming of storms, sometimes days in advance, based on nothing but the movement of the plants leaves and a metallic taste in the air, to the precise cycle of the stars in the small patch of sky available to him. The most prominent pattern, however, the one that concerned him most, was a little closer to home.

It hadn't taken Gavril very long to work out that there was something that he wasn't being told. Some unknown that was being kept from him regarding the world above. In particular, what his father actually did whilst he was up there and why in doing so, he sustained so many injuries.

Hadwin said that it was for supplies, but their home, as he often reminded Gavril, provided everything they needed to survive.

Over the past couple of years since Gavril's suspicions were first peaked, he had noticed several inaccuracies and contradicting aspects of Hadwin's stories.

His father would reminisce about his old home and tell him of how he had lived there most of his life after his mother had died, but when asked why they didn't live there anymore, he would offer little to no explanation saying only -"It wasn't safe!" before immediately changing the subject.

Then there was the question of his mother.

When teaching him, Hadwin often made references to her, who, like Gavril, it seemed, had taught him all he knew. But when Gavril asked questions about his own mother, these were once again deflected.

He tried time after time to prise the information from Hadwin, but nothing seemed to escape the ironclad prison that the man had created within himself.

Secrecy aside, Gavril was becoming worried about his father. Wherever his excursions above ground were taking him, the destinations were obviously dangerous. A limp, like the one Hadwin had exhibited today, was nothing new. It was just the latest in a long line of injuries that his father poorly tried to conceal from him.

Gavril had to prove that he was strong enough, fast enough and willing to help with whatever needed to be done up there. Anything, he thought, to help lighten the load for his father.

Taking a quick breath to prepare himself, which made him look like a man twice his age, Gavril stepped into the trousers and slipped on the steel coated jacket. After fastening the two pieces together around his middle with several buckles, an unbroken mesh of plating like the skin of a snake now spread from his neck all the way down to his small toughened boots.

Gavril quickly slid his serrated knife into a small sheath he had built into the waist then turned to face the remaining item that was staring up at him from the bed - two mirrored glass circles wrapped in leather strappings, forming his protective goggles. His stick-like silhouette was reflected back at him in each of the lenses. It was this thin, sinewy frame that gifted him with his most useful skill - speed.

Unlike his father's armour, which was bulky and restrictive, this gave him freedom of movement around his arms and legs, whilst still offering the plated metal protection, that judging from the dents that adorned his father's armour, it sorely needed.

In a daze, Gavril snatched the goggles up, made his way out of his room and started across the eerily quiet, dark space towards the largest tunnel.

His mind was elsewhere. Already above ground.

With the sun now set and no natural light to utilise, the mirrors high above hung camouflaged against the uneven rock face. Not that he needed them of course, they were for Hadwin's use, not his. With countless hours of free time and only the tunnels to wander, Gavril knew every twist and turn of their maze-like home like it was the back of his hand.

His footsteps were light and barely registered as a patter, but as he put a single step out of the atrium, one of his father's distant snores rang through air and made him halt momentarily.

It was almost as if subconsciously, even through his slumber, Hadwin was calling out for him to go no further.

"I'm ready, Father." he whispered quietly to the closed door before rushing cat-like down the passageway.

In a matter of moments, Gavril found himself standing face to face with the outer hatch, and just like earlier, his eyes burrowed through the metal to what lie beyond - a perilous and unliveable place plagued by storms so ferocious they could carry away someone of his limited size with ease. Gavril was sure that it couldn't be as bad as his father described, and in any case, he had chosen this night as he had calculated that the next storm was at least a few days away.

Gavril slid the goggles down over his eyes and felt his heart begin to beat faster in anticipation as he gripped his hand around the thick metal handle. As he rotated it, the heavy mechanism crunched, and the rusted hinges squeaked loudly before the latch finally clicked and unlocked. He wrenched the hatch open and a mass of cold air hit him square in the face.

After years of breathing in the same stale air, save for the odd wisp that spiralled down from the skylight, the sensation was a thing of beauty. It caused goosebumps to spread up his arms and prickle up the back of his neck.

On any given day, this small taste of the outside world would have been enough to satisfy Gavril's curiosity, but not today. Today, he had a plan - a plan that would prove to his father once and for all that he was ready to do more than simply tighten bolts and prune leaves day in day out.

Brimming with purpose, Gavril pulled himself cautiously through the opening and onto the soft, granulated floor. Solid stone still formed a canopy over his head but to his right, he saw light spilling down a path that meandered slowly upwards.

Drawn like a moth to a flame, Gavril stumbled towards the faint light as the passage began to inch wider. The unfamiliar terrain, which was composed of what looked like black sand and minuscule rocks, pooled around his boots as he pushed himself upwards.

He was filled with excitement.

Overflowing with a longing to see the place he had been denied all these years.

Without realising, Gavril had lowered his body to the ground and was pulling himself up the incline on both his hands and feet as the loose earth sprayed out behind him - he was an animal, brimming with bloodlust. His prey was finally within his grasp.

Finally, he emerged triumphantly from the cave mouth and was met with a sight that almost overwhelmed each and every one of his senses.

The strength he had mustered in the passage suddenly disappeared and his knees began to shake. Uncontrollably, Gavril slumped to the floor as the ground scraped against the metal plating of his legs and parted two perpendicular pits beneath him.

Kneeling there, as his heart pounded in his chest, Gavril allowed his quickly adjusting eyes to drink in every detail of what spanned out in front of him.

Bathed in a dim white light was the cold and barren landscape as promised. An unending, lifeless sea of grey and black, starkly contrasting the cosy and luscious home that he had left buried over a hundred metres behind him.

Skewed metal pillars, like the pikes and spears of a fallen army, stuck awkwardly skyward amongst the mounds of rusted debris, as the gentle, mournful grey wind whistled quietly over the ancient battlefield.

The wind not only brought the tang of rust rushing into his nostrils but also carried a new scent that was quite unfamiliar to him. It was an empty smell, completely devoid of life.

Gavril didn't know it then, but the smell was of death - this planet reeked of it.

Pulling his eyes up, as the lids tried relentlessly to close down on them, the vast masses of grey clouds that stretched for miles above careered silently past a barely visible black and blue sky.

The faint light that was still partially hidden behind one of the smaller clouds shone weakly through some of the less dense, opaque patches and as the wind blew towards the distant horizon, the source peeked into view and stung Gavril's wide and unblinking eyes.

It was a moon, quite unlike any he had seen in "Astrology Through the Ages". Those were depicted as beautifully bright floating orbs - their smooth ice white surfaces peppered with impact craters of all shapes and sizes after protecting their planetoid captors for hundreds of millions of years.

This one however, looked just like the planet that it circled above - defeated.

It was shattered into several greyish, angry looking pieces, like a dropped china plate against a pitch-black floor, with many of the continent sized fragments creating spiralled tails of rock that drifted into the darkness of space as they fought desperately against the planet's gravitational tether.

All of these sights, both above and below, should have struck Gavril as bad omens for the things to come, but somehow, they didn't.

He was looking at all of this with virgin eyes. The eyes of a ten-year-old boy who knew nothing but the cave behind him. Somehow despite the total destruction of this broken place, Gavril still found beauty in it.

As his breathing calmed and the anxious shaking of his extremities lessened, Gavril's gaze slowly drifted back down below the horizon's irregular line and his attention was drawn like a magnet to a collection of low-lying buildings in the distance.

With his six-hour window slowly ticking away, Gavril got tentatively to his feet and began to descend the hillside in their direction.

There would be time for more sightseeing, he thought, when he returned triumphantly at a later date with his father.

Gavril didn't know how long it had taken to cross the distance between the cave mouth and the outskirts of the collection of structures, but he knew it would have been shorter had living inside for all of his life not manifested as slight agoraphobia. As such, the open sky above shot fear throughout his body every time his brain focused on the vast nothingness swimming in his peripherals.

Gavril had no choice but to lock his eyes on the ground every few seconds as waves of anxiety came crashing down upon his shoulders. He tried to shake the nightmarish visions of his body floating up into the sky and being swallowed up by all that emptiness, but they clung on defiantly - ratcheting up and up until Gavril could see almost nothing else.

He was truly thankful when he finally reached the closest building and placed his hand upon the cold, solid concrete wall. Whilst artificially formed, the stone was familiar. It anchored him and calmed his racing imagination. Finally, his quivering legs steadied, and his back gave a sigh of relief as the weight of the empty sky evaporated.

With his confidence and composure regained, Gavril put on his determined head once more and spotted a nearby doorway, barely peeking above the blackened earth which led into the structures interior.

He dashed forward, dipping his head underneath the half-submerged archway and was bathed in the interior's darkness.

It took barely a second for Gavril's eyes to adjust this time.

He was standing in a large, enclosed space, with a buckled ceiling of concrete and steel that bowed downwards as it cupped the weight of the earth pushing down upon it from above. This, coupled with the black dirt and rocks that were blown inevitably through the open doorway, meant that the ceiling height was reduced, in Gavril's opinion, to a comfortable one and a half metres.

Hopefully, he scanned his eyes about the place; They were darting amongst each of the rusted and broken objects at his feet, looking for something or anything of value - for this was Gavril's plan. If he could find something useful and return it unscathed to his father, then surely that would be proof enough that he was ready to play a larger role?

Gavril believed so.

However, the longer he looked, the more Gavril realised that this structure was not going to be the keeper of such a treasure. If there were any objects that were worth salvaging here, they would more than likely be buried underneath the thick swathe of dirt that lapped up the edges of each of the four short walls and Gavril just didn't have the time for digging. He had wasted too much time already.

After kicking his feet defeatedly through the indistinguishable rusted items, as if searching for bones in the embers of a burnt-out campfire, Gavril abandoned the room and carefully moved through into the adjoining one.

A grin split across his face as he slid gracefully down the slope of earth at the entrance. He spread his arms wide like those wings of a bird and swooped downwards into the dark space, as a giggle threatened to burst from behind his lips. He was a child after all.

The squat room that Gavril descended down into did not have any other openings and the faint moonlight was barely able to sneak through the odd crack in the sturdy, thick walls.

Gliding to a halt, he scanned his eyes about and was pleased to find that due to the single sloping entrance, the place was not nearly as submerged as the former had been. The tops of time worn furniture could still be seen peeking out of the earth as if scrabbling for a last gasp of air before being pulled beneath the surface. The few survivors, several aged filing cabinets, leant at odd angles towards the back of the room.

Unfortunately, as he approached, Gavril could see that someone had gotten there first as each and every drawer had been pulled open and their innards, save for the perished piles of decayed paper, were picked clean.

Gavril knew instantly this was his father's doing - the scratches, hastily cut into the sides of the steel cabinet as he grabbed at the contents, were like a sign-off. A signature scribbled by the man's clawed gauntlets.

Feeling slightly disappointed, Gavril turned and retraced his steps back up the slope. He trudged his feet sourly into the earth displacing the playful sweeping lines that had been cut by his jovial entry, all the while a nagging feeling in the back of his mind kept thumping into the foreground. What if every building in the vicinity of their home turned out to be the same? Surely, his father had not been able to loot every single one of them?

But even as he tried to reassure himself, Gavril remembered that Hadwin had been doing this for years, not just a couple of hours like he had...

Slightly disheartened, Gavril stepped back out into the open air and gripped his hands around the jagged archway for support.

He focused his eyes on an edifice, towering high over the other roofs in the distance - with its multitude of floors and minimal number of windows, Gavril was able to reassure his doubts that he was bound to find something there.

With a deep breath, he lowered his head, determined to stop his mind from gravitating upwards into nothingness, and made his way forward, keeping one comforting hand running across the wall beside him.

The concrete was smooth under his fingertips; it was polished from centuries of minute rocks and grit being blown against its surface. He continued to skim the surfaces, jumping from building to building until his hand grazed upon something coarse. Something that threatened to cut at his thin digits as they scraped over the sharpened edge.

Gavril slowly rounded his head to see the full extent of the imperfection. Slicing through the steel rebar reinforcement and exposing the faint moonlight on the broken street beyond were two long slashes cut deep into the thick stone wall. Accompanied on either side by several shallower gouges, the criss-crossed lines cut across one another as if something had frantically struggled to claw its way through.

Instinctively, Gavril felt a surge of adrenalin rush up his arm as his hand disconnected from the wall.

Something summoned up from the bowels of his memories made Gavril feel like he had seen this kind of damage before, but as he stood there transfixed, searching backwards in his mind, he found that he could not remember where. All he knew was that an inexplicable fear had gripped him tight and squeezed the breath from him like the ringing of a sponge.

His father had told him about the damage that flying debris caused during a storm, and as his personal experience of this was limited to the muted clashes and booms that he heard as he lay in the safety of his bed, he settled on this as the cause.

That must be it, he thought to himself, high speed flying debris. The fact that they resembled long claw marks must have been purely coincidental.

Only partially satisfied with this conclusion, as that niggling feeling of familiarity in the back of his mind persisted, Gavril wrenched his attention back to the matter at hand and continued onward until he was awash by the shadow of the towering building.

Staring upwards, Gavril couldn't help but marvel at the architecture of this place. Yes, it's outer shell was pock marked from the elements and parts of the upper floors had clearly collapsed sideways reducing the adjoining building to rubble, but if what his father had told him was accurate? That it had been built well over one hundred years ago was an impressive feat of engineering by anyone's standards.

Gavril had always been fascinated by how things were made, which was something that his father had found to be immensely frustrating over the years, as almost every object that he brought back for him would be broken down into its individual pieces by morning.

Interrupting Gavril's adoration, however, was a loud crash that caused him to quickly whip his head around - a plume of dust was rising from a mound of newly fallen stone blocks a short way away. For all their resilience, the surrounding structures clearly had their limits.

After making a mental note to tread a little more cautiously, Gavril walked across the darkened street and entered the imposing building through the tall double doors at it's base.

The foundations of this place had obviously been positioned on higher ground than that of the others, as only a marginal amount of dust covered the smooth tiled floor.

Shielded from the gentle whistling of wind that flowed over the landscape, the grit crunched under Gavril's boots and echoed loudly around the cavernous entrance hall. Every sound could now be heard in deafening clarity - from the ominous creaking of the building to the breath rattling loudly past Gavril's teeth as he approached the central staircase.

As he took hold of the rusted bannister and rose his foot to the first step, Gavril decided that it was probably best to air on the side of caution and climb several floors before beginning his search. His father would almost certainly have stripped the low-lying floors and there was a chance, he hoped, that after climbing several flights of stairs that Hadwin's exhaustion would have contributed to a less thorough search.

After reaching the landing of what had to be the eighth or ninth floor, Gavril passed down a metal lined corridor as strips of light cut through the long darkness like swords.

Every few metres, the glossy floor was strewn with shattered pieces of glass which cracked and crunched loudly underfoot. The wide, empty frames that once housed them cut through the adjacent walls, giving Gavril a view of impressively large space that spanned almost the whole width of the building.

Ancient furniture lay upturned and mummified beneath thick layers of dust, and just as with the last building, Gavril could spot the tell-tale signs that these too had been pillaged.

The specks of white light from the moon were beginning to fade and Gavril could see the amber sun was hot on it's heels. Morning was coming and he was still no closer to finding anything of value in this place.

"Just a little longer" Gavril muttered to himself quietly, trying to quash the thought of not being back home when his father woke.

After reaching the end of the corridor, Gavril turned to the left and saw to his surprise an undamaged, closed door staring back at him from the end of the hallway. An unopened door was a good sign as he doubted very much that his father would have taken the time to close a door behind him, so whatever treasures the room may be hiding might be undisturbed and ripe for the taking.

Approaching the pristine doorway, Gavril heard a crash from what he could only assume was an upper floor - the building might not have been as stable as he had first thought and with that fresh in his mind, he hurriedly reached out and grabbed the rusted bronze handle.

With almost overwhelming excitement that prickled at his fingertips like electricity, he turned it counterclockwise and pulled the handle towards his chest which sent a cracking noise spinning along the frame. A small hiss rasped round the edges and the door swung open.

It took a small moment for Gavril's eyes to adjust to the pitch-black darkness that enveloped the room, as a stench of musty air poured out.

Gavril, who had experienced his fair share of wonders in the past few hours, couldn't help being bowled over by what lay before him. He had spent countless hours dreaming about the old world and the people that had once inhabited it. Now, here he was, standing in front of a room completely frozen in time, looking just as it must have over a century ago.

Gavril stepped into the room and felt his feet sink slightly.

Looking down, he saw that the floor was covered in a thick layer of deep blue fabric that seemed to swallow the sole of his shoes. Even to someone like Gavril, who had no concept of the finer things in life, this screamed of wealth and luxury.

An overwhelming urge to fall onto his front and bury his face into the soft pile tugged at his shoulders, but after a quick check of his internal clock, Gavril knew that he didn't have time for that sort of immature nonsense. At only ten years old, this level of control was impressive.

A solid granite table, covered in a thin layer of dust, wrapped around the entire back wall. It was encircling a single, deep brown leather chair that, unlike the rest of the room, was showing its age.

Stepping through the cushioned ground, Gavril reached forward and gripped his hand around the once supple backrest. The material, which was cracked and dry like the surface of drought ridden soil, perished instantly beneath his fingertips as he spun it round. Dishevelled fragments fell sympathetically to the movement, creating a sweeping arc of dust which floated down and disappeared into the depths of the decadent floor.

At that moment, Gavril felt utterly powerless to stop himself.

Begrudgingly, he gave into his childish urges and hopped into the chair, allowing the buried, ancient springs to wrap around his behind. The ancient leather continued to crumble and billowed up into a small cloud as he leant into the enjoyment and spun happily around, giggling wildly to himself.

This was as close as he could ever get to being one of those people that his father had told him about. Those who had squandered this planet and made the surface unliveable.

As the chair finally came to a stop, Gavril's thoughts snapped back to reality and he dragged himself forward to the desk's edge, his face now serious and purposeful.

A thin rectangular piece of glass sat atop the sleek surface and despite being masked by the thin layer of dust, it still was able to shine defiantly, reflecting the hints of light peeking in from behind Gavril's shoulders.

This could be it - the salvage that cemented the notion to his father that he was ready.

Gavril reached his left index finger forward and gently tapped the corner of the strange glinting object. What happened next made him instinctively push himself away from the desk with strength he didn't know that he possessed.

The chair keeled over immediately, sending him tumbling backwards into a heap upon the soft floor as the once dark room was now flooded with light. Gavril righted himself and peeked his goggled face cautiously over the toppled chair, feeling his pupils quickly shrink to the size of pin pricks as they struggled to contend with such an abrupt change in input.

Solid beams of white light were emanating from the thin slither of glass; It was almost as if the surface of the desk had suddenly become a window to a sun filled sky miles above.

The columns of light twisted and sharpened into various shapes that hung in mid-air like lanterns as their bluish hue shimmered across the ceiling like the surfaces were now made of water.

After a few moments of heavy breathing, as his heart beat unfathomably hard in his chest, Gavril tilted his head to the side and felt his body relax slightly. Somehow, he actually recognised some of the squiggles of light that were gradually scrolling in front of his face.

They were words. Lines and lines of them. Just like those printed in the several books he had back at home.

Captivated, Gavril moved closer and raised his hand to help him track the indecipherable letters as they moved sideways across the room.

Just as the complex words reached the rightest edge of the projection, Gavril's outstretched fingertip cut through the beam and, as if reacting to his presence, the images began to change. Suddenly, new lines of text and complex diagrams slid across the back wall. These were just as baffling to Gavril as the previous page had been. However, there seemed to be something urgent to the uppermost line which, unlike the others, flashed red every few seconds and drew uncontrollably at his focus.

"E...evac...evacua..." fumbled Gavril, trying to speak the unknown word aloud.

However, before he could get the full pronunciation out, a nearby crash shook the ground beneath his feet. It shivered up his legs and rattled the fragmented word from his lips and thoughts.

Quickly, Gavril slid his fingers under the edge of the glass device, and he lifted it from the table. As it separated, the light powered down with a faint whoosh, plunging Gavril and the room back into darkness.

The shuddering continued. Swelling in peaks and troughs of intensity as Gavril's heart beat frantically.

A loud drumming sound began to reverberate down the long corridor, causing the distant shards of broken glass to quiver and crawl towards one another like fear stuck beetles.

Louder and louder the noise grew. Like a blacksmith's hammer beating against an anvil. Over and over.

Someone, or something, was approaching...

Gavril hastily smuggled the device into a pouch on the inside of his jacket before springing effortlessly across the room and crouching behind a low metal cabinet.

A few of the tablets projected shapes still burned like darkened spots in his vision as he peeked over the edge and stared down the sparsely lit corridor.

At the end of the hall, visible only by the few streaks of light that cut across the space, a figure suddenly rounded the corner and came to a stop.

Almost instinctively, Gavril relaxed.

Though he could only see the towering form's outline, at this distance it was familiar in size and shape to that of Hadwin. But as he began to extend his legs and open his mouth to call out to his father, Gavril was suddenly frozen with terror.

The once squat form of his father began to stretch high into the air and, like a spider hidden within a hole, spindly limbs reached out from the darkness and stabbed viscously into the concrete floor.

This was definitely not his father.

Gavril's legs instinctively constricted and lowered him back down the few centimetres he had risen. With eyes wide, he watched as a further pair of arms protruded from the creature's back, seconds before a bright light exploded from it's centre, bathing the whole floor in searing red beams.

Gavril had seen enough. He slid down onto the soft floor and propped his back against the steel cabinet as the blinding lights reflected off the polished walls of the room's interior and into his eyes.

All the confidence that had been billowing inside him had suddenly disappeared. Now all that was left was a scared, helpless boy who knew that he should have listened to his father.

CHAPTER 6 - The Father

Hadwin found himself standing in the centre of their ransacked home, staring over the devastation that reached out into every corner of the cavernous curved room.

It was as if a bomb had detonated beneath the atrium's ceiling, vaporising the small reservoir and leaving a shallow, dried-out well in it's place.

Their garden was uprooted, and the leaves cracked loudly in smouldering, fiery piles that littered the charred floor in every direction. The columns of smoke rising from them looked like the many trunks and boughs of grey-barked trees as they weaved upwards towards the skylight. Hadwin followed them up to find the shattered mirror overhead, swinging silently under a cloud free, starless night sky. His many fractured reflections stared down at him; all pale and ghostly-white amongst the warm red of the blaze.

So, it had finally happened. They had found them.

But how? Hadwin asked himself.

He had always been so careful - covering every track and trace of his movements above ground.

It was then that he spotted the door to Gavril's room ahead, hanging awkwardly off its hinges with several large angry gouges cut through the plating.

The blame and guilt was promptly whisked away. It didn't matter how, only that it had happened.

Hadwin stood there, as still as a statue, staring at the mangled opening, knowing exactly what this damage meant.

He didn't need to see what lay beyond. He didn't want to either. However, despite his wishes, his legs seemed to have other ideas as they suddenly ushered him forward.

Prolonging the inevitable, Hadwin paused for a moment and reached out a hand to touch one of the jagged marks left by the machines.

As his index finger connected with the sharp metal, he felt a searing pain course through him like an electrical current that was desperately seeking the ground at his feet. Instead of instinctively clutching at the injured hand, however, Hadwin found that his other digits were clasped around the top of his thigh as a dull ache drummed at his flesh. But as quickly as the pain had come, it was suddenly gone, a passing thought amongst the many flooding his mind at that exact moment.

Without giving it a second thought, Hadwin pushed aside the beaten door and stepped into the shallow room.

Of all the things Hadwin had expected to find there, his son, alive, was not one of them, but there he was, cross-legged in the centre of the bedroom, his head hung low as his shoulders rose and fell with each of his small breaths.

It took a few seconds for Hadwin's eyes to move from the boy to his surroundings - a thick pool of red blood, creeping further and further outwards from beneath him.

As Hadwin watched the blood inch towards his toes, he saw Gavril in his peripherals, slowly raising his head.

His nose was the first to break through the shroud of hair. It parted the two sides revealing a cold, almost blue, visage.

Something was wrong.

The boy's eyes shot like daggers through the strands of brown, cutting a gaze that locked with Hadwin's just as they had done all those years ago as the machines waited just beyond his front door.

Unlike that night however, Gavril's eyes were not glistening with innocence or curiosity. The thin slithers visible to Hadwin were filled with unfamiliar and uncharacteristic emotions for the boy - hate and anger. Mirroring this was the scowl etched deeply across every feature and line of his miniature face as his hair blew aside.

Before Hadwin could speak, Gavril opened his mouth and let out a deafening cry that shook the room's furniture and sent ripples across the surface of the blood.

"HOW COULD YOU LEAVE ME?!" he screamed.

Every ear-splitting word was blown through the open doorway on a wave of wind that snuffed out all the fires and plunged the home into a cold, monochrome pallet.

Gavril's eyes seemed to be the only thing that retained any colour, bursting forth with bright green flames that licked out of his sockets and up onto his forehead.

As their light grew brighter, Hadwin found himself uncontrollably rising up off of the ground. It was as if an invisible hand had grabbed him round the waist, hoisted him into the air and proceeded to dangle him halfway between the stone floor and ceiling.

Helplessly, he thrashed his arms and legs around in mid-air but, as if he was trying to pull each limb through water, his motions were slow and subdued.

Hadwin wanted to reply, wanted to apologise, but as he opened his mouth to do so, a screech filled the space - a giant's mechanised screech that had haunted Hadwin for all these years - and he was sent hurtling backwards through the doorway like a human missile.

Streaking through the now deathly dark atrium, with Gavril's room now a fiery green inferno between his feet, he crashed into the surprisingly soft door of his own room.

Hadwin shuddered violently awake, gasping loudly, as if he was on the cusp of drowning.

He was drenched in a cold sweat that soaked uncomfortably into the uneven sprung mattress and his bed covers were wound so tightly around his body that they bound both of his arms to his side.

Hadwin rolled to one side, freeing the blanket and threw it back almost disgustedly.

He let out a long sigh and raised his hands to his forehead. Thick tails of sodden hair clung to his tepid skin.

As the shock of the dream faded, Hadwin looked down to see that a few droplets of rich red blood had splattered against the dirtied sheets and after shifting his body, he saw that one of the stitches had worked its way loose and now stuck out awkwardly from the wound.

Hadwin slid a cautious hand down and his fingertip brushed against the splayed thread. As he did, the searing pain from his dream flashed down his side.

At least that part of it could now be explained, but what about the rest. What about Gavril?

Rarely a night passed when Hadwin was not plagued by nightmares, but this one felt somewhat different. His dreams usually centred around some form of unending chase across the landscape above, culminating, as expected from such nightmares, in a variety of different gruesome and painful ends. But not once since that night ten years ago, when he had finally patched up the last tunnel with metal plating and covered the exterior with dirt and rocks, had Hadwin been worried about being found in this place. He knew that deep within the confines of their subterranean home that nothing like what his subconscious had just dreamt up for him, would ever happen.

However, lying there rubbing his thumb and forefinger against the bridge of his nose, Hadwin couldn't shake the feeling that something had changed and that the words that Gavril spoke in his dream were his mind trying to tell him something he had missed.

Maybe he had been too hard on the boy. Was that it? he asked himself.

Hadwin did sympathise with Gavril's longing to explore. The majority of his own life had been spent above ground and he was painfully aware that if the roles were reversed that he too might be acting the same way as his son.

But their childhoods differed greatly. Hadwin didn't have a target on his back like Gavril did. If he were to learn the truth about the horrors that searched for him night and day out there, he might not feel the same attraction to see more of it.

Maybe this was as good a time as any to tell the boy. Before he inevitably took matters into his own hands.

With a deep sigh, Hadwin hauled himself out of bed, pulled a heavily stained shirt over his extensively scarred torso and opened the bedroom door.

To his relief, he found the main cavern intact. A dim column of reddening sunlight danced across the undisturbed garden without a single fire in sight. At least this was proof that the dream had been just that.

He crossed towards Gavril's room, not really wanting to wake him, but he knew that he had to get this out of the way as soon as possible. His cautious mind had the tendency to populate itself with feelings of apprehension and doubt when this particular truth was hidden just behind his lips.

It was then, as Hadwin was still rubbing the evidence of his sleep from his eyes, that he caught sight of the open door to Gavril's room and the empty bed that lay beyond.

"Gavril!" he yelled towards the room as flashes of his dream sprung up in his mind.

There was no answer.

Hadwin quickly pushed his way inside and checked behind the door as hints of a nervous smile pulled at the corners of his mouth. He didn't want to scare the boy if he was just playing a practical joke on him. But the smile soon vanished when there was no sudden appearance or call of surprise from the boy.

"GAVRIL!!" he called out again, his voice louder and now with fear saturating every inflection.

The call echoed loudly around the chamber before trailing off backwards down the many passages. Yet there was still no response.

Hadwin knew that whatever frustration Gavril had been feeling towards him earlier, it wouldn't have stopped him from answering.

Where could he be? Hadwin asked himself.

"A couple of years!? I can't wait that long!"

The colour drained from his face as if he had been plunged into an ice-cold bath.

Like a man possessed, Hadwin shoulder barged the partially open door to his room, threw on his armour and sprinted back out. He was sure he felt another stitch pop loose as his legs scrambled him hurriedly down the nearest passageway, but he was so disconnected from everything to even care.

With both hands, he frantically tried to secure the fastenings across his chest and after taking his eyes off the tunnel for a fraction of a second, he felt his temple strike against something solid and a flash of light filled his eyes. A low hanging mirror was struck from its frame and it shattered loudly behind him, sending fragments of glass bouncing down the path. But Hadwin didn't even look back. Nothing else mattered to him in the world.

Manoeuvring his way down the corridor, Hadwin started to become more and more aware of a change to the air flow that was passing down the tunnel. The fact that his face was being brushed by a gentle breeze was a bad sign and when turning the final corner, his worst suspicions were confirmed - the outer hatch stood ajar and a chill air was blowing creepily through the opening.

"No, no, no…" pleaded Hadwin desperately and pointlessly as he approached the door.

In disbelief, Hadwin slowly placed his shaking hands upon the hatch, wondering whether or not he was still dreaming. The steel was cold to the touch and the hinges whined like a wounded animal as they moved under his influence. This wasn't a dream.

What was the boy thinking? Had his words of warning over the last ten years really fallen on deaf ears?

Hadwin could feel anger quickly creeping up inside of him until it throttled his senses. He clenched one hand into a fist and struck the hatch hard. The thick rim chipped violently into the tunnel wall and dislodged several stone fragments.

Now fuelled by frustration, Hadwin hurriedly clambered through the opening, all the while ignoring the small part of his brain that was attempting to remind him to shut the door behind him.

He bounded up the pathway with his breath blasting angrily out of his flared nostrils as he kept one eye fixed on the child shaped footprints stamped into the ground.

The familiar sight of the open landscape did not faze Hadwin, however, it did go some ways towards tempering his fury. He knew that with such a vast place to search, this was not a good time to lose his head or begin placing blame. Gavril was only a child after all. Clever, headstrong and sometimes petulant, but a child, nonetheless.

As Hadwin followed the small footsteps, innocently and

unknowingly twisting their way down the slope, the oppressive guilt that he had been feeling upon waking returned.

Hadwin realised quickly that the anger he felt only moments ago was warranted, just somewhat misdirected - he wasn't angry at Gavril, he was angry at himself.

He was the one to blame.

His selfish fear for the boy's welfare had led to him locking him away inside that mountain and keeping the truth of his origins and situation from him. Had he told the boy earlier instead of keeping him in the dark, this defiant act might have been averted.

Hadwin shook these thoughts from his mind for the moment and lifted his gaze from the gravelled earth. There would be time for remorse later, he told himself.

He stared down into the valley, looking for anything that might have piqued Gavril's interest - not that this really helped as Hadwin knew full well that everything up here would have been of interest to his inquisitive son.

In the distance, a small cluster of buildings sat in contrast against the sweeping smooth dunes of dust and stones. Hadwin, having combed through their innards on many occasions, knew them well. However, as he narrowed his eyes onto them, he saw something that was out of place. Something that flooded his body with eye popping levels of adrenalin and sent him careering down the hillside in swift, frantic bounds.

High in the remains of the tall skyscraper, dazzling brightly amongst the mass of grey concrete, was a singular sweeping red light.

*

On the eighth floor, in the windowless room, Gavril was crouched motionless behind the low cabinet as the lasers continued to scan across the pristine walls.

Fear had consumed every one of his muscles.

Even if by some miracle there was a chance that he could escape,

Gavril wasn't sure that his body would comply. His knees were pulled close to his chest and his lungs were helplessly holding on to the same breath that he had hastily gasped in at the sight of the creature's deadly bladed arms.

A drone of ear-splitting thuds boomed down the hallway and with each one, the ground trembled with growing intensity. This told Gavril one thing; whatever this bladed, mechanical creature was... it was getting closer.

The red light grew brighter and brighter until the room burned all around him like the inside of a raging fire. Blinded, Gavril clenched his eyes shut as tears began to run down his cheeks and pool at the corners of his mouth.

Despite knowing that it would probably give away his position, Gavril couldn't help but let out a tiny sob which sprayed flecks of saliva out from between his teeth and onto the fiery floor.

As expected, the sound didn't go unnoticed.

The mechanical figure let out an unearthly screech and judging from the chaotic noise that met Gavril's ears, began slashing those vicious limbs into the room.

Gavril cracked open his eyes and watched as fragments of plaster from the walls and ceiling bounced across the surface of the granite tabletop. Splintered wood from the century old door fell to the floor and stood up like miniature pikes amongst the carpet's deep pile.

The metal cabinet he was hiding behind suddenly gave a shudder, signalling that the creature was only steps behind.

The jig was up, Gavril thought. Within seconds, he would be joining the fallen debris on the soft floor. There was no point in hiding now. If this was to be his end, the least he could do was face it with an ounce of dignity.

And so, the ten-year old boy summoned up the last morsel of courage that he had left, wrenched his locked legs free and stood up shakily to face the monstrous creature and what he assumed would be his death.

However, what looked back at him wasn't the mechanical creature at all. To his surprise, all that stretched out before him was an empty corridor, the floor and walls on either side massacred by long swipes and slashes.

Standing there a little dumbfounded, his face pale and prickling, Gavril caught a momentary glimpse of the figure's long shadow disappearing from view at the end of the hall.

He let out a rasp of relief and his starving lungs quickly began to take in as much air as possible.

After a moment, his mind now brimming with oxygen, Gavril began to try and fathom what had just happened. Was this the thing that Hadwin had been keeping from him all along? And what was the reason for it's hasty departure when it had been just inches from him?

The answer to both of these questions promptly met his still throbbing ears.

Gavril flew out of the room, quickly ran towards the nearest window frame and craned his neck out as far as possible before his tiptoes began to slip precariously on the polished floor.

His father was below, clad in his thick blackened armour, standing like a boulder between two crumbled buildings and bellowing words that seemed to shake at every part of his body.

"HEY! HERE, I'M HERE! IT'S ME YOU WANT!"

Even at this distance, Gavril could hear the desperation ripping at his father's throat. It curdled his blood. His pain was discernible amongst every syllable.

Moments later, the entrance hall doors were blown off their hinges and sent spiralling high into the air. They landed amongst the ruins with a loud crash which sent dust flying in all directions.

Gavril watched as his father, just beyond the billowing mottle of grey and black, turned about-face and sprinted into the town's rubbly remains.

The machine, now fully visible in the soft moonlight, cut through the cloud like a shining spectre. It sliced after him with frightening purpose as the four bladed arms protruding from it's segmented body propelled it forward, ripping deadly gouges into the ground as it went.

Gavril tore back down the corridor and frantically began descending the numerous flights of stairs as if his life depended on it. But the fear for his own life was now a distant memory. He knew that without help, his father was going to meet the same end that up until moments ago, huddled petrified behind that cabinet, had been reserved for him.

As Gavril bounded down the stairs, the tears that he had managed to stifle in the office threatened to shake themselves free as every step vibrated up through his body. He knew that it was his childish obsession to prove himself that had gotten him into this situation and whatever the outcome of this chase was, the blame rested squarely on his shoulders.

Gavril tapped the waterworks back, focusing instead on his descent as he began to jump down three to four steps at a time.

He flew out of what remained of the battered entrance hall like a bull freed from it's pen and quickly sped along the street after the pair.

As Gavril passed down the darkened streets, however, clambering frantically over mounds of fallen bricks and debris, the tracks of the machine became harder for him to distinguish from the damage caused by the other recent collapses. Panting loudly, he reached a crossway between four of the tall buildings, then heard a scream that stopped him dead in his tracks. The deep pained howl reverberated down the alley; easily recognisable as Hadwin's deep guttural tone.

He didn't need tracks anymore. As painful as it was to hear, Gavril was able to home in on his father's location like a hound to it's master's call.

Rounding a corner, Gavril was welcomed by moonlight into a large flattened space between several clustered buildings. The other adjoining streets, all eerie and still, ran to this place like the spokes of a giant stone wheel.

Deeply pressed footprints guided Gavril's gaze to the opposite side of the clearing where the shining machine now stood with one of it's long, thin bladed arms pierced straight through his father's shoulder. It had pinned him high against the cracked concrete and like a long, ragged red cape, Gavril could see a river of his blood painting the stone wall behind him.

As Gavril rushed forward, his father caught sight of him, and he watched as his expression softened despite the blade continuing to cut at his chest.

Quickly, he gestured to Gavril with a slight raise of his palm.

This time Gavril did as he was told and slid silently to a stop next to the closest building.

All he could do now was watch as the face of the mechanical creature began to send the red laser beams across the contours of Hadwin's body, examining every inch of the helpless, writhing man.

It was torture for Gavril to be so close and yet commanded by such a small movement to stay away.

After a few moments, as the machine was seemingly finished with its inspection, the red lights diminished with an internal whirr and it pulled it's arm out of Hadwin's shoulder, sending him slumping awkwardly to the ground.

Hadwin let out a moan that pulled at Gavril's upper body as his feet shifted impatiently in the earth. He wanted to help but felt powerless against both his father's command and the towering machine.

A few seconds of silence passed as Hadwin clutched helplessly at the open wound and stared across the dawn filled space to his son. Unaware, the robot suddenly reared up on it's hind legs and raised both bladed arms up, ready to deliver the finishing blow to it's defeated prey.

"NOOOOO!" screeched the small boy, unable to hold the plea within his chest.

Once more, Gavril found himself disobeying his father as he tore forward to help.

As the machine hesitated and began to twist it's body to face the origin of this new sound, Gavril's legs shot him across the clearing at a speed that he didn't know he was capable of. He was now nothing more than a blur, streaking across the space like a comet.

Mere steps away, as he drew the small knife from his waist, the ground at Gavril's feet trembled before cracking audibly like the surface of broken ice as he pushed off and leapt high into the air.

Small glints of inexplicable green light glinted back at him across the machine's body as Gavril soared the distance at easily four times his own height. He raised the rather pitiful looking knife between his clenched fists - ready to do whatever he could to the robot who seemed intent on taking his father's life. But unfortunately, despite all of his determination, Gavril's catapulted body and drawn knife never reached their mark.

Suddenly, all of his forward motion was suddenly halted as if he had struck an invisible wall.

Gavril hung there, wide eyed and confused, suspended several feet from the machine's collection of sensors and lights as a white-hot pain shot through his chest.

A silvery arm, bladed and true, held him high off the ground as it had done his father.

Gavril let out a cough and felt blood splutter from his lips as the knife edge burst out the other side of his body.

Lowering his gaze, he could see his father's face full of despair as he screamed uncontrollably at the sight. But to Gavril, it was as if someone had turned down the volume of everything around him as all he could hear was the slowly diminishing thudding of his heart against his ears.

Blood dripped from his bottom lip as he tried to mouth an apology to his father, but the shape of the words wouldn't come - his face was slumping as his life inched away from him.

Weakly, Gavril rolled his head back towards his killer and watched as blood began to trickle slowly down it's unmoving metallic arm.

It didn't seem real, like he was watching it happen to someone else.

Just as the beating of his ear drums seemed to thump their last and his eyes began to close around the image of this silvery creature, Gavril felt something strange swell deep inside of him - a warmth that pooled around the angry wound beneath his armour and pulled itself to the surface of his skin.

Gavril felt his eyes widen as light doused his vision. He could now see those familiar bright flickers of green light reflected in the robot's polished plating again and Hadwin's quickly widening eyes beside him.

With energy that he thought had been snuffed out, Gavril lifted his head and watched as strings of this light began travelling up his arms and legs. They snaked their way upwards and wound around the razor-sharp slither of metal that still remained motionless in his chest.

Gavril wanted to speak, wanted to ask his father what was happening, but the metal impaled through the centre of chest continued to put a stop to that.

Silently, the individual sparks of what looked like electricity began to slither their way along the robot's arm, becoming intertwined like strands of matted hair as they burrowed between the gaps in the creature's metallic plating.

As they reached it's segmented body, Hadwin, who was still huddled on the floor clutching at his own injury, had to raise a bloodied hand up to cover his eyes as an aura of light exploded from his son's chest.

Through the minuscule gaps between his fingers, Hadwin could see the street was ablaze with green light. Where he expected such intense light to be accompanied by heat, he was surprised to feel a gentle breeze whisking past the palm of his hand, drying the thin layer of his blood that now clung there.

After a few seconds, the green light retreated back and returned the street to its former soft amber glow.

Hadwin dropped his hand cautiously and saw that his son and his attacker were frozen in the same position they had been before the light had swelled up around them, as if the scene had been carved out of stone.

Something about the robot, however, looked quite different.

The deep red that had glowed within the depths of its body had gone out and its armour seemed to have lost its shine. It now just looked like any one of the litany of scrap metal objects that covered the landscape. Statuesque and inert, standing above the flattened clearing.

Gavril let out a small cough which seemed to be just enough momentum to cause the machine to begin teetering on the edge of it's mechanical feet and the pair tumbled to the ground.

Gavril slid limply away from the arm of the now lifeless metal husk as it struck the floor and lay there, face down.

Darkness began to fill what vision he had left, but he felt his father grab hold of him and roll him over onto his back. As Hadwin's weeping face hung inches above his, he felt his father's hands wrap around the back of his head and pull him close.

Gavril mustered up the last ounce of strength that the strange light had provided and muttered what would surely be his final words into Hadwin's waiting ear.

"I am sorry, father."

CHAPTER 7 - The Wound

Darkness. Darkness was all that Gavril could see.

He could feel his eyeballs tugging weakly at the confines of their lids as they searched through the blackness for any shred of light.

He was comfortable, his body was without pain and surprisingly, he felt at ease.

Was this dying? He thought to himself.

With each passing moment, however, he started to become more aware of his extremities.

Perhaps it had all just been a dream and he was lying comfortably in the safety of his bed. The surface did feel soft and warm beneath his now moving fingertips, so it wasn't beyond the realms of possibility.

This hopeful optimism quickly began to fill him up and for a moment, Gavril became hesitant about the prospect of opening his eyes to face the truth. He wanted to simply lay there in blissful ignorance before the reality of his situation, whether good or bad, became something he had to deal with. Anyway, if it had all been a dream then what was the harm in having another five minutes in bed?

Despite this, whether intentional or not, narrow slithers of yellow light started to peek through the small openings that were forming in his vision.

As his eyes finally cracked themselves open, they were met with the softly lit ceiling of his room. The low curved stone, emblazoned with his coloured drawings, were a very welcome sight.

Gavril let out a sigh of relief. It had been a dream after all.

The sound of his escaping breath, however, seemed to stir something in the corner of the room and Gavril quickly became aware that he was not alone.

His joints in his neck were stiff and rubbed awkwardly against one another as he slowly creaked his head to the side to see what had made the sound - the image of his father, slumped low in a chair across the other side of the room, came sliding into view.

The hopeful dream was shattered as he spotted his father's arm hanging limply by his side. Blood, now blackened and thick, oozed slowly from the hastily bandaged wound on his shoulder.

Gavril traced the flow of blood with his eyes which ran down the length of Hadwin's arm in small streams before dripping from the tip of his fingers into a small puddle on the stone floor. Even in the dim light, Gavril could see that the edges of the pool were beginning to coagulate into a solid disk that shivered slightly with each subsequent drip.

How long had they both been lying there?

Gavril stared down and noticed the top of his own arrangement of bandages peeking from above the hem of his threadbare blanket.

He winced slightly as his mind flashed back to the bladed arm that had plucked him out of the air. The feel of the cold metal as it tore through both his armour and flesh alike.

He shouldn't be alive. His bones had been splintered, his skin flayed wide open and his organs easily punctured beyond repair.

It had almost certainly been a killing blow.

But here he was, pulling himself upright and running a hand gently across his bandaged chest - the fabric ever so slightly blood stained yet dry beneath his palm.

Bracing himself for a sharp pain, Gavril pressed his hand gently against the site of the injury and to his surprise, felt nothing. There was no spreading ache at the pressure. No sensation that even acknowledged the existence of an obscured wound.

Without another thought, Gavril threw back the covers and frantically began to grapple with the wrappings. He spun the bandages round and round his small frame until, at last, the tail end slid away to reveal a smooth and unblemished torso.

Gavril sat there staring down at his body, poking at the pinkish skin quite roughly in disbelief. Not even a scar remained to tell the tale of what had happened, only a few patches of dried blood clung on - imprinted to his skin like a wax etching of the bandage's overlapping folds and lines.

Could he have imagined the injury to be worse than it had actually been, or had that strange green light had something to do with why he was still alive?

As his mind raced, his eyes crossed to the slumped figure of his father leaking blood from a still present injury and the gravity of his condition immediately snapped Gavril back to reality.

The bed let out several high-pitched squeaks as Gavril scrambled feverishly across the covers and leapt down to his feet. He rushed to Hadwin's side, a stagnant smell of copper pounding his nose, and clenched gently at his shoulder to wake him.

Nothing. Not even a stir.

Gavril grabbed the slumped figure under the crook of each arm and heaved him up into a more upright position as his head lolled on a neck seemingly made of jelly.

The old man's eyes were like pits of black and cast deep shadows in the soft light of the room's single candle.

Flecks of dark blood coated the wiry hair protruding from Hadwin's chin, and his face was a pale chalky white beneath the matted spirals.

Gavril knew that he had to stop the bleeding, but the question was how he went about it. He had had no experience of deep, life threatening injuries like this. In fact, the only person he knew who did, the only other living person on this planet, was currently in no fit state to do anything about it.

"Father! Wake up!" he exclaimed loudly, coupled with a light shake in a further attempt to rouse Hadwin from his unconsciousness.

This time, his father stirred, and his eyelids began to flutter. His eyes spun around almost independently from one another, shifting in and out of focus until they finally met with the vivid green of Gavril's irises. After a few moments of processing, they widened, and his mouth inched open in sheer bewilderment. Clearly, he had not been expecting to see the face of his son looking back at him.

"Gavril...how?" Hadwin croaked weakly.

His eyes, bloodshot and dilated, darted from the boy's face down to his uninjured chest.

"Never mind about that," Gavril said dismissively.

One thing at a time, he told himself.

"We have to stop your bleeding!"

In his semi-conscious state, Hadwin looked for a moment like he was not willing to let this issue slide, but instead followed his son's suggestion and lifted a shaky finger towards Gavril's bed.

"The box, on the table. Urgh... bring it to me"

Judging by the pained expression and the tensing of the muscles in his neck as he spoke, every word was clearly agonising.

Hurriedly, Gavril dashed to the bedside table and swept up the small, unassuming metal box lying there. The tin was covered in different coloured bloodied fingerprints, some obviously older than others judging by their dry and darker tone.

Rushing back to Hadwin, Gavril popped the lid to reveal a number of thin curved metal needles and a spool of thread. He recognised it quickly as the set that Hadwin frequently used to repair his toy animal.

As he continued to stare from the immobilised man down to the collection of items now cupped in his hands, Gavril suddenly realised what his father was about to ask him to do.

"Now son, it is time for you to practise your sewing." Hadwin mumbled, before letting out a stifled laugh.

It was plain to see that even this short-lived laugh was immediately regretted, as his face contorted in pain and his body constricted.

Succumbing, Hadwin fell limply back into unconsciousness and his breath fell back to a weak rattle that brushed visibly past his scraggly beard.

"No, father!" Gavril pleaded.

"I don't know what I am doing with this!"

He shook him again, but it was no use. Hadwin was completely out cold.

Gavril pocketed the metal box before pulling on his father's uninjured arm and heaving him up over his shoulder.

It was a sight to behold - this barely four-foot boy carrying the bulky, towering man across the room with seeming ease.

Gavril, too, was slightly surprised with how effortless this task seemed to be for him but chalked his surprising strength up to the adrenalin that was undoubtedly coursing through his veins given the situation.

Gavril knew that if he was going to have to attempt to sow the torn pieces of flesh back together, that there would have a greater chance of success on a flat surface rather than awkwardly slouched over a chair. So, crossing to the bed, as several of the stone beads from earlier dug uncomfortably into his bare feet, Gavril lowered Hadwin gently onto the covers and straightened his legs.

Had the circumstances been different, Gavril may have found the rather awkward way his father hung over the end of the child sized bed to be quite funny, but there was no chance of happiness being derived in this room - not right now, in any case.

The petrified boy inched his hands tentatively towards the mass of sodden, maroon bandages and peeled back the first layer.

Each of the overlapping strips became redder and redder until a nauseating squelching sound ripped through the room as the full extent of the gouge cut into Hadwin's shoulder was laid bare. If Gavril was intimidated by the task before, it was nothing compared to what he was feeling now, looking down upon the congealed and angry looking wound staring up at him.

Using the wound ball of bloody rags, Gavril rubbed at the surface of the broken skin until most of the freshest blood was cleared away.

With a gulp, he removed the sewing kit from his pocket, popped open the lid and raised one of the curved needles up until it hovered between his eyes.

This was the only way to save his father and he knew it.

Gavril had seen him repairing the toy animal many times over the years but wished now that he had paid more attention to the act rather than planning his next attack against the innocent creature.

As the light of the flickering candle slid back and forth across the slither of polished metal clenched between his slightly shaking thumb and index finger, Gavril took a deep breath and began to sew.

He wasn't sure how long it took him to complete, having had to roll his father over halfway through to tend to the exit wound on his back, but once finished he noticed the small candle in the centre of the room had almost halved in size; the milky, yellow wax now formed a winding river through the numerous blood spatters that decorated the floor.

Gavril gazed down at the now sealed wound. He was sure his father would have done better if he had been up to the task but at least the crisscross of stitching ran somewhat evenly down the cut and pulled both sides of skin tightly together as was intended.

Gently, he wiped the dried blood from around the injury with the edge of the bed covers and watched as only a few fresh spots pulsed out from in between the sutures. All he could hope for was that the internal injuries, now hidden tightly from view, would knit themselves together over time.

Gavril slumped to his knees, draping his small body over the side of the bed and rested his head against Hadwin's arm.

The skin that pressed against his cheek was clammy and pale but looking sideways up towards his father's face, Gavril optimistically thought that he could see a hint of colour returning to his cheeks. This was a good sign, he thought.

Gavril suddenly felt the heaviness of his eye lids weighing down on him again. Only time would tell whether the stitching would be enough to help his father, so residing himself to that fact, Gavril joined him and fell asleep curled up at the end of the bed.

*

Both Gavril and Hadwin awoke at the same time. Neither of them could be sure who had shaken who, but the stirring vibrations travelled through the bed frame into each other's bodies simultaneously. Only one of them, however, was immediately alert and jumped from the bed to their feet.

"Father, are you okay? How do you feel?" Gavril cried, his voice teetering on the edge of shouting.

Luckily, the sun had now come up and it sent an ambient greyish hue from the atrium pouring through the open door. The light twinkled almost mockingly over the melted remains of the candle which now lay in a solidified puddle in the centre of the floor.

"Awful! Awful, but alive" Hadwin grumbled.

His face winced as he fumbled around trying to rearrange himself on the bed.

"You seem to have found yet another talent for yourself" he said, noticing the multitude of neat stitches running just below his collar bone.

He shot Gavril with a small smile.

"Not bad at all!"

There was a brief pause where it seemed like, even if only for a moment, everything in their small home had returned to normal. Caught up in it, Gavril threw himself forward and flung his arms around Hadwin's neck.

"Ow! Ow! Owww! Be careful, boy!" he exclaimed.

"Sorry… sorry!" sobbed Gavril.

His face was buried deep into Hadwin's neck as a fresh stream of tears doused his face.

"I'm sorry for everything! I shouldn't have left! I… I should have listened to you. If I had, none of this would have happened!"

A few moments passed whilst Gavril continued to cry into his father's neck before he pulled away and saw that tears were also streaming down Hadwin's face.

"Yes, you should have listened to me." said Hadwin weakly, as Gavril's face screwed up even tighter.

"But you are not the only one who should be sorry" he continued, as a sombre tone now heavily layered his words.

"If I had been more honest with you, then you wouldn't have gone looking at all"

Gavril's sobs and sniffs began to diminish as he stared into his father's eyes. The man looked exhausted - both physically and mentally.

Hadwin patted the bed softly and suggestively with his hand to which the boy eagerly obliged by sitting cross legged on the spot.

What then proceeded was the conversation that this father should have had with his son years ago.

Hadwin told him everything.

He detailed everything from the arrival of his mother's spaceship to their ongoing evasion from those vicious robots. All the while, Gavril sat on the edge of the bed, transfixed by what was coming out of his father's mouth.

Every few minutes, he would try to interrupt Hadwin with a question, but was quickly silenced by a wave of a hand. However, without being able to ask them, Gavril's confusion and disbelief seemed to turn inwards.

It was almost too much for him to take.

His face prickled with shock as more and more blood was pulled downwards into the pit of his stomach.

Once Hadwin had finished unloading the truth of the last ten years, silence hung between the pair like an impassable and dense fog.

Gavril just sat there slowly massaging his hands over the tingling skin of his face as the millions of questions that were swirling around his mind, fought over who would get to be asked first. The most important, the one that took pride of place at the front of the queue, was why had this all been kept from him.

The room was quickly becoming filled with Gavril's mounting anger as he realised that being kept in the dark about such important aspects of his life was almost as painful to him as a bladed arm ripping through his torso.

When Gavril finally dropped his hands and raised his head to speak, only the first angry syllable managed to escape his mouth before he noticed that Hadwin had once again passed out. His head was slumped awkwardly to the side and his arms were limply crossed in his lap.

Clearly dredging up the past and relaying it so quickly had sapped what little energy his body was not diverting to repairing his shoulder.

Gavril's rage quickly subsided at the sight and he darted across the bed to catch his father as he began to topple sideways towards the floor.

Carefully, he shifted him back into a lying position and pulled the blanket up under his chin. There would be time enough for answers and anger, Gavril thought, once his father had regained some strength.

Dropping his gaze, Gavril noticed Astronomy Through the Ages peeking out from under the bed, undoubtedly pushed under when Hadwin had rushed them home.

After picking it up, Gavril wandered into the atrium leaving Hadwin to rest and began turning the pages over in his hands.

He had stared at the images for years, but now they had an all new meaning to him. His eyes rose skyward, and he stared through the lunette in the centre of the ceiling. Past the haze of debris, past the thickening grey clouds and into the endless space beyond, somewhere out there, amongst all that vast emptiness was where he came from.

*

Gavril had spent the rest of the day at his father's bedside.

The thick book that he had been flicking through most of the afternoon, wondering if any of the planets that it pictured could possibly be his homeland, laid open in his lap.

He creaked the book gently shut and placed it down by the side of the chair, before standing up and leaning over to study his father.

Beads of sweat were glistening across his brow and his face had an almost greyish hue to it which promptly and correctly alarmed Gavril.

He placed a hand on his father's forehead and felt a burning fever throbbing against his palm.

As fear shot through his body, Gavril felt Hadwin's hand brush weakly against his. He clasped hold of the clammy digits and brought them up to the side of his face.

"I'm here, Father."

Gavril watched as Hadwin's eyes slowly inched open. His pupils were heavily dilated, filling almost the entirety of his ragged irises.

"How do you feel?" said Gavril hopefully.

However, judging from the distress in his father's eyes, he believed already knew the answer.

"Not good, son. Not good at all!" he gasped.

Gavril let go of his father's grip after hearing his raspy voice and seeing his dried tongue flick past his slightly yellowed teeth.

He quickly reached over and began to unscrew the lid of a metal bottle before pouring the cold liquid tentatively into Hadwin's waiting mouth. Unfortunately, he was unable to take down more than a few drops before beginning to cough and splutter. Hadwin's outstretched hand, that had been gently cupped around the bottle as he drank, was suddenly clasped against the bandages at his shoulder.

Gavril could do nothing but watch as his father writhed in pain, tears ready and waiting to return.

Once it had subsided, Gavril laid his father's head back on to the pillow and began to awkwardly unravel the layers of bandaging so that he could inspect the wound. As he pulled back the final layer, Gavril recoiled slightly - it was not a pretty sight.

An acrid smell met both of their nostrils and Hadwin, who had caught sight of his son's gaze staring horrified down at him, craned his neck so he could see in his peripherals what warranted such a reaction.

After a few moments of looking at the blackened wound, with angry coloured bruising spreading out across most of his chest, Hadwin dropped his head back on to the pillow and let out a sigh of anguish.

Seeing the defeat written across his face was almost too much for Gavril to bear.

"What do you need to make this better? Just tell me what you need!" Gavril pleaded, frantically looking around the room as if some miracle cure would be simply lying around.

"Stop." he said softly, whilst giving an almost unrecognisable wave of his hand.

The words had little effect on the boy, who proceeded to crawl under his bed, throwing various useless items across the room from its depths.

"Gavril st...!"

Hadwin's slightly raised command was cut short by the returning cough which caused him to wince and convulse.

His tone, however brief, still had the desired effect and the boy was now still and positioned once more at his side.

Once the worst of the pain had passed, Hadwin fell back against the headboard and let out a short raspy sigh.

"In my bedroom… by the back wall there is a chest. Bring it… to me!"

His speech was rushed, as if Hadwin was afraid that his voice would fail him any second.

Without any words of protest, Gavril leapt from the room and after noisily tearing through their home, he returned a few moments later with the small metal box in his arms.

Resting it on the bed, Gavril slid it forward across the rippling linen until it knocked into Hadwin's side.

Hadwin, whose eyes were briefly shut, clenched his jaw, revealing slightly blood-stained teeth before shaking his head.

"No Gavril… this is for you."

Gavril hurriedly threw open the lid to reveal the contents, expecting to find some sort of instrument or medicine, however, all that lay at the bottom of the chest was a bundle of leather secured tightly with a length of rope.

Gavril shot his father a confused look, before Hadwin gestured to him with a weak spin of his wrist for him to continue.

Carefully, Gavril began to unwind the ancient rope as directed and quickly felt a sense of anticipation rising at yet another mystery obscured from him. The material audibly cracked and creaked as the partially solidified knots that bound the roundish package began to loosen. Once it was untied, the leather bundle, which turned out to be a jacket, fell open to reveal two metallic orbs and a small beaten book nestled in its centre.

A singular word was embroidered into the chest of the supple garment - Gavril.

He flashed his eyes upward at Hadwin who gave him a small smile.

"It seemed only right to name you after something of your mother's."

A faint chiming sound bounced around the room as the two spherical objects rolled and knocked into one another in the brown leather basin now hanging between Gavril's arms.

"I found those with her. I... I could never get them to work..."

Hadwin's face tightened and thin tears began to seep amongst the aged lines of his cheeks.

"I am sorry that it is all I can give you of that life." he breathed raggedly, looking up at Gavril.

The silvery orbs shone like marbles in Gavril's eyes as he stared down at them. He reached down a hand which hovered momentarily over the spine of the small notebook, before throwing a look back at his father who was now beginning to turn a shade of white.

"I tried to remember the way back so that one day, when you were older, we might return to the crash site... but now..." his voice trailed off as his eyes gazed down at the blackened skin by his chin.

Without another thought about the untold mysteries of his existence, Gavril bundled the leather jacket and its contents together and threw it rather carelessly onto the floor beside him.

"What can I do father? Please tell me how I can make you better!"

His voice somehow seemed to have dropped an octave, as if this small child had been aged by the situation.

After a long pause, his father opened his bloodshot eyes.

"There is nothing that you or I can do."

Hadwin smiled, almost blissfully, and studied the carvings and pictures etched into the ceiling above.

"No amount of needles or thread can fix me now." he said calmly, before turning his gaze to meet Gavril's.

Solidifying this damning conclusion was the small trickle of vivid red blood that began to ooze out of the side of Hadwin's mouth. The sight of this overwhelmed Gavril with a sorrow that dragged every positive emotion out from beneath him. He began to sob quietly, clenching his fingers tightly around his father's hand.

Hadwin raised his free hand and placed it on his son's head, rustling his hair slightly as he usually did.

"But it seems you are even more special than I already thought you to be…"

His eyes drifted towards the boy's chest and hovered over the exact spot where he knew the injury had been.

"Those things will try to find you Gavril, but you mustn't let them! Promise me you will run, promise me that you will stay alive!"

Hadwin's voice was beginning to fail, as if his lungs were squeezing out what little air was left within them.

"I promise father. I promise…" wept Gavril.

And then Hadwin said his final words to Gavril, the very same words that his mother had told him all those years ago, as if it were some terrible destiny for both parent and child to endlessly repeat.

"Gavril, don't let this planet defeat you."

CHAPTER 8 - The Risk

An eerily calm breeze whistled over the ashen grey hillside as the faint clink and clank of metal echoed sympathetically some thirty feet below.

Six long years had passed since Hadwin's untimely death and in that time, the cave had become almost unrecognisable.

All visible wall space in the atrium was now lined with a multitude of metal objects piled on top of each other, giving the room an almost scrapyard feel - albeit a very neat and meticulously organised one.

The same choice of decor - or lack therein - could be found in the rest of the small rooms that spurred off of the main cave. All had been repurposed for storage and contained thousands of different rusted objects hanging from their ceilings or secured in orderly stacked metal crates at their base.

The only room that had been left untouched amongst the twisting, dusty mirrored labyrinth of passageways and chasms was Gavril's.

In the years that had passed, when all the other chambers had begun to overflow with salvaged items, Gavril had kept a promise he had made to himself that this place would remain as it was. After his father had died, it had become a sort of shrine to the man - not filled with candles or mementos in some ritualistic manner as one might expect, but a room frozen in time. With every drop of blood, every instrument and item in exactly the same position as it had been that day. Only the bed - Hadwin's body having been removed and laid to rest in a distant passage - had been renewed with clean sheets.

Gavril wanted it to be a reminder of sorts. Somewhere that he could go to reflect on the simpler life that he used to have, and more poignantly to remember how his actions had cut it abruptly short.

Even though it was now the only room with a bed, Gavril never slept there. He much preferred to curl up in the atrium on a mossy patch of earth next to the shimmering water's edge, surrounded by the ever-expanding greenery that weaved its way between the stacks of containers and various other salvaged objects. He found the abundance of life around him soothing in this otherwise cold and dead world.

Hadwin would never have let the plants grow so unchecked and out of control had he still been alive - having constantly reminded Gavril that their small source of water had to be rationed sparingly between themselves and their small garden to limit the risk of it drying up all together. But now that there was only one mouth to feed, Gavril had relaxed this, allowing the small oasis within the mountain to flourish - untamed and unbound - regardless of the consequences.

Lying stretched out in the centre of the room, with his eyes pointed in their usual upward direction, a vaguely familiar looking Gavril spun his small serrated blade aimlessly between each of his fingers - seemingly unaware of the thin lacerations that it was cutting into his digits.

As the blood tickled at his palm, he finally clocked the damage and gave an almost disinterested sigh before throwing the knife high into the air.

The silvery slither spun round and round, sending the faint traces of the blood it had acquired along it's razor edge spiralling away like strands of flowing auburn hair. The blade was finally tugged downwards by gravity, as if for a moment the force had paused interestedly to watch the pirouetting display before remembering itself. It stabbed, hilt deep, into the ground next to his head with a small thud.

Gavril raised himself up onto one elbow and stared down at his bleeding hand. His expression was blank and unconcerned, almost as if he was somehow disconnected from the pain all together.

Continuing to stare, his brow furrowed, and his eyes narrowed on the minute gouges made by the knife's pirouetting blade. Seconds later, his irises began to glow with a greenish hue and a singular spark began to flow down the length of his arm. The green stream briefly wound around his fingers creating rings of pure light before disappearing beneath his skin as quickly as it had came.

Gavril flexed his hand; the skin was healed as good as new and not even the droplets of blood that had begun to briefly seep from the cuts remained.

With a grunt, Gavril absent-mindedly pulled himself to his feet and walked forward as if what had just happened was nothing out of the ordinary. But ever since he had been skewered by that machine six years ago, nothing about Gavril could be considered ordinary.

Nothing in Hadwin's death bed confession had hinted at an explanation as to the powers that had unlocked within him that evening. Gavril had therefore settled on the answer that it must have something to do with his heritage. He knew now that he came from somewhere amongst the stars and who was to say that these abilities were not commonplace among his people? Maybe he wasn't as special as Hadwin had thought and there was a world out there, full of people who could do the same things that he now could.

The only thing that threw shade on this conclusion, however, was that his mother had died during childbirth. If he had inherited these powers from his biological parents, then why had she not used her own to save herself?

It was questions like this that had plagued the rapidly approaching adolescent during the countless days and nights of the past years. Recurring like clockwork, they were the first thing he thought of when the dim sun finally rose and the last thing that occupied his waking thoughts as darkness blanketed this lonely place.

As Gavril crossed the room and the reflected moonlight rippled around the room, the changes to his body were now clearly evident. He towered at a height of nearly seven feet, almost as if his body was purposely pulling itself skyward like the many plants that grew around him.

His physique, whilst now somewhat extruded, was still that of his much younger, slender self. However, stretching across every part of his body and pressing out subtly from underneath every inch of his unblemished skin, were dense, sinewy muscles. They tore across his frame like metallic fibres, weaving each joint and bone together with what looked like an unbreakable mesh.

Gavril's unkept hair was now below shoulder length - a thick and greasy tangle that swung wildly in front of him as he leant forward and reached out for the handle to his old room.

Stooping low through the opening, Gavril was quickly enveloped by both the deep darkness and the sombre atmosphere that this place imbued in him.

His mood wasn't all sunshine and rainbows the rest of the time, mind you - the isolation had eroded away most of his positivity long ago.

Wearing every ounce of his current mood on his face, Gavril lowered himself down onto the blackened stone floor and crossed his legs as if in prayer. Several spots of old blood that had curled away from the cold surface long ago cracked and crisped away under his knees.

"Hi Dad." he mumbled glumly.

In stark contrast to his seemingly untarnished and chiselled body, the condition of Gavril's mind was far from perfect. His face was solemn, and his still young eyes stared blankly towards the bed as if he was addressing someone that only he could see - but that was, in fact, exactly what was happening.

A couple of years ago, in a last desperate attempt to give Gavril some form of companionship, his mind had triggered its final and most desperate defensive mechanism. The real Hadwin was buried deep at one of the cave system's many dead ends, but the spectre of the man that now sat opposite him silently offered an ear to any matter that he wished to discuss.

"I was almost seen again last night" Gavril said tentatively to the empty room before pausing for a moment as if expecting a scolding. But the ethereal version of his father simply sat there passively - hands crossed together in his lap with an expression that looked more like interest than disappointment.

"There are just too many of them out there. I... I don't think I will ever be able to make it"

Gavril let out a small rasp of air and felt his eyes beginning to well up. The place that he was referring to was the one detailed in Hadwin's old journal - the book held within his mother's jacket along with those orbs. It showed the location of the ship that had brought him to this planet and his only chance of escape.

Over the years and as his body got stronger, Gavril had ventured out further and further into the landscape, following the roughly scribbled directions on the hand-drawn maps. But every time that he did, he found the way blocked by intensifying robotic search parties.

The only piece of advice his father had told him regarding these mechanical creatures was that if he should ever see one of these machines again, that he was to turn, run and never look back. Since the first day that he had plucked up enough courage to step back into the outside world, he had followed this advice to the letter. However, after thousands of excursions, all Gavril had to show for his time was the scavenged materials and objects that he had amassed from the return journeys. Ultimately and quite unfortunately, none of this expansive collection offered any clue or alternate means in which to escape this planet.

The one item that Gavril had, that held any hope of revealing any such information, was the glass pad that he had found on that night six years ago. But unfortunately, after looking through the bloodied remains of his punctured armour, Gavril had found that the same bladed arm that had skewered him through the chest, and brought these strange powers to the surface, had also clipped the edge of the device and shattered it into several useless pieces.

A single tear slithered its way free and tracked downwards along Gavril's nose.

He was that tear. Alone. Gently slipping towards a precipice.

"I don't know how much longer I can take this," he said plainly, before raising his head to face the invisible ghost sitting on the bed.

Six years ago, an admission like this, whilst meeting his father's eyes, would have resulted in a torrent of tears, but now there was only one.

The droplet finally fell, leaving an unnoticeable blot on Gavril's trousers as he clawed back his hair into a rough ponytail. His eyes widened and he flexed his jaw open so as to banish the remaining liquid from his eyes.

"I'm sorry, father." he said whilst looking everywhere but the bed to avoid the man's gaze.

Before waiting for an imaginary response, Gavril stood and left the room. The harsh truth was that he was at the point of wanting to be caught, or at the very least pushing onwards to his mother's ship whatever the risk or ultimate cost may be.

Gavril had become sick of the repetitiveness of his daily life - even more so than the one he used to live when Hadwin had been alive.

He was holed up inside the mountain, leaving once a day to see how close he could get in the direction of the ship, only to have his path cut short by those machines. Then to return home defeated, scavenging materials and trinkets left over from a world that he knew was not his own.

No, either by ship or by blade, he had to be free from this place.

Gavril crossed back to his small sleeping area and began to gather a few items for the journey. He threw them to the bottom of a large rucksack, his father's, which was more often used as a pillow rather than something to carry things.

Optimistically, Gavril decided to fill two canteens of water. For some reason, a glimmer of hope that he might make it all the way to the ship had begun to fill him up. Perhaps it was simply the prospect of change or that in one way or another this period of his life would be coming to an end?

The prospect of pushing behind the machine's lines wasn't that daunting to Gavril now that he had a better grasp on what his unusual body was capable of. He knew the damage that he could unintentionally cause one of those machines, having replayed that instance over and over in his mind.

As Gavril absentmindedly rubbed a hand over his chest - the mere memory of that night invoking a prickling sensation across his sternum - an idea began to blossom into something that could help turn the tide should he become overwhelmed above ground.

He strolled over to a nearby storage container that was slightly isolated from the rest and flipped off the pockmarked and dented lid. Inside lay the shimmering yet slightly bloody remains of the robot that had taken his father's life and set the last six years in painful motion. Recovered long ago, it now lay in several pieces having been dismantled by his younger self's intrigue and curiosity.

Reaching down, Gavril slid a long-bladed arm from the makeshift coffin and turned it over in his hand. Most of the blade glowed in the dull grey light of the cave but the blackened blood that still caked the tip did the exact opposite and drank in every ray.

Holding the arm aloft in both hands, as if he were holding a giant tentacle that was about to wriggle free, Gavril crossed to a small workbench and began to work on the limb with several complicated tools.

Minutes passed as he darted about the atrium, pouring over the many rows and shelves, whilst selecting various bits of scrap and returning almost excitedly to the work bench.

After a short while, Gavril clasped the hilt he had attached to the machine's wrist joint and raised it high in both hands. The arm, now repurposed into a long gleaming sword, sang in the soft moonlight.

Aside from the blood, the surface still bore the spiral engravings where the energy within his body had coursed through it and seared an almost beautiful pattern of lines as it went.

Somehow, the blade now held some skewed sentimental value to him. Gavril knew that it had been this arm that had pierced his chest all those years ago and it seemed only fitting that it would accompany him on what could be his last trip.

Clipping the bag shut, Gavril rested both it and the sword up against the passageway opening before lifting his armour from the nearby hook on the wall and climbing into it.

Over the years, he had been forced to construct a number of sets due to his ever-increasing height. But last year, as his growth seemed to level out, he had fabricated what he hoped would be the last.

The armour was a culmination of the different sets that he had worn over the years. A mishmash of all the salvageable parts including the addition of metal plating which he had taken from the body of the dead robot - it was an immensely tough material which Gavril had focused on applying, quite rightly, to the chest area. So that he always kept a piece of his father with him, he had also chosen to weave the ruptured shoulder piece of Hadwin's old armour into the construction.

Gavril clearly made a habit of constantly reminding himself of that night, which judging by his current state of mind, might not have been the most beneficial practice to follow.

Like his old bedroom, the armour served in part to torture him, but Gavril chose to see it as something to learn from, even if subconsciously, it was slowly compounding his guilt.

Finally, ready to leave, Gavril turned and surveyed the cavern.

It was a strange feeling, knowing that this may be the last time that he lay his eyes on it. Sure, every time he left could have been the last time but now, staring over the culmination of the last six years of his life, it felt more significant.

Gavril looked to the door of his father's now sealed tomb and closed his eyes almost in prayer.

He was seeking forgiveness just as he had when sat on the bloodstained floor moments ago - not from a god or higher being, but from the father that had implored him with his dying breath to not let this planet defeat him.

Gavril turned, secured his plated metal helmet onto his head and without any more twitches of hesitation, left the atrium.

Almost effortlessly, Gavril lifted several small boulders and placed them into a pile in front of the rounded entrance. They masked the steel door and blended it perfectly amongst the rest of the misshapen rocks littered there.

Gavril had no intention of returning here, but that didn't mean that he wanted those machines to find and ransack the place. Just like that plush office he had found high in that skyrise six years ago - he wanted this place to be preserved in more than just his memories, but in time itself.

He gave a small smile at the idea of what that place might look like in another hundred years without him holding it back, then turned and walked up the passage to the surface.

As he stared out over the darkness, Gavril pulled out a thick piece of paper and then gazed down at it's crumpled surface. It was Hadwin's crudely hand drawn map of the area.

Having been annotated so much over the years, the long spiralling routes amongst the dotted structures were almost an illegible mass of intertwining lines. To Gavril, however, it made perfect sense. In fact, he didn't have much use for it anymore - every path and obstacle was already ingrained into his memory - but checking this small piece of his father had left him before setting out had become a force of habit.

As he stood there with his father's map in his hand, Gavril knew that he wasn't going to get anywhere by playing it cautiously. For six years, he had been documenting search routes, no-go zones and waypoint markers. None of which had managed to provide him with an entirely safe route.

In one last act of defiance against the cautiousness instilled in him by his father's dying words, Gavril screwed up the map in his fist and let it flutter to the ground. It came to a rest on the blackened soil briefly before a gust of wind snatched it away.

Where he went now was his decision. Along a path that he alone would decide.

Setting off at a run, Gavril silently and effortlessly sprinted down the weaving natural paths cut into the dust dunes.

Since the healing power that lived inside him had awoken on that night, Gavril had found that it could be used in a multitude of different ways. As he sprinted across the landscape, a useful application of this power came into fruition.

Beneath him, his legs had become a greenish blur, propelling him forward at a speed that would be impossible for any normal human.

Crumbled buildings swept by in an instant; vast peaks and troughs of debris swam past him like waves rippling past a speeding ship. He was a bird - swooping around corners and soaring across the hillside - carried along by the powerful beating of his limbs. This was how the journey between the ship and their cave, that had taken a normal man like Hadwin nearly a month to complete, could be reduced to a matter of days.

Gavril could no longer see the mountainside behind him that cradled their subterranean home and a small piece of him felt saddened. However, this small part was overshadowed by the much larger feeling of desperation that wrenched his head back around. He had said his silent goodbyes, now he had to get off this rock and find his people. If not, he was going to die trying.

It wasn't long before the first real test of Gavril's conviction shone through some ruins up ahead.

He slowed his pace, allowing the gentle glow of his legs to simmer back below the armoured carapace, and watched as two of the machines crested over a small cliff face ahead of him.

Usually, this was when Hadwin's command was heeded and a plume of frantically kicked up dust would signal him trailing away in the opposite direction, but not today. Today, Gavril did not shy away. He moved forward and found cover amongst the debris at the cliff's base.

Gavril's heart felt like it was several times too big for his chest and beat thunderously in sync with the stabbing of the machine's limbs as they sent faint vibrations through the unsteady earth.

He drew the sword from his back and brought the hilt to his chest so that the flat side of the blade floated millimetres from his lips.

The leather grip depressed and wrapped around each of his clenched fingers as the machine's search lights seared from left to right over the precipice, casting long uneven shadows across the opposite elevation.

Leaning his head back, Gavril could see the remains of a small building leaning precariously out and over about ten metres above him. Half of its foundations - thick piles of steel and stone - were visible, pressing fruitlessly upon the empty space that now stretched out beneath them.

Gavril waited breathlessly as the building itself was scanned.

A few seconds later however, the lights diminished and the slicing sound of those vicious arms and legs could be heard moving away.

Once the footfall had faded amongst the soft haze of wind, Gavril stood and sheathed the sword once more. Now only the night sky above framed the outline of the crumpled and structurally questionable building.

Ambitiously and before giving it too much thought, Gavril silently rocketed himself upwards in a single bound and reached forward with one hand for the slight window ledge that jutted out from the building's first floor. Unfortunately, the state of the foundations should have given Gavril some hint as to the probable condition of the rest of the building, as he felt the stone almost instantly begin to loosen beneath his fingers.

"Ah…!" exclaimed Gavril involuntarily as his vice-like grip proved too tight for the century old concrete to contend with.

Swinging his other arm over his head, Gavril quickly gripped the crumbling ledge with both hands and catapulted himself even further up onto the building's flat roof.

Beneath him, the ledge that had become dislodged from the wall as his fingers left, fell with an almighty crash amongst the rusted metal piled at the base of the cliff.

Lying face down on the roof, Gavril flipped himself over so that his chest could heave in deep breaths as adrenaline coursed through his veins.

How could he have been so stupid he thought to himself. Why hadn't he waited longer before moving? Surely those things must have heard all the commotion that he had just made.

Sure enough, as Gavril lay there trying to calm himself, a shrill noise rang through the night sky, bringing back memories of an obscured shadowy figure and a long-darkened hallway. The pair of robots that had been moving away could be heard cutting their way frantically back, the clattering of their legs forming white noise as they got closer and closer to him.

Gavril was frozen. Gripped with the same fear as that night six years ago as he sat huddled behind that low office cabinet.

The structure trembled and then fell still.

After the crescendo of noise, the silence felt like a punch. Hitting him hard and disorientating his other senses.

Then amongst the emptiness, he heard it - the machine's inner workings, a complex ensemble of whirring and clicks, less than three metres from where he lay.

They were going to find him.

All of a sudden, the mechanical noises intensified before two loud clashes rose up to him from a lower elevation.

Crawling cautiously to the edge of the building, Gavril looked down to see that the mechanical hunters had just dropped themselves to the bottom cliff and were combing viciously through the disturbed debris that lay there.

Sensing the opportunity, Gavril got steadily to his feet and sprinted along the flat roof top in the opposite direction before propelling himself effortlessly across to the next building some twenty metres away.

He ran further and further across the congregation of rooftops, silently and calculatedly, until he was happy to find that he was alone once more. The machines and their red searchlights were barely visible over the protruding rooftops.

The fear that had threatened to consume him before was now replaced by a proud sense of triumph. For the first time, he had not retreated back to the cave's safety, but pressed forward to achieve his goal.

Gavril was suddenly swelling with happiness which flushed his face with an unfamiliar warmth. It was a sensation that, given his isolation, had become almost forgotten to him. It was like greeting an old friend that time had all but pushed from your memories. He let his face pull into the smallest of smiles as he tightened the straps on his rucksack and stared forward across the dunes.

With a swell of green and a sudden burst of dust, he was gone.

CHAPTER 9 - The Sight

Gavril could feel the terrain moving unsteadily beneath his feet. Like a frozen lake the surface shattered like glass under his footfall. Frantically, he struggled to keep himself upright as the earth crumpled and tore with each step.

Looking down he saw that the ground was no longer ashen in colour but a soft yellow that was stained darker in some places.

Lines of varying colours and thickness tangled across his feet like faceless snakes, weaving their way between blurred markings and away from him towards the horizon. Inexplicably, Gavril felt a longing to chase after them. He wanted to know where they were going - needed to know. He chased and he chased but they somehow managed to keep just ahead of him.

Then, just as he was about to give up, the line of the horizon rushed to meet him, and the coloured lines disappeared altogether as if they had never been there in the first place.

He was standing at the edge of the world, looking out across a boundless starry space. Except it wasn't the world at all on which he stood, but Hadwin's paper map.

Beyond the crumpled and frayed edge was the unknown - vast and uncharted.

Gavril's eyes crept open and they were greeted by the intense purples and oranges of a readying sunset. Through the cracked ceiling of the small bunker in which he lay, the mottled sky looked beautiful.

He continued to lay there - watching, as the faint shards of the distant moon began to peek around the concrete and gouged angular shadows across it's dense debris field.

After all his years exploring, Gavril was still amazed by the enormity of this place. It had been years since his agoraphobia had reared its ugly, breath-stealing head, but laying there beneath the starry sky, watching darkness steal the miles of amber skyline, it was hard not to feel dwarfed by the scale of it all.

When it was finally dark enough, Gavril finally brought his gaze back down and pulled himself off of the rubble strewn floor - which was not nearly as comfortable as the mossy water's edge he was used to. He re-secured the sword to his back before jumping up to grab hold of the ceiling's misshapen opening.

Gavril pulled himself up slowly until his eyes crossed the threshold and he could see across the now dark, monochrome vista. The depth of the coming night was signalled by a frigid rush of air that lapped across Gavril's face and stung his narrowed eyes.

Having run the rest of the previous night, Gavril had but no choice to retreat here along with the disappearing darkness as the machine's red lasers became almost impossible to spot in the daytime. This decision was validated almost immediately as the sight of several beams shining in the distance cut across the slither of the horizon.

Gavril cautiously spun his head around several more times before clambering to his feet and tightening the straps on his pack.

Building after building. Wreckage after wreckage. This journey didn't feel like it was going to end. How Hadwin had managed it whilst simultaneously caring for a child, he would never know.

As if sensing his increasing uncertainty and doubt, the landscape threw him a lifeline - dead ahead, a warped, complex structure of spindled steel that was silhouetted against the deep blue sky. The distinctive shape of the framework lit up like a spark in Gavril's memories. It was a marker from Hadwin's map and a clear sign that he was going in the right direction.

A few minutes later, Gavril circumvented the colossal amalgamation of steel and fragmented stone, briefly allowing his eyes to count up the near endless number of collapsed floors.

The building's height intrigued him. How far would he be able to see from its highest point he wondered? Possibly, if he was lucky, all the way to the sunken gorge and his final destination.

Gavril threw himself quietly upwards towards the mangled

arrangement of metal girders and slowly began to crawl up the rusted bars like they were the branches of some ancient tree.

Through busted floors, up broken stairwells and over vast overpasses of wrought steel, Gavril expertly traversed each of the structure's challenges as if he'd done it a thousand times.

He finally reached the roof with barely a hastened breath clutching at his chest and straightened to a stand.

With no aid from his powers he walked the length of the uneven terrace that swept upwards towards the clear, moon-lit sky.

Over the lip of the building's highest edge, a sight grew wider and brighter with each of his steps. It was like he was watching a new sun cresting around the periphery and that the structure on which he stood had now become the whole world.

Illuminated ahead was a vast flattened plain, reaching from one end of the horizon to the other like an ocean of white.

There were no buildings. No discernible formations of any kind. Just smooth piles of rubble here and there, like hastily dug graves for former structures that had once pierced the skyline.

The edge of this strange and barren place formed a slight downward curve a few miles ahead and through the slight haze of dust, Gavril could make out some familiar spots of light - hundreds in fact - all equally spaced apart along the perimeter like a halo of twinkling rubies.

Behind Gavril, several rocks began to tumble through the building's levels creating a flurry of noise that grappled at the end of each of his muscles. Whether it had been caused by something he had dislodged during the climb or by some threat unseen, he was not waiting around to find out.

Without reservation or thought of injury, Gavril leapt forward from the rooftop and plummeted down the hundred or so metres to the ground below. It was easily the tallest height he had ever fallen from, and the sight of the fast approaching earth made him whisk a quick shot of air into his lungs to ready himself for the inevitable pain.

"Arghhh!" groaned Gavril.

Both his legs and the concrete floor shattered loudly in several places as he touched down, but within seconds, before even gravity had a chance to collapse his limbs like the bellows of an accordion, the pain was gone, and a flash of green told him that the breaks were healed.

After a quick shake of his thighs, he was in flight again. A green shimmer across the night, tearing away from the echoing noise towards the moon-lit plain.

Gavril racked his brain but knew that no part of the map had been described as what he had just seen. Had Hadwin neglected to mention it because it was a void, and that this space was so empty and desolate that it was beyond description? Not likely, Gavril thought to himself. Whatever this place was, it had to be new, and judging by the perimeter being lined with hundreds, if not thousands of machines, it must be important.

At this speed, it didn't take long before Gavril heard the familiar sound of bladed limbs ahead, so he instantly dialled back his speed and made his way forward to cover under his own steam.

The culprit, another mechanised replica, stood beside the boundary line, not on four legs but on two, in a stance that he had seen them do only once before - when they were readying themselves for a kill.

However, if there was something at its feet worth killing, Gavril doubted that there would be anything left for him to tell what it was; the machine was sweeping through the debris at it's feet in menacingly quick strokes and throwing up a shroud of dust that masked the ground from view.

As Gavril continued to watch, the robot moved two steps sideways and started sifting through the new patch in the same calculated manner. Behind it, like a snail's trail, the earth mimicked that of the landscape beyond - smooth, shattered and picked clean.

Just like this morning's transitioning sky, Gavril was entranced by the sight. He had been in awe of something so beautiful then, whereas now he was astounded by the brutal nature of what this thing was doing.

Gavril's eyes flashed first from the machine to the plain, then back towards the now distant structure behind him. His mind's-eye drew an arching line across the sky, intersecting with the shattered moon and back down to the pale horizon beyond. If his bearings were correct, then his destination was ahead, somewhere amongst all this emptiness.

The machine moved sideways once more with an earth-shaking thud and a sudden prickling sensation rose up the back of Gavril's neck as all the pieces of this puzzle fell into place. Every inch of ground for as far as his eyes could see, was being methodically searched, not for materials or sustenance, but for him.

For sixteen years, they must have been relentlessly combing for any clue or sign of his whereabouts and now this far-reaching decimated landscape that stretched out in front of him was the result of that process.

When Hadwin had first told Gavril of the machines and their unrelenting yearning to get hold of him, it had scared him - who wouldn't be scared by a mechanical force hellbent on finding you? But presented with this swathe of land that had been reduced to dust on his behalf, filled him with an all-encompassing dread that shook at his very core.

The sound of the machine's swipes had become distant, occupying the same small place in his mind now reserved for the present. The majority of Gavril's focus was on the past and of the home he had left behind.

Hadwin had been right to hide them there. What could he have hoped to do against such an unrelenting force such as this? Machines unburdened by fatigue or time.

Gavril shook his head and brought his focus back squarely to reality.

Just because fleeing had been the right thing for his father to do, it didn't mean it was for him. Gavril knew that he didn't belong here and had made it too far now to even think of turning tail and retreating.

The nearby scouring machine was moving off - continuing on it's preordained track around the outskirts of the search area - leaving the path clear behind it to the space beyond. After shaking the anxiety from his limbs, Gavril crept in a spider-like crawl across the beaten earth to the small perimeter line.

The moonlight, now unobstructed, reflected up all around him and dazzled his eyes. Finally, his irises managed to slowly filter it back until the gentle peaks and troughs of the landscape became clear, but still no hint or marker of his position jumped out at him from the whiteness. Hadwin's map, noting the structures and formations of importance to help him retrace his steps, was now useless. Its surface wiped clean like the miles of earth before him.

Gavril continued defiantly on all fours over the flattened ground until the sound of the robot's slicing arms were barely audible behind him.

He straightened himself up and scanned all around as the winds whipped up glistening clouds of fine dust that spiralled and crashed into one another. Yet again, Gavril paused to drink in the unexpected beauty of this place, but the view suddenly soured as he realised his surroundings for more than their aesthetics. He had been so obsessed with his destination that he hadn't given much thought to how visible he was now. Not only that, but for the same reason he had sought shelter from the daylight the previous morning, the machines' lasers would be as equally as difficult for him to spot.

Gavril funnelled the fear that both of these facts brought down into his legs and shot forward, creating his own sparkling plumes of dust behind him as he went.

He breathed sharp and shallow as his eyes darted from side to side, somehow faster than his footfall, but still they found nothing. No sign of approach. No sign of anything at all.

For miles, the moonlight now shone around him and the fear of the machines finding him was quickly replaced by the uncertainty of where he was.

He continued to run in what he hoped was a straight line and thankfully began to see a pillar of rock slowly beginning to protrude from the horizon. It reached higher and higher until it filled his field of vision and he was thankfully draped in its long shadow.

As Gavril gained on the jagged miniature mountain, reaching proudly towards the sky above, it's form once again began to feel familiar to him somehow.

Something told him that not only did he know this place, but also that it deserved his respect. Gavril obeyed without rhyme or reason, dropping his speed and rounding the uneven base at a walk.

The ground at his feet began to fade from a coarse, silvery grey into the deepest black as thousands of sliced sections of dark metal replaced the uppermost layer.

Gavril twisted his head to the side and saw that two arching shapes were imprinted on the ground. They swept out from the rock formation's base and at their crux sat a black chasm, gouged out of the rock like a giant's mouth. A singular cloud drifted across the sky and in the dull light of the now half-concealed moon, Gavril could see scorch marks that lapped up out of the space, charring the rising stone of the cliff face like a furnace.

He stopped for a moment as his eyes drank it all in, then he finally realised what it was - this was once Hadwin's home.

This bleak and empty shell had kept his father safe for so many years and with its dying breath had even given them a chance to survive a bit longer.

"Thank you", said Gavril softly to the memory of the home that the machines had tried, yet failed, to erase.

It also seemed that this place was not finished with lending a helping hand to Hadwin and himself, as the significance of discovering it suddenly blinked on like a light bulb in Gavril's mind. This towering cliff was just the marker that he needed to get his bearings and point himself in the right direction.

Gavril felt a rush of excitement as he turned his back flat against the burnt-out home and bound forward in the direction of the gorge.

His mother's ship was now almost within reach.

After only a few minutes of running, Gavril slid to a halt at the edge of the precipice, his heart racing faster than it had in all years avoiding the machines.

He looked down into the gorge, described by his father as a mass of towering buildings, huddled together tightly on the fallen earth. But of course, just like the rest of this plain, none of these structures remained. Instead the wide spanning sunken area was filled with the same piles of broken stone and steelwork - so much so that the basin's surface, with its many ripples and undulations, looked like it was filled with liquid rather than thousands of tonnes of rubble.

Gavril felt a sudden surge of panic at the thought of the ship being buried underneath it all or shredded into tiny pieces like everything else here, but thankfully, towards the gorge's centre he saw something metallic winking at him from above the surface.

Gleaming and beautiful, Hadwin had described it. Shining steel that didn't look of this world - which on this occasion was undoubtedly true.

Gavril dropped down the cliff face and proceeded forward at a run. He no longer cared for caution, no longer feared the machines of this world. Within mere steps was his ticket away from it all.

As he dashed further, however, an unfamiliar noise echoed over the clearing and instilled caution back into him like a red-hot poker on either side of his head.

He climbed, cat like, up onto a taller pile of rubble to get a better view of the origin of the noise and felt his heart sink lower than he could have ever thought possible.

The glint of moonlight that had been reflected back into his eyes had not been from the spaceship's hull, but by the polished carapace of a large humanoid shaped robot, unlike any that he had seen before, standing statuesque above the rubble.

Gavril heard the sound again. It was high pitched and not unlike the shrill alarming noise that the machines created. However, as he continued to listen, he started to notice that there were subtle changes emerging amongst the coarse noise.

There was repetition. Emotion. Words.

The screeching noise was a human scream. Possibly that of a child.

After moving himself into a better position, Gavril focused his eyes down towards the robot's feet and saw that cowering in fear was not a child but a girl, roughly his age, her arms stretched out in front of her as she seemingly pleaded with the mechanical figure standing over her.

The sight of another person caught Gavril completely off guard. He forgot about the ship and the imposing machine that was in its place, then managed to forget where he was entirely. He rose to a standing position with his mouth hung wide in disbelief.

It didn't seem real. Was this another dream? Had he finally lost his mind to this place?

Whether she was real or not, the girl caught sight of Gavril framed between the robot's towering legs and locked eyes with him.

"HELP ME! PLEASE!" she screamed.

CHAPTER 10 - The Girl

The girl's words echoed within the gorge and around the inside of Gavril's skull. They also seemed to collide against the part of his brain that was responsible for sending commands to his muscles as he found, not for the lack of trying, that he was unable to move.

He looked like a statue standing atop the plinth of rubble - his eyes frozen wide as they stared unblinkingly ahead.

It was not until the girl cried once more that he managed to regain some control and shake himself from his paralysis.

"PLEASE! HELP ME!" she pleaded.

The robot didn't seem to notice that the girl was no longer speaking to it or even that she had shifted her body, so that her line of sight to Gavril was no longer through it's reinforced legs.

Her words were a call to action.

A plea to him from another flesh and blood human being which, even when Hadwin had been alive, hadn't happened to him before.

Gavril sprung down, unsteady and foal-like, from the mound of rocks with a little more force than intended which sent a landslide of rubble cascading down behind him.

This, the mechanised Goliath, did not miss.

It's head began to swivel around. Clunking and thudding, it's inner workings echoed almost as loudly as the girl's screams as the rest of it's monstrous body began to rotate as well.

Not wanting to lose the element of surprise, Gavril sprinted forward faster than he had ever thought possible. His legs glowed bright green and a warm feeling pooled at his toes as the immense pressure that he was putting them under plateaued.

To the robot, and the still cowering girl, he must have looked like a blur as he flew towards them, creating a wake of flying dust and debris behind him as he went.

Completely abandoning the silver sword still slung across his back, Gavril raised a clenched fist, launched himself forward and swung a lightning fast roundhouse punch straight into the robot's midriff, some six feet above the ground.

As his hand connected with the solid metal and sparks began to fly, Gavril's vision was suddenly flooded with images - streams of indecipherable text, numbers cascading over one another and a twisted black form, spiralling like a tornado in an ice white hall.

Time seemed to stand still, then move backwards with the motion of the cloud-like entity as it morphed back and forth before settling into an angular version of a face. It was a face Gavril had never seen before with cold and unnatural features. It was one that he hoped he would never have to again.

The face strobed several times like static, overlaying the reality that was his fist disappearing amongst the robot's armoured shell and in a flash, Gavril was back in the gorge.

He could feel his fingers breaking apart but, like the images, the pain seemed unfamiliar to him. Sparks of green light obscured within the machine's innards instantaneously wove the fractured bones together, so that despite what seemed like the shattering of every joint and ligament, his hand kept up it's momentum.

Finally, and rather triumphantly, his fist punctured straight out the other side as the sheer power and speed of the punch split the robot clean in two and sent it's top half flying off sideways in a lifeless heap. The legs however, remained upright, standing almost comically as a few sparks of electricity crackled around the torn metal at its waist.

As the electrical cables fizzled their last, the girl peeked her head around the frozen legs and Gavril saw that her mouth was now the one hung in disbelief.

She stared bewilderedly from him to the two dismembered parts of the machine, repeating the process a few more times for good measure, before finally speaking.

"H...Ho...How did you do that?"

Her voice was now quiet and soft, but Gavril wasn't listening. More accurately, he couldn't hear her over the booming sound of the blood beating against his eardrums, downing out all noise but it's own.

Gavril might not have been able to see those images any longer, but their effect and the confusion they had caused was still reeling inside him. He looked down at his still clenched fists, as their green hue slowly began to fade, then across to the machine.

After a few seconds, the girl repeated her question. This time her words managed to cut through the swell of his thoughts and Gavril's voice cracked to life in reply.

"I... erm... I don't know" he stuttered weakly.

He knew full well how ridiculous that truth must have sounded to her.

For a moment, the girl looked confused, but like a mirror, Gavril was reflecting an equally perplexed look back at her.

This confusion must have gone some way in proving to her that he was telling the truth as her face relaxed before spreading into a wide smile.

"Well, however you did it, thank you!" she exclaimed, before stepping forward and kicking the robot's backside with the sole of one of her boots.

The tiny impact was enough to send the legs toppling to the floor with a loud thud.

"Nice to meet you, my name is Gaia." she said, approaching Gavril with her hand outstretched.

This was not met.

Gavril instead stared at it, slightly bewildered, as his cautious mentality returned once more.

There was also something rather puzzling about her voice, something which Gavril had never heard spoken before. Her words were clear; with every syllable defined in a way that was quite unlike the hurried mumble that he was used to from Hadwin.

"What do you want?" he asked, gesturing to her outstretched hand.

Gaia looked at her hand and turned it over in both confusion and embarrassment.

"Erm...nothing, I only wanted to introduce myself"

Gavril watched as the girl pulled back her hand and the perplexed expression returned to her face. He was not used to introductions, this of course being his first.

"Gavril, my name is Gavril." he said gruffly.

A smile returned to her gaunt, yet pretty face and she let out a small laugh.

"That wasn't so hard was it?" she asked rhetorically.

Her smile turned out to be quite infectious, as Gavril felt for the first time in five years, one of his own beginning to spread across his cheeks.

"So, what are you doing here?" she asked keenly and inquisitively.

This question was like a slap across Gavril's face. It smacked the slight smile clean off his face and replaced it with an expression of panic. He had gotten so caught up in the robot and the rescue that he had completely forgotten the reason he had travelled so far.

Rather manically, Gavril began to scan his eyes across the rest of the sunken gorge in search of the ship. He spun around manically and began scrabbling up nearby mounds to get an elevated view. But it was useless, the ship was gone, evidently moved or stripped down to its elements by the machines.

Whichever gutting scenario turned out to be accurate, the ship was forever out of his reach.

"It's gone..." whispered Gavril hollowly as his knees gave way and he crashed to the floor beside the powerless machine.

After several moments, the despair Gavril was feeling quickly turned to frustration and he began to pound his fists into the ground in anguish.

Large plumes of dust were thrown into the air from the impact points, until Gavril was completely shrouded by a haze of grey.

It was then that Gaia, a girl he hardly knew, stumbled through the cloud with one arm cupped around her face and placed the other on Gavril's shoulder.

This unexpected human interaction sent a warmth spreading from the point of contact and Gavril immediately stopped his bombardment. The cloud of dust fell slowly around them and the beating sound was replaced by the exasperated heaves of Gavril's lungs.

"Are you okay?" she asked softly.

Gavril turned to look at her, his eyes flooding with tears as spittle dripped from his bottom lip.

"It's gone" he sobbed.

Clutching both hands over the back of his head, Gavril buried his face into the ground as his fingers dug white-knuckled into his scalp.

No words were spoken from either party. Only Gavril's patter of cries broke the otherwise silent gorge.

Gaia, obviously deciding that it was not best to press the issue until Gavril was ready, shuffled awkwardly on the spot beside him.

After a short while, Gavril sniffed back the tears and straightened himself, so he was in a kneeling position.

"I was looking for a ship that landed here a long time ago. It... it was my only chance to escape this place."

As the last words left his mouth and the tears threatened to return again, Gaia's hand returned gently to his shoulder and settled him once more. He had all but forgotten what the touch of another human being could feel like.

He turned to look at her, half expecting to see a confused expression waiting for him after the mention of a spaceship, however, her dirt splattered face was pulled into one of concern that Gavril knew was for his well-being.

As they looked at one another, Gavril decided that it might be best to change the subject - sobbing away like a helpless child was clearly not the best first impression to give someone.

"I thought I was the only person left alive out here!" he said, rubbing the back of his hand against his slightly bloodshot eyes.

"You and me both!" she replied.

The contagious smile returned to Gaia's face once more as she circled back to the machine's remains and looked down at it with intrigue.

"What even is this thing?" she asked innocently as she tapped at the inert wreckage of metal with her boot.

Gavril looked at her confusedly. How could she not know about these creatures? Was there somewhere on this planet where the machines did not go?

Gaia caught sight of his bewildered expression.

"I mean... this one looks different to the others I have seen in the past." she said quickly, almost as if hurriedly trying to hide something.

Gavril opened his mouth to reply but before the words had time to take form, a number of shrieks began to echo ominously over the landscape.

Springing to his feet, Gavril felt Gaia's back knock into his as the pair instinctively began to scan their eyes in a semi-circle around the edges of the gorge's high cliff walls.

"Do you see anything?!" snapped Gavril, with a glance backwards at her.

"No, nothing!" she replied.

Her voice was now noticeably higher in pitch.

The processed, artificial cries rang out once more. However, this time they were louder and clearly much closer.

"What shall we do? Where shall we go?" panicked Gaia.

A gentle whistle of wind spiralled between them interjecting briefly before Gavril had a chance to reply.

"I know of a place..." he started before realising the stretch of treacherous terrain that lay between the pair and his subterranean home.

The distance itself wasn't daunting to Gavril, the problem was that after glancing down at the five-foot-nothing girl behind him, he knew that it wasn't going to be an easy feat with her in tow.

"But to get there it might take a while, for you at least" he said rather unapologetically as he gestured down at her stumpy and rather scrawny legs.

It was apparent that Gavril still needed more time to get back into the swing of conversing politely.

"Well, what do you suggest?!" Gaia retorted as she processed Gavril's thinly veiled criticism and the screeches became louder still.

Then an idea popped into his mind, something that he and Hadwin had done quite a lot of years ago around the tunnels of their home.

"Climb on" he said, bending his knees slightly and issuing to his back with a jab of his thumb.

Without hesitation, Gaia, who seemed to understand what he was inferring to almost immediately, jumped on and wrapped her arms tightly around Gavril's neck. He, in turn, linked his arms around her thighs and hauled her up into a comfortable yet secured position. Her petite frame was light, and barely registered as a burden to Gavril's muscled physique.

"Hold on tight and try to stay quiet." he commanded.

Gaia opened her mouth, possibly to serve up a rebuttal, but the words were thrown back into her throat as Gavril set off. She let out a small squeak and pulled her head forwards, burying it deep into Gavril's neck to shield her face.

In that briefest of moments, Gavril felt the hairs on the back of his head stand on end and a warmth spreading from the point where her lips touched his bare skin. But as quickly as this sensation came, it was gone; dashed by the leaping motion as he soared high into the air and out of the sunken gorge.

Gavril's eyes began to sting as they were dried by the cold air rushing past his face. However, Gavril resisted the urge to blink; not daring for a moment to close his eyes until he either spotted the source of the noise or was far enough away from the gorge that it did not matter.

Thankfully, after a few minutes, as he passed the stone obelisk of Hadwin's old home, the screeches became more distant and Gavril allowed his lids to skim the surface of his eyes with a fresh coat of moisture.

The rest of the journey across the now eerily quiet, flattened plain went without incident, that was until Gavril spotted the perimeter line fast approaching in the distance.

The robots, who had been positioned along the edge outwardly searching through the debris, no longer had their backs to the open space. Instead, as far as Gavril could see, their red searching beams were pointed inwards, fixed perpendicularly to the edge of the scoured landscape.

Sliding behind a low mound of rubble, the pair conversed quickly in hushed tones.

"What are they doing?" asked Gaia, her voice barely louder than a whisper.

It didn't take long for Gavril to work it out. The close-knit pattern of their positions, forming a barrier between them and the untouched land beyond.

"They are waiting for us."

He didn't need to know Gaia very well or look sideways at her face to know that she was as petrified as him. He felt her fingertips clench harder around the plates of metal that covered his shoulders, pressing the corners into the tightly woven fabric beneath.

They were caught in a trap and the machines were slowly closing in on them from behind would soon be there to spring it.

There was only one option available to him.

"Pass me my sword… please, Gaia?" he said nervously, stuttering over the niceties of politeness.

Gaia obliged, drawing the blade from between them and passing it over carefully as if worried it might burst into flame at any moment.

"What are you going to do?" she asked timidly.

Gavril decided that it might not be best to tell Gaia for fear that she may try to talk him out of it.

"Just hold on, okay?" he said, as confidently as he could muster.

Gavril clutched hold of Gaia's legs as tightly as humanly possible without shattering her bones and sprinted forward once more in a streak of green.

As he neared the perimeter, he let go of one of Gaia's legs and raised the sword high.

The point of the blade gleamed in the mix of moonlight and red laser beams that were now sweeping round to face it.

The machine only had time to raise one of its arms slightly before Gavril swiped the blade through the air with deadly accuracy, rending both it and its head clean from its shoulders. The lasers emanating from the various decapitated instruments momentarily spiralled in large arcs as the head spun through the air.

As the lifeless scrap metal clashed into the floor behind them, swathes of crimson lights began to focus on it's location and Gavril could only assume that the other robots guarding the perimeter had immediately become aware, through some invisible communication, about their fallen comrade. However, he did not turn around or pause to confirm this, opting instead to dig the balls of his feet into the earth and shoot them forwards into the familiar wasteland.

Shrieks whistled past their ears like bullets as Gavril sped on.

After several minutes of listening to the crunching of Gavril's boots on the harsh ground, Gaia briefly removed her face from the confines of his neck, but quickly realised that her timing couldn't have been worse.

She let out a drawn-out scream as her stomach lurched and the ground suddenly disappeared beneath them, for it was at that exact moment that Gavril had decided to launch them up from the uneven dune of blackened earth onto the roof of a nearby high-rise.

Unaware that this was the cause of Gaia's cry, Gavril skidded to a halt on the grit covered concrete roof and looked frantically behind him, raising the sword once more.

Had she seen something he hadn't, he wondered.

Looking through the darkness that surrounded them however, Gavril could not see anything but the endless derelict buildings and scrapped metal structures.

"Is everything okay? Did you see some..." he began before his voice trailed off.

In the distance, from the direction that they had just come, was a sight that made the blood drain from his face.

From the elevation of the building's roof, the horizon, as far as his eyes could see, was ablaze with red lights. It looked like a forest fire, ferocious and unyielding, spreading wildly across the earth towards them.

Now that they were back on solid ground, Gaia, who was still reeling from the jump, removed her face and her eyes were met with the same terrifying sight as Gavril's.

Somehow, she kept her mouth shut at the sight, but Gavril again felt her arms grip even tighter as the machines let out a chorus of mechanical cries. Whether by fear or by Gaia's arms constricting his throat, he gasped loudly.

Looking down at the sword, Gavril realised that even with this and his powers, he wouldn't be able to contend with that many of them. The only hope that the pair had of surviving was if he could outrun them.

He passed the sword backwards without a word of instruction to Gaia, who somehow knew exactly what was being asked of her, then gathered himself up to full height.

He dashed quickly towards the edge of the rooftop and launched them from the roof onto the ground below, as a splash of green and bits of debris sprayed up from around his legs - Gaia decided that it was best to keep her eyes shut from here on out.

Apart from the almost chanting-like sound of their pursuers behind them, the far-reaching land in front of them was oddly quiet. But Gavril knew better than to let his guard down, choosing to jump from rooftop to rooftop where possible.

His body felt like it was on autopilot. Just like Gaia was riding on his back, he too felt like a passenger - carried along inside his own skin as his mind wandered.

Gavril tried to designate most of his concentration to his surroundings, but a part of his mind was inescapably sifting through the nights events.

The ship is gone, and you are never leaving this place.

He had done the same in the early days after his father had passed by repeating the facts over and over until he came to terms with them.

However, even after he tried to convince himself, he began to think of the numerous possibilities that could have befallen the craft. Could it have been moved? Could it still be intact? Judging by the robot's decimation of the structures inside the gorge and the vast circular search area surrounding it, the chances of this being either case were slim at best.

An even larger portion of his thoughts were wondering about the person straddled across his back.

Over his entire lifetime, and most of Hadwin's, they had never seen another living soul. Not even a sign that anyone else was or ever had been doing what they had - surviving.

Now, not only had he discovered somebody in this empty place, but that someone was looking to him for protection. Like a child to an unknowing parental figure. The similarities to Hadwin's situation years ago were not lost on Gavril.

There was also something strange about her, something that he quite couldn't place. Perhaps it was how she had been able to survive with only the thin clothes hanging from her back, or how in an instant she had come to trust him? Without spending any time together or a shred of explanation as to how someone so fearful of the world around them could have survived, he somehow trusted her, too. More than likely, he thought, because she was a living, breathing person and that gave them something in common.

The night flitted past just as the miles of ground did and for the most part Gaia respected Gavril's wishes for her to stay quiet, save for a few involuntary noises as he bounded in an inhuman fashion from the dunes to derelict buildings.

There was no time for rest - for him, at least.

"We are almost there." he said softly, turning his head to the side so that Gaia could hear him.

However, when there was no response, he began to feel slightly alarmed.

He could feel her chest filling and contracting against his armoured back, so he knew she was still breathing. Without looking, he suddenly realised that she must be sleeping.

Rather unexpectedly, Gavril found himself consciously keeping his movements smooth and fluidic as he carried on. Like a sleep deprived parent holding a restless new-born. This was how Hadwin must have felt, he thought.

Thankfully, after spotting a few familiar landmarks in the distance, Gavril was relieved to find that they were not too far from the cave.

He sped softly to the top of a mountainous dune that he remembered passing when he left his home the previous day and decided that it was best to check back to see if the legions of robots, he had seen from that rooftop earlier were well out of sight.

Gazing back, however, Gavril was shocked to see that even at the incredible speed he had been tearing across the landscape, it hadn't been enough to shake the horde of robots that had been hot on their tail. If anything, they seemed closer.

Even now, as he stared through the failing night, a few of the lights began to break formation and speed ahead of the crowd.

All thoughts of moving silently for the benefit of Gaia's slumber evaporated and before Gavril knew it, he was sprinting frantically down the dune towards the mountain ahead that he knew housed his home.

As his eyes flitted around the base, Gavril thought about the main hatch that he would need to uncover before they could enter and was unsure whether he had the time. Also, if the machines were to find the uncovered doorway then all would be lost anyway.

No, Gavril knew that he needed to use another entrance, one that up until now had never been used before by either him or Hadwin.

"What is happening?" asked a rather confused Gaia over his shoulder.

Gavril did not have enough time to answer but felt Gaia's body twist around on his back and the sudden snapping motion informed him that she had found the answer to her question.

Instead of summoning the energy down to his legs, through fear of the green light alerting the robots to their final location, Gavril climbed up sheer rock face using his regular muscle's strength.

He kept climbing and climbing as his feet slid awkwardly over the uneven rock face until he reached a small hole cut irregularly into the stone.

Finally, he lowered Gaia, who almost reluctantly slid off of his back.

"Why are we stopping?!" she screeched, as she looked alarmingly back towards the visible beams of light fast approaching in the distance.

"We are here, get in!" Gavril replied, equally as alarmed.

Gaia looked down to the hole and then back to him. Somehow, the unspoken trust that had been built between the pair of them didn't seem to stretch this far.

"Go, trust me!" he shouted, pointing a finger down towards the blackened hole.

Thankfully, these words and their tone seemed to do the trick and the last thing that Gavril saw was her mass of dirty blonde hair disappearing into the darkness.

After one last look towards the fast approaching lights, as the slashing of blades ricocheted through the air, Gavril lowered himself into the hole and plummeted down to join her.

CHAPTER 11 - The Partnership

Gavril's elbows knocked painfully into the tunnel walls as he dropped awkwardly through the skylight. He felt one of his outstretched arms connect with something solid as he fell downwards into the atrium, causing his body to rotate uncontrollably in mid-air like the blades of a turbine.

Plunging backwards into the pool of water with a loud splash, Gavril felt a few of the plants that had been calmly drifting across the surface crumple beneath him.

Half submerged, Gavril began thrashing around frantically, trying to get himself up out of the water. When he finally managed to haul himself out, he found Gaia huddled by the water's edge, her drenched hair clinging to her face as she flashed her eyes around the darkened cave.

"Where are we?" she panted loudly, as the water continued to stream over her lips and down onto the dry earth.

"Shhhh!" breathed Gavril, as he raised a finger to his mouth.

After he was sure she understood, Gavril removed the finger and slowly gestured upwards to the hole in the roof through which they just fell.

Seconds later, the ground around them began to shake violently and miniature ripples formed across the surface of the small pool.

As the pair stared silently up through the skylight to the dimly lit sky above, flashes of red and silver streaked past, partially obscuring the limited light around them. The vibrations grew and grew until Gavril could feel his teeth jarring up and down within his skull as thousands of robots stampeded relentlessly across the hilltop.

All around them, the darkened collection of salvage shuddered and shook. Cases upon cases and rows upon rows, with their contents knocking together gave the impression that the machines were right there with them in that very room.

Gavril looked sideways at Gaia, as the repeatedly broken light from above created a strobe effect and burnt the image of her terrified face into the back of his eyeballs.

The minutes dragged by and Gavril's body did not relax for a moment. His muscles were taut, and he felt like his face was tearing as he winced at the possibility of each one of the machine's legs happening upon the hole or hearing the cataclysm of rusted instruments clanging below. All it would take was one false step, or one noise to reach them amongst the clatter, and the entire metallic rabble would descend upon them.

Thankfully, however, after several more minutes, the shuddering began to diminish until finally, silence encapsulated the pair.

Cautiously, Gavril opened his mouth to speak - still fearful that a robot from the back of the pack might still be nearby.

"I think we are okay..." he whispered, not entirely convinced of this himself.

The concerned expression that Gaia gave him hardly hid her hesitance at believing him either.

They continued to remain motionless and silent for quite a while until Gavril was satisfied that they were finally alone.

"This is my home. Don't worry, you will be safe here."

Gaia said nothing in response, but Gavril could see that her shoulders had relaxed slightly as she took in the last of her panicked breaths. She looked down at the cascading moonlight, now dancing over the crumpled leaves and the still water of the spring, and a small smile began to tug at the corners of her mouth.

"This place is amazing!" she said, looking around.

"Thank you" he responded, whilst replicating her expression.

Finally, Gavril relaxed completely and settled back into the home as if he had never left.

"My father found and built this place." Gavril stated, gesturing with both hands around the room.

When his eyes finally grew accustomed to the reduced light, they gave him a clearer view of Gaia who was busy passing up and down the rows of salvaged items like it was an exhibition.

As she re-emerged and the moonlight shone brightly across her face, Gavril was reminded of her skinny frame and gaunt complexion.

"You must be hungry?" he said, moving towards the small garden in the centre of the pool.

He bent down and plucked a couple of large red tomatoes that had managed to escape being crushed and passed one to her.

Gaia turned it over in her hands, seemingly perplexed but equally amazed at its form.

"What is it?" she asked.

"It's a tomato" responded Gavril before biting into his own, slurping the juices as they began to run down his slightly stubbled chin and onto the floor.

Gaia giggled at this sight before promptly biting into her own. Her face was filled with elation and her eyelids flew back into her head.

"No...Th...This...is amazing" she said hurriedly through the mouthful of tomato innards.

This time it was Gavril's turn to laugh.

The pair giggled together as they hastily polished off both of the tomatoes in record time.

"Sorry, but you would have the same reaction if you had eaten some of the food I have!" said Gaia, hurriedly trying to justify her amazement.

In an effort to impress her further, Gavril grabbed a cup from a nearby shelf, bent down onto one knee and scooped up a glass of the crystal-clear water before passing it to her. Despite being still drenched head to toe in the stuff, a similar expression of elation spread across her face.

This time, as she took the cup from his outstretched hand, Gaia didn't waste time giggling and gulped it down. Her throat soaked up every drop as if she were a sponge.

A twang of pity dashed across Gavril's face - he could only imagine what sort of things she been forced to drink out there in the rest of this unforgiving world.

He quickly stifled the look as her eyes met with his once more.

"Thank you" she said, her voice brimming with sincerity.

Gaia dropped into a cross legged position on the ground, her eyes transfixed on the pool and the abundance of plant life that surrounded it.

"I never imagined that I would live to see plants again..." she said absentmindedly, as a glazed over film that could easily be mistaken for tears covered her eyes.

Gavril couldn't hide his intrigue, even for a second.

"Again? Have you seen them before?" he asked quickly, as if unable to hold the question back.

It was his turn to peel his eyes wide with excitement. What if beyond the limits of what both he and Hadwin had explored there were places on this planet where plant life grew above ground. Maybe she could take him there now that the ship was forever out of reach?

Seeing the excited look on Gavril's face, Gaia quickly spoke in a rather apologetic tone.

"I saw them drawn on the side of an old building when I was younger, probably an old advertisement of something."

Gavril's face fell instantly, and Gaia looked down towards the moss surrounding her dirtied boots, knowing that she had disappointed him.

"Oh, okay..." he replied solemnly.

His ambitious daydream had been dashed in an instant.

Gaia returned her attention back upon the miniature oasis of vibrant colours positioned in front of her and she opened her mouth again to fill the slightly dead air that was lingering from Gavril's disappointment.

"Anyway, what is your story then, really?" she asked, gesturing with a nod of her head towards him.

Gavril presumed that she was referring to his powers, which of course he didn't fully understand himself and had already indicated to Gaia as such back in the gorge earlier that evening.

For a moment, he calculated whether it was best to tell her the truth, or to hold back some small portion of himself until he knew her better. Gavril decided that if they were to have any form of friendship moving forward, then it was best for him to be open and honest - his father had regretted not telling him the truth of his origins sooner and it had cost him dearly.

"Earlier, when I told you that the spaceship in the gorge was gone..."

Gaia shifted herself so that her focus now rested solely on him.

"What I should have said was that it was my ship, or at least it was my mother's."

Gaia's face changed into one of confusion.

"You see, my mother was pregnant when she crash landed here."

However, Gaia's unsure and perplexed expression remained.

"But you said it was your father that built this place..." issuing a finger in a circular motion above her head as she spoke.

"He wasn't my real father... he... he found me in that gorge sixteen years ago. My mother died giving birth to me. I had no one else and neither did he, so he decided to raise me as his own"

Speaking the words aloud brought the emotions of his foster fathers loss to the surface. It was a feeling that he struggled to hide behind the facade of strength that he wanted to convey to Gaia.

Gavril shifted uncomfortably on the spot and felt his eyes drawn towards the dark doorway of his old room. He could feel Gaia's gaze and wondered what she must be thinking of him.

"So, what you are saying is that you are a spaceman?" She said with a stern face.

"Erm... I guess... if that's what you want to call me" he replied.

Her pursed lips softened to a grin, then to a smile, then to laughter.

Gavril felt the sadness of his past dissipating as the giggles gripped him also.

Laughter - this home hadn't heard it in years.

As their last chortles bounced away down the adjoining passageways, Gaia pulled her face back into an attempt of seriousness.

"But that still doesn't explain how you can do the things you do; I mean you are human, aren't you? I mean for the most part we look the same."

Gavril swallowed the small amount of moisture retained in his mouth and took a deep breath before answering.

"I think so. I mean maybe out there, or wherever I am from..." he said as he pointed a finger up towards the opening in the ceiling.

"...these powers are normal?"

Gavril finished the sentence in a rather unsure tone, which correctly relayed his lack of confidence in this conclusion.

After a few moments, he could see Gaia's own brain trying to work it out. She made several attempts to speak, which saw her mouth opening and closing silently, but she too was left with a perplexed look upon her face as a definitive answer did not come.

"Well Spaceman or whatever you are, if it wasn't for your green arms and legs, I wouldn't be alive"

"You and me both!" he said jokingly.

The pair smiled in mutual acceptance of this fact.

Gavril refilled Gaia's cup and handed it back to her welcoming hands.

"What about you? My father told me that there was no one else left alive on this planet" said Gavril, now taking on the inquisitive role.

"Oh, my past is nowhere near as eventful as yours. No outer space origins for me, I'm afraid to say!"

Gavril looked at her curiously and waited in anticipation for stories of the world beyond what he knew. But as it turned out, his small corner seemed to be just like every other.

Gaia explained how she had been constantly moving since being orphaned herself at a very young age. Her family's home - the basement of some derelict skyscraper - had collapsed one day after a violent earthquake struck and had claimed both of her parents' lives in an instant. She didn't go on to describe her parents any further and Gavril could see that, like him, their loss was a sensitive matter that she didn't wish to pry open.

As Gaia spoke, Gavril was reminded of Hadwin when he had explained what his life had been like prior to finding this cave: scavenging for food, digging for water in the barren earth and picking desperately at the bones of this world's long dead inhabitants.

Before every new part of her story, Gaia hesitated for several seconds. It was as if the memories were a long-forgotten thing that she locked away years ago and only now was she able to find the key. He knew that feeling all too well…

"I thought that I had found another person when I saw someone moving down in that gorge, but unfortunately it turned out to be that monstrous machine" she said finitely.

Hadwin had told him to be cautious of everything growing up. At that time, unknown to Gavril, he had obviously tried to instil this quality in him to help him survive the dangerous, robot infested, world outside their cave walls. Consequently, every part of this upbringing was telling him to be suspicious of the girl sitting in front of him, as he should be of everything above ground. But he just couldn't do it. Everything she said felt genuine and just listening to her voice soothed any reservations that he might have had about her.

"Well it looks like we found each other at just the right time!" exclaimed Gavril, without realising what he was saying.

"What do you mean?" she replied, slightly perplexed.

"Never mind…I just meant that… erm forget about it" Gavril stuttered nervously.

Perhaps the truth that this had been a do or die excursion for him, rather than one of returning in defeat and facing longer isolation, was something that he would keep from Gaia. In any case, with her there, it was certainly not how he was feeling anymore.

If Gaia was thinking about pursuing this comment, her expression showed no intent. In fact, Gavril suddenly noticed how hazy Gaia's eyes looked and remembered how she had fallen asleep during their journey above ground.

Without hesitation, Gavril marched forward and creaked open the steel door to his old room.

"There is a bed in here, if you would like to get some rest?" he asked politely, thankfully starting to get the hang of it.

Clearly the prospect of a bed was just as enticing as food and water to Gaia, who proceeded to dart through the now open door as a look of glee spread across her face.

Gavril followed and was surprised to see her already laid out on the bed, stroking the soft fabric between her fingertips.

He crossed to the small stubs of candles that stood on a nearby table and struck one of the few matches left in the slightly perished paper box.

Away from the distractions of the outside world and the busy background of the atrium, Gavril was able to see Gaia clearly in the yellow candlelight. In some bizarre and unexplainable way, she almost looked familiar to him, but that was impossible - he had only met one other woman in his lifetime and wouldn't have been able to remember her face, even if he tried.

Chalking this up to coincidence, Gavril turned and walked back towards the doorway.

"Okay well, I guess I will see you in the morning?" he asked hopefully as he reached the threshold and pulled the door to his chest. The question hung there for a moment as he waited for a response that never came.

Gavril turned around and saw that Gaia was fast asleep, the small smile of content still adorning her surprisingly pretty and unblemished face.

After smiling to himself, Gavril turned and crept, soft footed, back across the stone into the atrium, not wanting to disturb her any further.

He crossed to the opposite side of the cave, returned the makeshift sword to the storage container and then fell back to his patch of bare earth next to the spring, feeling his body creak and extend. His singular determination to get them both to safety had obviously masked his own exhaustion as his muscles began to shut down.

As he lay there with his eyes pointed towards the moon lit sky, he noticed the main reflection mirror was swinging limply and its metal bracket bent awkwardly off at an angle. It must have been this that he had caught himself on as he fell, he thought, and luckily Gaia's small frame had somehow weaved past the mechanism.

Just before falling asleep himself, Gavril used his remaining energy to briefly summarise the evening's unexpected events in his mind: up until several hours prior, he had been ready to risk his life in an attempt to find his mother's ship. Now he lay there, knowing with almost complete certainty that he would never find it and that his chances of ever getting to find his real home were dashed.

But there was a glimmer of hope. Something that quelled this overwhelmingly heart-breaking fact… he was no longer alone. The crippling isolation and loneliness that he had been willing to die for to be free of, had been remedied in any case by the small girl resting in the next room.

*

When Gavril awoke the next day, he found himself almost unable to move. His limbs felt as if they were glued to the atrium's floor and it was a struggle to even raise his head from the surface. Dropping his eyes, he promptly noticed that he had neglected to remove his armour before falling asleep last night. He began to unclip the chest piece and slipped his still heavy arms out of the plated sleeves as the morning wind blew a deep melancholic note above him.

Gavril stood and shook some life down into his fingers and toes, then stared at the number of crushed plants, half submerged in the pool's waters. He knelt down and begun to pull out the ones that were beyond salvage and place them in a small pile upon the moss. As he did so, his eyes flashed to the bedroom door and the darkness that still enveloped it. The events of the previous night felt like both a dream and a nightmare that he couldn't wake from.

Once the mess of the pool was remedied, Gavril crossed over to his old room and took a deep breath before crossing the threshold.

His eyes fell onto an empty bed, with the bed linen stretched so tightly and neatly it was as if it had not been slept in.

"Morning, sleepyhead!" said a voice behind him.

Whipping his head around, he saw Gaia's outline, her face masked slightly against the daylight pouring in from the atrium behind her.

Gavril was relieved to see her, for a moment he had taken the empty bed as a sign that she had already left or even that he had imagined her existence entirely.

"M... Morning" stuttered Gavril slightly in response.

"How did you sleep? You passed out almost immediately!"

Gavril watched as Gaia wrapped her arms around her chest, holding herself in a tight embrace as she gently rotated her shoulders from side to side. Her eyes were closed, and her cheeks almost swelled with colour as she replied softly.

"Oh, it was wonderful, thank you!"

The dreamy reminiscing of her sleep disappeared a few moments later as Gaia must have realised how immature she looked. It seemed that Gavril wasn't the only one concerned about making a good first impression.

"Good, I'm glad to hear! he said with a smile.

There was a silence between them for a moment before the wind blew another tone through the open doorway.

After a small scoff, Gavril crossed back through the atrium and side stepped his way down the corridors of salvage before bending to pick his armour up off of the floor. He threw it around his shoulders and began securing it tightly across his chest before Gaia caught up with him and interjected.

"W... where are you going?" she said rather nervously, almost as if the idea of being alone was now something new and otherworldly to her.

"I'm going to go check the perimeter and the outer hatch before it gets dark again" he said plainly.

Gaia narrowed the distance between them until their boots were almost touching.

"Why?! Do you think those things are going to come back?"

Gavril didn't answer right away. His senses had carried him elsewhere.

"Erm... no, maybe, I don't know. That's why I need to check."

Gaia took a few steps back allowing Gavril to compose himself.

"But what am I supposed to do?" she asked.

However, as the words left her lips, her eyes began to look around the room at the miscellaneous treasure trove of items and Gavril could see the smile on her face widening as they darted from shelf to shelf, each lined with more interesting objects than the last.

"Actually, I think I will be fine!"

Her eyes beamed back at Gavril.

Strangely and against his expectations, the thought of someone else rooting through his organised stock did not faze him. Prior to what had happened in the last couple of days, Gavril had taken pride in keeping the items ordered and collected - having spent countless hours obsessively sorting and resorting every item into a system that only he could understand. But Gaia's arrival seemed to be having more of an effect on him that he realised and was clearly softening him to the prospect of sharing this place with her.

"Just one thing" Gavril said, turning around to face her as he reached the mouth of one of the cave's passageways.

"Don't eat anymore of the food today. We will need to ration and plant more if you are going to stay here..."

The words had left Gavril's lips before he even knew what he was saying - translating thoughts to words was clearly another social cue that had been lost to him.

Before Gaia could respond or see his rapidly reddening face, Gavril whisked himself away down the passageway. His cheeks were burning like hot embers as he snaked his way towards the exit, swelling with each pulse and beat of his heart.

What had he been thinking, abruptly blurting that out after only a matter of hours together?

As the smell of metal replaced the dull mustiness of the stone passage, Gavril forced the uneasiness he was feeling behind a layer of responsibility. There would be time to reflect on his words, however presumptuous they had been, once his checks were complete.

After unlocking the steel door, Gavril applied enough pressure with his shoulder to send the pile of rocks outside tumbling over one another. They made a gentle clopping sound that bounced away up the heavily trodden path.

Cautiously, Gavril followed the winding track until the sunlit landscape filled his view.

It was a sight to behold.

Cuts and slices were etched into every obstacle that rose out of the blackened ground. Like the bark of a tree, new paths made by the horde were incised in meandering patterns upon everything's surface as they had rambled over the mountainside.

Quietly, Gavril checked all the exterior passageways to see if any had been uncovered or damaged during the stampede, but thankfully all remained hidden. For now, at least, the cave would remain just as it had for the past sixteen years.

Even though his checks were now done, Gavril couldn't quite bring himself to head back inside right away. It was as if his misspoken words had reversed the steps he felt he had made to make a friend in this lonely world. He decided to repeat the checks several more times before finally finding the courage to head back inside.

When Gavril stepped into the atrium, he was met with quite a different scene to the one that he left. Where once there had been an organised catalogue of salvage, there now lay chaos. Almost every storage container had been haphazardly opened, with their contents thrown to the floor in messy piles.

His life, his record of the past several years, was splayed out like a storm had torn through the place. The storm - Gaia - was nowhere to be seen.

An all-consuming sadness washed over Gavril.

She was a scavenger, just like him. To her, his home and all he and Hadwin had made here was just another place to be picked clean.

Gavril didn't know why he had expected anything different from her - she who lived in the same harsh world as him and had obviously suffered far worse without a place such as this to call home.

Once again, Gavril was all alone and it was his doing. He had been disarmed by her trusting nature and just for good measure, pushed her away by stupidly presuming that she would want to stay there with him.

However, as he stood there on the verge of collapsing with the weight of his own sadness, he heard footsteps in his old bedroom before Gaia suddenly stuck her head around the corner.

"Oh, you're back, finally! I thought you had run away or something!"

Gavril sucked back the teetering tears and rubbed his face with both hands trying to look natural.

"No, nothing like that. I just wanted to be thorough."

"And.....?"

Her face, framed by messy strands of hair, hovered next to the door frame, a worried expression plastered across it as if waiting for bad news.

Gavril stood there with a rather confused look on his face, still reeling slightly from the surprise that she was still there, but he finally managed to realise what she was waiting for.

"Oh yeah, no, we are okay! No sign of any machines as far as I could see."

Gaia let out a large sigh before her usual smiley face returned.

"That's good then! Sorry for the mess by the way, I will clean it up! I just couldn't help myself, there are just so many amazing things here!"

Her head disappeared back into the room and out of view. Gavril used the time to let out an exasperated sigh - he had never been happier to be wrong.

Just as Gavril began to remove his armour once again, Gaia strolled out of the room with a familiar locked box in her hands. His heart stopped momentarily at the sight of it as he had not seen it for a number of years.

"What is in this one, I wonder?" she said.

Her eyes were locked curiously on its surface and she had not noticed the now tense look that had sprung up upon Gavril's face.

"Be careful, please!" he pleaded, holding both hands out in front of him as he rushed forward.

Gaia, who had now looked up from the box, passed it over quickly to his waiting hands. Gavril snatched it away and held it close to his chest as if he was worried that she still might somehow damage it.

"I'm sorry" she said, although not fully aware of what she was actually apologising for.

Judging from Gavril's demeanour however, she knew she had obviously crossed an unspoken line.

Awkwardly, Gavril shifted back to the water's edge.

"No, it's okay." he said, as his hand gripped tightly around the sharp metal corners.

"Sorry, but this is all I have left of my mother."

He stared down at it then waved a hand, inviting Gaia to join him. She was still standing by the doorway, half frozen, as if worried to do something else to offend Gavril. But at the gesture, she crept over and knelt down next to him.

Pulling a small key from an obscured chest pocket, Gavril unlocked the box and opened the lid so that the inside was now visible under the diminishing sunlight.

A dark brown leather jacket, folded neatly into a little parcel, looked back up at the pair of them.

Gavril gently slid it out from the box and held it up by each of it's shoulders.

"No need to guess where your father got the idea for your name!" exclaimed Gaia.

Gavril let out a small chuckle and ran his fingertips over the embroidery.

"My father found it with my mother all those years ago. He thought that it was fitting to name me after something of hers."

He continued to stare at the name in silence as a warmth pooled in his eyes.

Then, almost involuntarily, and very uncharacteristic to how he had reacted to seeing Gaia with her hands on the box a moment ago, he tossed the jacket over to her.

She caught it with both hands and clenched the soft material beneath her fingers.

"Try it on, it looks about your size." he said fondly.

Whether he was speaking to the jacket or to Gaia herself, it was a bit unclear.

Gaia obliged hesitantly, sliding her arms down the wonderfully silky sleeves and pulling it close around her chest. It was a perfect fit.

"It suits you!" said Gavril, with an even larger smile now on his face.

Gaia did not respond at first, choosing instead to hug the arms of the jacket and reciprocate Gavril's warm smile.

"Thank you." she murmured truthfully.

Looking down, her eyes fell on the spherical metallic items that sat at the bottom of the box.

"What are those?" she asked inquisitively, stretching out an arm to point at them.

The aged leather jacket creaked slightly at the movement.

"Not a clue" Gavril replied as he pulled one of the orbs from that container and tossed it a couple of feet above his shoulder.

"Hadwin told me that they were around my mother when he found me. He said that they gave off some form of light, but he never managed to get them working."

Gavril offered the orb for Gaia to take and she carefully obliged, raising her hand to meet his.

As her fingertips clenched the orb, Gavril felt her fingers press awkwardly against his and suddenly, with a burst of light, it began to whirr and spark into life. Both Gavril and Gaia snatched back their hands which sent the device falling to the floor with a small clunk.

Now visible beneath a layer of spiralled markings, the orb's centre began to twist and spin, before suddenly projecting hundreds of thin beams of white light outwards as the centre unlocked.

Gavril was unable to peel his gaze away from the slowly shifting sphere. It was beautiful. A miniature sun trapped in a revolving steel casing.

Finally, a tap on his shoulder made him break his eye contact with the spinning piece of metal and he turned to look at Gaia. She, however, wasn't looking back at him. Instead, she was sat slack-jawed, her neck craned backwards whilst pointing a solitary finger upwards towards the atrium's ceiling.

Gavril raised his head and instantly understood her bewilderment.

Above them, the entire dome shaped roof was lit up with a projection of hundreds of stars and planets. It was as if the mountain and the miles of thick clouds above had been wiped from existence and they were peering up into the cosmos beyond. Comets streaked across the jagged rock like fireballs, swirling masses of colour pulsed from miniature nebulas and gas giants complete with vast stone rings careered around distant blue suns.

The pair looked down and across at one another, their faces full of wonder as the twinkling of the stars danced in their eyes.

CHAPTER 12 - The Beacon

A harsh wind could be heard rattling against the outside of the hatch that now covered the atrium's skylight.

Each time a stone or piece of metal was whisked down the channel, a sporadic gonging sound filled the cavern below and echoed away down the adjoining passages. Like church bells, it had almost become a comfort to the cave dwellers - reminding them of the security which this place gave them, whilst also helping them to realise the procession of time without the sun or moon to guide them.

The storm above had been raging on for few days now and unfortunately, without the daylight's nourishment, the crops drifted limply across the surface of the pool. They looked defeated as they brushed gently into one another and tickled against the shoulders of the two human inhabitants lying next to the water's edge.

For the past six months, both Gavril and Gaia had been tirelessly studying the information that the orbs cast upon the ceiling of this cavernous room.

In an effort to aid them in unlocking it's secrets, the first thing the pair had done together was to clear the entirety of the atrium. As such, there were no more shelves topped high with relics and rusted machines, and all the containers that had lined the arching walls were now squirrelled away into several of the unused passageways. The only things now standing in the way of all that emptiness were the leaves and stalks of the vegetable garden that still reached hopefully up from the small oasis, and one of the orbs - sitting proudly atop a small metal stand that Gavril had placed in the room's centre.

Now that the deep green moss that crept amongst the shelves was uncovered and every inch of the room's lofty ceiling was filled with the orb's projected stars and planets, the place now resembled a luscious clear glade beneath a beautiful night sky. It was a sight to behold.

At this very moment, the pair were both lying on their backs amongst the grassy shore of the water, deep in a rather one-sided discussion that had been going on for quite some time now.

"What else could it be?" Gaia asked passionately, as if her voice was on the brink of crossing into frustration.

The question seemed half directed towards herself as she stared intently up at the ceiling, so Gavril did not answer. He decided that it might be better to stay silent until he knew a question was one hundred percent aimed at him.

Instead, he continued to absentmindedly rub the tips of his fingers into his palms - a feeble attempt to clean the coloured ink that had somehow and inexplicably found its way beneath his fingernails.

Gaia let out an exasperated groan that seemed to shake all the way down her body to her toes.

In the early days, Gavril had almost forgotten what it was like to have someone real in his life. How conversations and interactions quickly shortened the once long, silent days into unexpected moments that challenged his dormant personality.

It had scared him at first, the thought of sharing his home and himself again, but Gaia turned out to be exactly what he needed - in this dead and dark place, she was a light, bursting with life. She had an enthusiasm for discovery that rivalled that of his younger self and with each passing day, he felt more of it creeping back into him.

"It has to be here, Gavril!" Gaia cried.

He could see her in his peripherals as she continued to whip her head back and forth, first from the ceiling and then back to face him as she waited impatiently for his response.

Gaia jumped to her feet and with her forefinger leading the way, she rushed bare footed to the atrium's wall. As she approached, she separated her thumb from her outstretched fingertip and the entire projection above stretched outwards into a more detailed version ahead of her.

Gaia, who had a particular affinity in the orb's use, had

discovered that the star map was interactive almost immediately after it had burst into life six months ago. She had placed an inquisitive digit upon the wall where a small star had been glinting at head height and to their surprise, the entire projection had begun to expand outwards from that point until a much larger, blazing ball of fire, accompanied by several swirling planets filled the room.

Every waking moment since then, it had been impossible to prise her away from the thing - which of course Gavril had no intention of doing. It was captivating for him to sit there day after day, watching the different planets of all shapes and sizes drift silently across the ceiling. In a place that had once stifled adventure, they had become explorers, and the silver orb was their ship.

Gavril could see Gaia's face reddening with frustration and knew that he could not remain silent any longer.

"Could it just be a coincidence?" he asked rather despondently, meeting her eyes with a mock-disinterested expression.

Exactly what Gaia was referring to was the small cluster of circular bright lights that she had found earlier that evening.

This particular planet had caught her eye whilst she had been performing one of her usual searches throughout the galaxy. Unlike any she had seen before, it sported a glowing aura that outlined its circumference and every few moments it would give out a small flashing pulse that radiated outwards. Zooming closer and closer, she found three further glowing lights situated upon the surface of a large continent - two were grouped tightly together whilst the other was located far to the north.

Inquisitively, Gaia had widened her arms even more, so that the terrain of the surface was now visible as a topographical map wrapped backwards across the entire cave wall.

It was the sight of a familiar shaped gorge between the lights that had caught her eye and led her to her current hypothesis.

"Just take a closer look, will you!" she said angrily.

When he did not move, Gaia pitter-pattered her way to his side and gave him a swift kick in the arm. Gavril, who was now lying with his eyes closed, hardly felt the kick, but remembered being at the receiving end of her terrible tempers before and did not want a repeat of that experience.

"Okay! Okay!" he cried.

Gavril raised himself up and gazed at the multitude of lines detailing the various contours and elevations of the grey landscape.

She could be right, he thought, as he looked at the familiar misshapen form of the terrain.

He craned his neck to the side trying to see if there were any other markers that he could marry up.

"Can you turn it slightly?" he asked, whilst indicating his hand in a twisting motion in front of him.

Without any help from Gaia, however, the orb responded to his commands and began to slowly spin ninety degrees to the left.

Before it had even come to a full stop, Gavril knew that she was right. There was no doubt that what he was looking up at was a bird's eye view of the local area. It was all there.

Gavril turned to face Gaia, smiled, then gave her a nod of approval.

He watched as her expression changed almost instantly from one of apprehension to one of elation - her big blue eyes scrunching up in happiness as her cheeks swelled with colour.

Prising his eyes from her, Gavril returned to the map and traced the route from memory with his outstretched hand until it settled on the glowing lights, directly positioned above their cave.

"So, what are those?" he asked, pointing at the pair of white lights.

Gaia did not respond right away. Her brain was obviously working in overdrive whilst her eyeballs darted around the cave, trying to figure out this unknown.

Since their meeting, Gavril had developed a deep respect for her and her intellect. He used to consider himself gifted, but compared to Gaia however, he felt overwhelmingly dim. Amongst countless things, she had been able to increase the yield of their crops by utilising the suspended mirrors to focus the daylight and even use the information in his copy of Astronomy Through The Ages to figure out the names of certain star systems by comparing them to that of the orb's map. So, he knew the answer to his question, like so many before, would be found any moment now.

She clapped her hands together as she evidently arrived at it.

"The orbs!" she exclaimed.

"It has to be, it is the only thing that makes sense!"

He knew she was right, nothing else within these walls was of modern technology, except maybe - his face beginning to drop - the robot wreckage that now lay discarded in one of the other rooms amongst the other unorganised items.

Gaia caught sight of Gavril's sullen face and somehow, as if she had peered into his thoughts, put two and two together.

"No, I ruled out the robot's remains. If it had been that, then surely we would be able to see the others crawling over the place" issuing a sideways thumb shake to the map covering the atrium walls.

Gavril let out a sigh of relief that up until that moment he had not realised he was holding on to.

"So, if these lights are the orbs, then what...is that?" as he pointed a finger at the remaining lonely light blinking in the northern hemisphere.

But before Gaia could respond, an answer and an overwhelming feeling of optimism began to flood through him, reigniting a part of him that he thought had all but burnt out six months ago.

Gaia was already smiling as Gavril turned to face her.

"The ship!" he blurted out, almost uncontrollably.

"It has to be!"

Gavril scrambled to his feet and ran towards the dot as if the craft was parked upon the rock face itself. He clutched lovingly at the stone behind the projection, allowing his fingertips to wind around the coloured notes that Gaia had scribed into the wall. His eyes were full of tears and happiness clutched at his innards.

A minute must have passed before Gavril composed himself and began to pace the distance between the two points. The deep-seated smile that was pulled across his face froze for a moment, then began to melt away as he realised the distance between their collection of lights and the one that was now blinking almost mockingly from the opposite wall.

Gaia's face, unbeknownst to him, followed suit and dropped to one of disappointment as she too worked it out.

"It's too far." Gavril groaned.

"Maybe a month's journey, at a push"

He lowered his head and his long hair fell down in front of his anguished face.

"Is that with or without me?" Gaia asked plainly, her face returning to its serious problem-solving stance.

Gavril turned his head to the side, his hair swaying limply from the movement, with a look of dismay clearly written across his face.

The question hung there verbally unanswered for a few seconds whilst the two exchanged opposing expressions.

"I'm not going without you!" he said finitely, accurately predicting where Gaia's next question was heading.

"How long would it take though, if it was just you?"

"It doesn't matter. I. Am. Not. Going!"

Gavril said the last few words in a punchy finite manner, signifying that the matter was not up for discussion. However, he knew Gaia better than to think that this would stop her. He turned and walked angrily through the closest opening to the tunnel network, needing to be alone with his thoughts, even for just a short while.

Gavril knew that if he had stayed there a moment longer, then Gaia would inevitably begin trying to convince him to go, and from experience, he knew that it was a losing battle trying to argue with her. She had a way of always figuring out the rational answer to almost every problem and, much to Gavril's annoyance, this answer tended to lean towards her original solution. So, stomping down the passageway, away from this inevitability, was his only choice.

After a few minutes of navigating mindlessly down the twists and turns of the path, Gavril slumped down in a small widening of the tunnel. He rested his back against the stone and pulled his legs close to his chest.

In that brief stroll across the atrium, between the two lit up points on the map, Gavril had worked out that the trip would take less than a week without her in tow. But to him, this was insignificant, there was no way he was going to abandon her - in saving her that night six months ago, she had in turn saved him.

Discovering that the spaceship had disappeared from the gorge that night had ended a six-year long obsession - an obsession that had made him fall into discontent with the life that Hadwin had built for him here.

This, however, had all changed since the introduction of Gaia into his life. Having her there had washed away all those negative feelings of a future on this planet and the way he now saw it was that as long as they were together, life in this place no longer seemed daunting at all.

What worried Gavril, and had fuelled his misdirected rage, was that this new information could change all of that. Not just within himself, but within Gaia as well.

She knew how much the understanding of his origins weighed on him, having on numerous occasions found him staring longingly into the starry sky through the atrium's roof. If she became the reason as to why he never found answers, then it would only lead to guilt on her part and resentment on his.

After several minutes of silent contemplation, Gavril reluctantly got to his feet and returned down the path to face Gaia and her inevitable persuasion.

As expected, she was waiting for him, cross armed and stern looking.

"Are you quite finished?" she said seriously.

Gavril did not feel the need to answer and simply reflected her serious face back at her.

"So, what did your tantrum down the tunnel reveal?" Gaia said rather mockingly, her face now sporting a small grin.

Gavril however, seemed immune to any humour being derived from this situation and so did not answer. He decided instead to stroll back around the room, past the glowing projected lights, as if he hadn't heard her in the first place.

"Gavril, you have to do this! You said yourself, the robots above had increased their search parties since the night that you saved me. I wouldn't last a day out there anymore, let alone a month. I would just be a hindrance."

Gaia finished talking, but at the sight of Gavril seemingly ignoring her as he continued to wander round the room looking at the lights, she let out an angry grunt and crossed the room so that she was blocking his path.

Unable to ignore her any longer, Gavril pulled his eyes from the wall so that they met hers.

"There has to be another way, Gaia. I will not leave you behind." he said softly.

For all his contemplation in the corridor, he still couldn't justify it to himself. Regardless of logic and how the resentment would affect their friendship in the long run - leaving her here on this dead planet, whether by flying off in the ship or being killed by one of the robots, would end their relationship entirely.

"So, why don't you use that big brain of yours and figure it out" he said finally, smiling slightly in an attempt to lighten the atmosphere.

For a moment, Gaia stood there rather dumbfounded, then after a long exhale that seemed to deflate her entire body, she returned to the grassy pool and lay down in defeat. Gavril hesitantly joined her, and the pair lay in silence for what seemed like hours.

As the minutes passed, Gavril heard the sound of Gaia's mouth popping open as if she had the solution on the tip of her tongue and was about to speak it aloud. However, all that followed was more silence.

Finally, it seemed that Gaia had given in, as after rolling over to face her, Gavril found that she was sound asleep. For a moment, he debated picking her up and carrying her to bed, but instead decided to quietly marvel at her beauty as she slept.

It was in that moment, as the reflections of the projected stars bounced silently from the water onto her smooth pale skin, that Gavril realised the true reason that he could not be without her; it was staring him plainly in the face.

Not only had Gaia saved him from the isolation, but she had given him something to care for again. It was a completely different type of feeling to that which he had felt towards Hadwin; one that made him want to cross the small space and hold her close so that they would never be apart again.

Gavril resisted the urge tugging at his chest, knowing that a foolish action or admission on his part could, and probably would, jeopardise what they had; a strong friendship as the last two remaining humans on Earth.

The internal confession of his feelings towards Gaia did have one concrete ramification - it quashed even the tiniest notion that he may have had about making the journey without her.

He would never leave her.

Gaia shifted slightly and her expression, visible through the faint light, now somehow looked disappointed.

With his focus still on her face, Gavril raised a hand overhead and pressed the hidden switch within the orb's mechanism. The light sucked backwards, draping the atrium and its inhabitants into darkness.

As Gavril closed his eyes, he hoped that Gaia's dream had not been about him.

*

The next morning came just like any other.

Though his eyes were still closed, Gavril could see a low light - a lamp or the orb, he thought - obviously lit by Gaia who had a tendency to wake up earlier than him.

Gavril's internal clock told him that it must be nearly mid-morning and he knew any moment that the sound of her, going about the place without much care for the noise she made, would reach his ears.

The sound, however, did not come and an eerie, hollow sort of emptiness clung to the air in it's place.

Gavril pulled his eyes open and saw daylight, not firelight, rippling across the poolside next to him. The moss-like vegetation across from him, bright and sumptuous in the much-needed rays, showed no indentations to imply that anyone had been lying there recently and echoed the emptiness of the morning.

He continued to stare at the green space as the drumming of his heart quickened it's pace just a little. He could almost feel the flow of extra oxygen pooling around his eye sockets as they pulled at his irises and focused his still sleepy vision on the patch of undisturbed earth.

As his vision cleared, he saw an orb, sat, almost gravity defying, upon the centre of the mossy patch. Beneath it, sandwiched between the undergrowth and the silvery metallic shell, lay a yellowed piece of paper. Crumpled and torn, as all things were, the folded slither swayed a little in the gentle breeze that the skylight brought down.

What game was she playing? thought Gavril, as he reached an arm forward and allowed a small, curious smile to creep across his face.

He lifted the orb and took the paper in his hand before opening it to reveal Gaia's curvaceous, yet orderly writing, in several neat rows.

The smile, born of intrigue and excitement, had fallen before Gavril had even finished reading the first line.

I don't want to become your burden, Gavril. You will never leave this place without me, so I have made the choice easier for you. When you are ready, come find me.

Gaia

Gavril quickly rolled himself over and gazed upwards at the skylight.

Determined, the sun continued to dazzle his unfocused eyes, but as a distant cloud crept in front, a blurred structure began to sharpen and form between them. It climbed from the opposite side of the atrium up to the hatch, twisted and arching like the body of a snake - it was a ladder, hastily cobbled together from several mismatched items with no obvious care for stability.

In half a heartbeat, Gavril was on his feet, disbelief inhabiting his every molecule and draining the warmth out of him like a cold bath.

Before he knew what he was doing, both the orb and Gaia's note had fallen from his fingertips and his hands were pulling him upwards in a frenzied blur of limbs.

As he gripped the lip of the hatch and a burst of energy sent him rocketing skyward, the sound of the ladder crashing to the stone floor below barely fell on his deadened and otherwise occupied ears.

A chill wind raced over Gavril's bare skin. It sent a crackle of energy swirling across the soft membrane of his eyes as they fought back against the ingress of both daylight and metallic that dust were both attempting to bore its way into his skull.

He scoured the grey mass of twisted metal and stone, but try as he might, she was nowhere to be seen. The only things puncturing all that stillness were the hundreds of search lights swaying back and forth, here and there, as far as his eyes could see.

A turmoil suddenly exploded within him as his body pulled him this way and that. His feet slipped in the unsteady earth - Gaia could be miles away by now, in any direction.

But even as this prospect formed in his mind, he remembered the kind of person Gaia was and how she wouldn't have willingly left him without a way to track her. After all, her note had said "come find me."

Gavril tamed his breathing, allowing his more rational thoughts the space they needed to read between the lines that Gaia had left him. An image of her note re-entered his mind - the yellowed ancient scrap of paper held in place beneath that silvery orb...

He shot downwards into the atrium like a falling tombstone and landed with an almighty crash amongst the twisted metal of Gaia's ladder and the remains of their vegetable garden.

Gavril sloshed through the pool and tore towards the orb. With a flick of his thumb, the atrium was suddenly alight with the undulating lines of the area's topography.

Wildly and with as much uncertainty as he had exhibited above ground, Gavril sprinted round the room looking for any sign of her.

"Come on, come on, please!"

He cried exasperatedly.

Then, as he rounded the fallen ladder, a small yellow light flashed above him, sending a fading aura slowly outwards. Gavril raised his arms and with a surprising amount of efficiency, that would have had Gaia applauding him, motioned for the image to enlarge and rotate so that it was now hovering at head height on the opposite wall.

A small sigh of relief quickly escaped his lungs - of course she had taken the other orb!

Gavril continued to watch as fear ebbed from his shoulders, but as he did so, something strange struck him about the beacon's movement.

Slowly, he drew his fingers and thumbs together which zoomed his view further and further from the planet's surface.

This couldn't be right, Gavril thought, as he continued to stare at the pulsating yellow light. He had to be reading it wrong. If he wasn't, then somehow, with only several hours head start, Gaia had managed to travel several hundred miles towards the beacon that she believed to be his mother's ship.

Gavril continued to stare unwaveringly at the light from Gaia's orb as it edged further and further across the landscape. There was no way she could move that fast, even he, aided by the energy inside him, could barely have made that trip in such a short amount of time.

But if she wasn't travelling that fast, then what was?

The answer came crashing down upon him with what felt like the weight of the entire mountainside.

His breath was gone.

His face was numb.

All thoughts sat in limbo, trapped somewhere between action and understanding, as if his head had been wrenched from his neck halfway through the process.

Gavril fell to his knees, cold and alone, as slithers of the truth made their way through - the machines must have the orb, and they weren't going to be taking either passengers or prisoners.

After several moments, seemingly without care for what he may alert to his location, Gavril let out a cry that shook his body like the strongest of earthquakes.

"GAIA!!"

His voice echoed around the chamber and out of the skylight as tears fell in torrents onto his thighs. Despite his call - that a desperate part of him had hoped could summon her back to him - nothing arrived.

Gavril sat there silently sobbing as the minutes became hours and the beacon above tore across both the ceiling and half the continent. By the time he finally raised his head, the sun had set, and the flashing icon had come to a stop.

With bloodshot eyes, Gavril looked up at the blinking light hovering above the exact same spot that Gaia had told him they needed to travel to.

This place, whatever it was, had now taken two things from him.

The pain of Gaia's loss was immediately replaced with another emotion entirely, one that caused his fists to clench, his brow to furrow sharply and the blood vessels in his eyes to glow a vivid green.

CHAPTER 13 - The Base

It had been three days, but still the rage that was fuelling Gavril burned like a blaze.

Sleep was now impossible; he did not want the severance from reality that he knew it would bring. He needed, above all, to remain in control and have a grip on everything that was going on around him.

To submit to sleep was to surrender his safety to chance and risk everything that had been sacrificed to get him to this point - his mother, Hadwin and now, Gaia.

However, he could feel that without rest, his reactions were slowing and the rage that he had bottled up deep inside himself was beginning to overflow.

Every red laser that now crossed his eye-line goaded him. They wrestled with his lessening control and tugged him towards a violent path. He could feel his teeth clenching and nostrils flaring, but a deep exhale settled him.

It would have been easy for him to lash out at the first machine he had seen when he had left the cave, but where would that have gotten him. Every one of those things, between him and his destination far to the north, would have known his location and it was unlikely he could fight his way through them all.

No, he had to remain in control.

"You need to rest." said a familiar voice inside his head.

Gavril ignored it as he continued to run.

It would have been easy to blame hearing things on his sleep deprivation, but Gavril knew what it really was, having experienced it before when conversing with an imaginary version of Hadwin.

Somehow, he knew that in acknowledging the ghostly voice, it would cement it in his mind that there was no chance of finding Gaia alive. This was something that only in that moment he realised that he was subconsciously clinging on to.

He buried this thought, like he tried to with every other, and focused back on the world around him.

It wasn't until a day later, after crossing hundreds of miles of broken earth, that the spectral voice returned.

Gavril had decided to catch a few moments to rest atop a half-submerged skyscraper. He knew that he had two power reserves within him - one that could heal him and bless him with inhuman speed and strength and the other, his normal human energy, that was depleted just the same as anyone else. He could count on one hand how many times he had used his powers in the past six months whilst inside that cave, yet he still suffered with fatigue and needed rest, just the same as Gaia had.

"You are making good time, Gavril" whispered the spectral voice reassuringly.

He knew it wasn't her. Just as he had known that the figure of Hadwin hadn't been real. But as the voice and form of Hadwin had been of comfort to him in the oppressive loneliness of those years, this voice almost seemed to antagonise him.

He didn't want to believe it.

Gavril jumped to his feet, not feeling remotely well rested, and bounded from the roof of the building. He did not want to give his mind another second of silence to play with.

The journey continued on like this for a couple more days, with Gavril travelling continuously on a northern trajectory and avoiding the mechanised patrols as his body screamed for rest.

He tried to keep as close to the planned straight-line route as possible, but found that it proved rather difficult, what with the towering obstacles that pock marked the landscape constantly throwing him off his bearing as he circumnavigated them.

As night approached, the wind began to tease of an oncoming storm and after entering what looked like a half buried bunker protruding from the side of a large gravel dune, Gavril was forced to give into his body's wishes.

After unbuckling his pack, Gavril slumped to the floor and felt every ounce of his body pull itself downwards.

He could feel his eyes failing, but in one last attempt to keep the reins of control in his hands, he slid out the orb and filled the room with light.

As the light spun around the room, just as it used to do in the cave, Gavril let out a small sigh of relief. He had only managed to veer off the path slightly and furthermore, judging by the small gap between the lights, the projection revealed that his journey was almost at an end.

He clutched the orb in his hand before powering it down and to his surprise, the small piece of the metal surface that was visible between his clenched fingers continued to project upwards. He traced the fine beam of light up onto the cracked stone ceiling and saw that a condensed version of the map shone there. Gavril was slightly amazed that even after six months of use, both he and Gaia had never thought to check if the light could be focused.

He imagined the grumpy face that Gaia would have pulled if she had been there to see him make this discovery and not her. With a smirk, he powered it down and pocketed it back amongst his gear.

Looking round the darkened room, with its solitary opening at the far side, he almost felt like he was back in their cave.

Gavril dragged himself to the opposite of the door and let his head rest against the steep incline of gravel that swept up into the corner of the room. No longer fighting, he felt his eyes slide shut and sleep encircle him like a blanket.

For the first time in six months, Gavril's dreams were haunted by the terrifying images he had seen on the night he had saved Gaia.

The white hall.

The segmented and angular lines of something poorly mimicking a human face.

"Wake up" said a voice loudly, which shook him abruptly.

The words were still echoing in Gavril's ears as he looked frantically round the bunker.

Daylight now poured brightly through the doorway in a large solid column.

A moment later, something moved past the door, breaking the beam and plunging the space back into darkness.

Gavril looked hopelessly around the room for somewhere to hide, but there was nothing but the smooth sloped gravel lining every wall.

There was only one other option available to him.

Hurriedly, he began to sweep the mound of black dirt and gravel that had moments ago supported him as he slept, down upon himself.

Gavril fitted on his helmet and pulled the last of the stones towards him so that he was completely buried.

In the last moment, before the stones blotted out what little light was illuminating the room, Gavril caught sight of the footprints he had made on the soft floor when he had entered the bunker last night.

He could feel the robot's powerful legs approaching, vibrating through the ground and sending the gravel rattling against his metal armour. Gavril closed his eyes and hoped that this movement wasn't enough to shake the disguise off of any part of his body. If it did and the robot saw him, then he would have to act quickly and take his chances with it's inevitable reinforcements.

The clashing feet stopped with a thud and a whirring sound filled the room.

Gavril opened his eyes a fraction and looked through the minuscule rocks that were resting upon the glass of his helmet as a search light was passed around the room.

Closing his eyes once more, he prayed that it didn't spot him or the footsteps he had left foolishly dug into the ground beneath its bladed feet. But thankfully, after a moment, he heard the laser power down and the vibrations of the robot's footsteps resuming once more. The steps slowly began to diminish until only the sound of the wind whistling past the doorway remained.

Gavril brought his torso out of the stones and pulled his helmet off frantically, gasping for air. He quickly cast a look downwards at the floor where his footprints had been, only to find that they had disappeared. Luckily, it seemed that the vibrations from the robot's stomps had caused the ground to level out and fill them.

After a few long breaths to calm himself he pulled the rest of his body out of the ground and got to his feet.

This encounter had struck a note of fear into Gavril and as he pulled his bag and sword out from the earth; he vowed to himself to be more cautious in the last leg of his journey.

With that in mind, he waited in the bunker for a further few hours until the sun had set before warily continuing onwards; his pace now drastically and cautiously reduced.

As his legs carried him expertly over the uneven ground, closer and closer to what he hoped would be his final destination on this planet, he began to see a glow of red swelling along the horizon. It almost looked as if the reddish sun was rising already, but Gavril knew that this was impossible as it had only set a few hours ago.

For a split second, his mind threw up the images of the chasing army that he and Gaia had narrowly escaped. However, this worry was quashed after Gavril realised that the light was spreading wider and higher into the sky as he gained on it, thankfully not across the landscape as before.

The silhouette of a jagged structure was beginning to emerge in front of him, carving its way upwards from the horizon like a knife piercing through blood red flesh.

As Gavril got even closer, he felt a gradual incline in the ground beneath him which grew steeper and steeper, until he found himself clawing at the ground with his fingers in an effort to stop himself from slipping.

Soon, a sheer rock face that seemed to arch back on itself blocked Gavril's path.

Plumes of green sparks lapped around his fingers like lightning before it strengthened his arms and catapulted him up to a footing high above.

The searing red light he had seen against that angular black shadow scorched his retinas like hot pokers as he pulled himself over the mountain's crest and an intense heat bathed every part of his body. As his eyes grew accustomed to the fiery light, a prickling sensation swept across every part of his skin as disbelief rippled through him.

Gavril was standing on the edge of a vast impact crater that was several miles wide and arched out either side of him like two sweeping mountain ranges. The peaks of these stone giants seemed to cower away from the ginormous, city-like structure that sat in the craters basin.

With hundreds of blade-like buildings, the hauntingly brutal piece of architecture scraped at the sky, whilst several spires in the centre sent out beams of red light that seemed to ignite the distant clouds.

The sheer scale of the thing was staggering and struck a fear into Gavril that caused him to clench at the hilt of his sword.

Gavril hastily withdrew the orb from his pack and cupped it tightly between his two hands. He activated it with his thumb and cracked open the bottom of his palms as if he was letting out a pair of recently rolled dice.

The projected image of the map fell through the inch-wide gap onto the dirt floor and showed the circular crater complete with the flashing dot of light representing his location.

Strangely, however, the bird's eye image did not show any signs of the structure and just displayed the hemisphere shaped impression, cut deep into the landscape. Thankfully though, the glowing dots of Gaia's orb and the ship continued to shine brightly in the crater's basin.

Carefully compensating for perspective and the position of the dots, Gavril saw that one of the lights was close to the edge of the outer wall directly in front of him. There was no way for him to know which light corresponded to the ship, so he would just have to pray that this was the right one, otherwise he would have to go traipsing across half the city to find the other.

Gavril stowed the device into his breast pocket this time, knowing full well that he would probably need quick access to it when he reached the structure below, then took the time to scan the crater's edge and it's smooth belly for any movement before starting his descent.

Satisfied, his back foot pushed off and propelled him downwards through the gravel. Almost instantly however, Gavril spotted a steady stream of faint red dots cresting over the lip of the crater, thousands of metres away from him on the other side of the mountain range.

He teetered for half a second, but his hesitation at the sight of them coupled with his backwards stretched foot, caused him to fall awkwardly forward onto his front and the orb he had just tucked away against his chest dug painfully into his rib cage. He felt a sudden rush of energy; it was flying instinctively across his skin to repair the bruising it had caused.

Gavril continued to lay on his front as he watched the machines moving slowly in single file down the sloping earth towards the structure. Their convoy was some way off and were only visible due to their red lights shining through the night, so Gavril did not consider them to be an immediate threat but remained cautious all the same.

After summoning up the courage, Gavril climbed carefully down the jagged rock face until he reached the smooth surface of the crater some thirty feet below.

Staring down the steady decline, Gavril noticed something that made him pause for concern, something that he had not thought about when he had been surveying it from above. The crater had a uniform, curved surface, with no obvious places to seek shelter or hide if the robots caught sight of him. To make matters worse, this also threw up another issue. Even though the robots who were making their way down the crater were far away from him, they would clearly be able to spot the glowing green light that he emitted whilst sprinting, just as clearly as he could see their red lasers through the darkness.

There was only one choice of action, he would have to run unaided by his abilities and hope that in the time it took him to reach the outer wall that no other problems cropped up. It was a risk, but looking at the line of lights, it didn't seem like he had much of a choice.

Gavril took a deep breath and began to run.

It didn't take long for him to realise how much harder this was without his powers.

Heaving deep exasperated breaths as he ran, Gavril felt exposed, almost as if the green light of his powers might be the stealthier option.

Almost halfway down the crater's basin, Gavril glanced sideways at the stream of red lights and felt his foot catch beneath him. Without enough time to react, a small rock that was protruding from the crater floor sent him rolling forward and he fell flat on his face with a loud crash.

Gavril pulled himself up onto all fours and looked sideways; his face was flushed red with a mixture of anger and embarrassment as he stared for any change in the robot's movements.

For a moment, it seemed that he was in the clear, but then a second later, as the dust cloud around him began to settle, the leader of the pack's laser beams began tracking along the ground in his direction.

He scrambled to his feet, aided by a surge of adrenalin, and sprinted as fast as his normal coloured legs would carry him.

Gavril cast a look back and saw the laser pausing at the disturbed ground and the small plume of dust that his feet had just made. He snapped his head back and heaved his arms back and forth in front of him, willing every part of his body to help him in generating more speed.

Breathless and sweaty, Gavril finally slammed into the tall outer wall and placed both hands on its surface before spinning himself around.

The short-lived feeling of relief that had fallen over him evaporated almost instantly as he spotted the red beam of light scouring towards him across the ground in front of him. The inquisitive robot had obviously decided that these further small disturbances of dust were worth investigating.

There was nowhere for him to hide. The wall was smooth and offered no refuge between any of its large overlaid metal surfaces.

Gavril spun around again and tilted his head up so that he could try to judge the height of the wall. It was tall. Definitely higher than anything he had ever jumped, at least in a single bound, but what choice did he have? If he hesitated any longer, the beam would locate him, and he would find an army of robots cascading down upon him in seconds.

Reluctantly and fully aware that he was about to create his own beam of light through the night, Gavril channelled energy down into his legs before crouching deep and rocketing himself up into the air.

Gavril stretched both hands out in front of him, reaching for the ledge at the top of the wall, but it was simply too far.

Almost in slow motion, Gavril watched as the ledge began to move further away from him as he careered back down towards the ground to where the waiting red laser surely sat.

Instinctively, Gavril reached across to his waist, drew out the silver sword and plunged it deep into the wall. The blade groaned and bowed under his weight as it stopped him dead in his tracks.

Hanging there limply, like some playful monkey, Gavril looked down and watched as the red light hovered on the patch of ground below him.

Before it had any ideas of following him up the wall, Gavril pulled himself up so that he was balancing gracefully on the hilt of the sword and as much as it pained him to do so, knowing how much he would likely need it's services inside, Gavril knew that had to leave the sword behind.

The slightly flexible blade bowed slightly beneath his feet as he launched himself upwards again. This time, however, his jump sent him clear over the edge and onto the solid parapet where he landed painfully, his arms flailing into the unknown.

For a second he lay there, his ears poised for any noise from the troupe below that might be cutting their way towards his tracks, but all he heard was the wind rattling past his helmet.

Regardless, Gavril gathered himself up and frantically looked around for a means to move deeper into the structure. A short way away, the answer stood, cut out of the towering wall of one of those staggeringly tall spires, was a doorway.

White light spilled invitingly out from the opening as the wind brought the sound of slicing metal from below.

He wrestled the orb out of his breast pocket and flexed his free arm, readying himself for a fight.

CHAPTER 14 - The Discovery

A brightly lit, metal lined corridor rushed to meet Gavril as he darted quickly through the open doorway.

His dirt encrusted boots crunched loudly on the floor and echoed ominously down the eerily quiet passageway as he trundled forward.

Stretching out in front of him, the walls, ceiling and floors looked as if they had been cast out of a single piece of metal. Except for the bright white strip of light that shone down the centre of the ceiling, there seemed to be no imperfections; no doorways, no twists or turns, just an endless corridor that disappeared out in front of him as far as his eyes could see.

As Gavril crept hesitantly forward, he ran a singular hand across the smooth surface of the wall and could have sworn that after a few seconds, he began to feel the solid material vibrating slightly under his fingertips.

All of a sudden, as if the wall had also become aware of their contact, the shuddering seemed to intensify, and Gavril heard a faint rattling noise coming from behind him. He turned to find that the grit which had loosened itself from his boots was bouncing loudly across the polished floor, diving a few feet into the air before ricocheting off the walls with a clatter.

As quickly as the sound had begun, the corridor fell silent once more and the dirt dropped lifelessly back onto the ground.

Whilst the juddering of the corridor had stopped, the same couldn't be said for Gavril's racing heartbeat, which continued to pulse loudly and sent his breath rushing hastily back and forth in his chest.

Just as he was beginning to compose himself, the doorway that led to the darkened parapet, some ten metres in front of him, slammed shut.

The speed in which the thick door, which mirrored the corridor's metal composition, struck the ground sent a deep clanging noise booming away down the seemingly infinite corridor behind him.

They were sealing him in.

He stood there, his carapace of armoured chest plate scratching against each other as his lungs heaved his chest against the inside of the armour. His ears tried desperately to filter out the thumping of blood, as they waited for the sound of approaching foes to reach them. But somehow, and very unexpectedly, the sound, or their makers, never came.

Hurriedly, Gavril activated the orb and the half of the sphere that was not pressed against his palm shone brightly against the nearest wall. He could see that he was almost on top of the nearest beacon now, but unfortunately, because the map projected a bird's eye view, it did not give any indication of elevation.

As he stood there, Gavril realised that he had a simple decision to make. Up or down?

Frantically, he tried to rationalise where it was most likely that the robots would have kept the ship but drew up a blank.

Of course, Gavril had no way of knowing if the light indicated on the map was that of the ship or of the orb that the machines had taken from Gaia that night, but he allowed himself to optimistically believe that it was the former.

Thinking logically, and as if the roles had been reversed, Gavril imagined that he would have kept something of such importance deeper within the safety of the city's depths. But these were machines, not human like him, so their methods of keeping something safe might be completely different to his.

Gavril decided to go with his gut instinct and head downwards, but finally choosing a direction and actually achieving it were two completely different matters.

Now that his only means of escape had closed behind him, his only choice was to press onwards down the seemingly unending corridor and hope that he found some stairs or other means in which to descend.

As he walked forward however, Gavril couldn't help but think about the vibrations and the door that had slammed rapidly behind him. Had it just been a coincidence that it closed moments after he had passed through it, or did the machines know he was there and were making efforts to stop his escape?

"Don't worry, Gavril" the voice said quietly in his ear.

The abrupt return of the disembodied voice after so many days made Gavril jump, causing him to instinctively throw himself flat against the nearest wall in a feeble attempt to hide from the speaker.

To his surprise, the wall reacted to his presence, just as it had to his fingertips moments ago and began to vibrate ever so slightly.

A small hissing sound began to escape from the seam where the surface met the floor and ceiling as Gavril, readying himself for anything, clenched his hands into luminous green fists.

Slowly, the wall began to inch backwards and once it had drifted a metre or so away from him, it slid quickly to the side to reveal another identical and equally long passageway.

Hesitantly, Gavril entered through the opening and stepped cautiously down it's similarly sleek interior.

He couldn't have gone more than ten paces when he heard the hissing sound again and caught sight of the wall sliding back into place with a small click.

As he continued forwards, Gavril ran his hands along the walls, pushing every so often in an attempt to discover other accesses seamlessly hidden from view. It was his hope that one would lead him downwards instead of along the endless perpendicular corridors that he had encountered so far.

After discovering several new doors, which revealed several similar paths, Gavril was beginning to get the distinct feeling that he was trapped in this maze-like web of unending passageways.

However, just as his heart began to race once more at the prospect of being lost in this place, the wall he had just pressed against moved aside to reveal what at first seemed like a small room, no bigger than his own had been back in the cave.

Gavril, who was so overcome with elation at seeing something of a different shape in this place, rushed forward without fully taking in the room's contents and as his foot crossed the threshold, he felt his stomach lurch as the ground did not meet it. He teetered on the spot, as if time had ground to a halt and saw to his horror that the room had no floor at all.

Fighting against every instinct to flail his arms around helplessly, Gavril shot out both arms behind him, staking them through the metal doorway before it moved too far away. Helped along by green sparks, his fingertips punctured through the plating like large rivets and crumpled it into footings that his hands could clench on to.

Gavril froze there for a moment, his body arched backwards in a large curve whilst his arms spread widely behind him like wings. He looked like the figurehead of some grand old ship, overlooking the course downwards into the city's depths.

He drew back his foot, pulled himself straight and released his hands from the small pockets they had created in the walls either side of him.

Cautiously, Gavril approached the edge and peeked his head over to look down into the darkness. As ominous and unknown as this bottomless chute was, it was the first place that seemed to lead anywhere else other than horizontal.

Gavril knew that he could keep searching along the unending corridors for another, more promising, way down, but he would be risking forgetting this one's location the further in he went.

No, this was his chance and he was going to take it.

The next problem was how to get down there. The shaft's walls were made of the same smooth metal that made up everything in this building.

Living in that cramped cave, Gavril had always thought of his height as a hindrance, but now, looking from one wall to another, he thanked his lucky stars for it - if he was right, then he might be able to stretch himself out between the two walls and shimmy down, using the friction of his hands and boots to stop him from free falling downwards into the unknown.

However, before he began the climb down, Gavril riffled through his backpack, looking for something heavy and more importantly, something that he didn't mind losing.

At the bottom of the canvas he found a number of small black stones that had managed to worm their way inside when he and the bag had been buried earlier. Taking one in his hand, Gavril held it out in front of him, positioning it as close to the centre of the small room as possible, before letting go.

The stone dropped silently into the darkness and Gavril craned his head to the side, listening intently for the sound of it striking the bottom. If it ever did, however, it was so far away that he was unable to hear it.

Gavril gulped slightly before positioning his feet so that his boots hung slightly over the edge and raised his arms to shoulder height.

Even though Gavril was used to heights, the sensation in the pit of his stomach as he fell forward still made him hold on tightly to the breath that he had just taken into his lungs.

Like a piston releasing, Gavril slapped his palms against the smooth metal surface of the opposite wall and pushed his legs out so that he was locked securely in place.

The act of holding oneself in this horizontal position for any length of time would be nearly impossible for any normal person to undertake, but the green sparks pulsing down his limbs allowed Gavril to hang there with apparent ease as he stared into the dark depths.

Slowly, he began to inch his way downwards, releasing each limb one by one until he got into a comfortable yet safe rhythm.

Above him, the small room that had been filled with the white light which spilt in from the corridor beyond fell dark and a small and familiar hissing sound confirmed to Gavril that the doorway had shut behind him.

Swallowed by this dark metallic throat, Gavril found quickly that it was almost impossible to work out how far he had travelled or for how long.

Every once in a while, the energy that was no doubt coursing continuously underneath his armour in an effort to help him, would ripple up out from his collar and sleeves and the brief flashes of light gave Gavril a glimpse of the immediate area below him. Unfortunately, just as the plummeting stone had done, the light did not reach an end.

As he descended further and further into the abyss, his mind threw up another problem, as if it was concerned that he was getting off easily.

If the ship was down here and intact, how was he going to get it out?

In his imagination, whilst staring dreamily up at the stars and planets projected on the cave walls, he had pictured himself flying out into space on the ship to join them. Weaving amongst all the fantastic colours, drifting past planets and gigantic flaming stars, all the while piloting a ship that he knew exactly how to fly.

It couldn't be that hard, could it?

He buried the thought and focussed on one problem at a time.

After several more minutes, or perhaps hours, Gavril decided to pause for a moment to check the map.

After spreading his legs wider and positioning one of his arms straight in line with the centre of his body, he loosened his other arm and reached carefully into his pocket for the orb.

Luckily, the map still showed that his orb and that of the ships were almost directly on top of one another. However, to his delight, something about the light had changed. The frequency of pulsing light around the beacon had increased rapidly and Gavril couldn't help but let himself believe that this signified that he was now in closer proximity to the ship.

Brimming with optimism, Gavril continued deeper and descended what had to be another hundred metres or so before his eyes began to pick up faint spots of light, pin pricking their way through into the void below him.

The closer he got, the more the light began to focus in his eyes until the silvery outline of the chute was burned into his retinas.

It was a small grate, replacing one of the wall panels, that led into somewhere bursting with white.

As he squinted, he was sure he could see the floor of a room edging out from between the lattice of metal.

That was good enough for him.

Gavril was done with being cautious, and at that very moment, he felt so full of vigour that he cared not for what lay on the other side. All he knew was that he just wanted to be out of this shaft.

So, positioning himself directly over the opening, he daringly let go of the wall with his hands and as the front of his body fell, he sent a surge of energy down into his calves as he kicked off the wall behind him. The resulting momentum sent him crashing straight through the metal grating and into the polished room beyond with an almighty crash.

"GAVRIL!" exclaimed Gaia's voice inside his head.

He lay there for a moment with his eyes closed as the muscles in his arms and legs throbbed slightly.

"Please leave me alone, I don't need you right now" he said aloud to Gaia's ghostly voice whilst he raised himself onto all fours.

"Fine! But you're the one that burst in on me!"

Gavril snapped his head back and felt his face flood with rapture as he realised that this was not a voice of his own creation, but a voice that had come from the other inhabitant of the room.

As his eyes quickly became accustomed to the light, he saw the blonde haired, thin form of Gaia raising herself up off of the floor on the opposite side of the room and before he knew it, his legs were glowing green and rocketing him towards her.

Gavril threw his large arms around her, heaved her off the ground and began to spin her around in his tight embrace as tears of joy began to fall from his screwed-up eyes.

"Easy! Easy!" she said loudly, her voice slightly pained.

Even though he heard the concern in her words, Gavril found it almost impossible to abide by them. He never wanted to let go of her again.

When Gavril finally released her and pulled his face from neck, his eyes clocked what was causing her face to tighten as she feebly tried to pull her tattered jacket sleeve down to conceal it.

A bluish black patch of skin was stretched across her upper arm.

It crept up her sleeve and out of sight. Gavril then saw his mother's jacket was torn in places and stained with a familiar blackened substance.

Gaia obviously saw the sudden change in Gavril's expression as it was wiped clean of all its happiness.

"It's okay" she started, pulling a weak smile across her pale face.

"Just a little scratch that one of those robots gave me."

Gaia tried to pull the arm from Gavril's grasp, but there was no point in her trying to save face now. He was already rolling back her sleeve and revealing the full and horrifying extent of her injury.

"No, it isn't Gaia! This is a deep cut and I... I think it's infected!" he stuttered.

Worryingly, his prognosis was confirmed by slightly yellow tinged liquid that was pooling in the centre of the wound and the burning temperature of her skin beneath his fingertips.

It was going to happen again, just as it had with Hadwin. She was going to die and there was nothing that he could do to stop it.

As he looked down, Gavril noticed that his fingertips, which were still clenched gently around Gaia's arm, began to spark. The energy began to flow down from his wrists and gently tickle its way across her skin.

Almost unaware of what he was doing, Gavril placed his free hand on the other side of the bloodied wound and closed his eyes.

"W... what are you..." began Gaia before falling silent to watch.

His palms began to glow brightly and the droplets of sweat that clung to Gaia's skin sparkled as they reflected the escaping light.

Between his two hands, the sparks began to jump, weaving themselves over Gaia's arm before diving into the weeping laceration.

She suddenly took in a massive inhale of air before releasing it slowly and calmly.

When Gavril finally opened his eyes, he saw the wound was in the final stages of stitching itself back together. He smiled sideways at her and saw the paleness of her face beginning to fill with colour.

Slithering back into Gavril's fingertips, the green light faded, and

Gavril let go of her.

"I didn't know you could do that!" exclaimed Gaia loudly.

"Neither did I!" replied Gavril honestly.

"...but I had to try something"

Gaia stuck out her bottom lip and nodded in mock approval as she inspected her now healed arm. Her eyes flitted back to Gavril and the pair began to laugh, almost forgetting about their surroundings and situation.

"How did you find me?" she asked, as Gavril paced back across the room and stuck his head through the ruptured grating where he had made his entrance.

Turning back to face her, Gavril pulled out the orb from his pocket and tossed it over to her.

"I followed the one that you took with you when you left the cave!" he said, hardly trying to mask his disapproval of her tactics.

Gaia had noticed the change in Gavril's tone but decided to press on. Whatever Gavril was meaning to ask would likely come out soon enough.

"It was taken from me by those machines"

"Well it must be nearby, as it's what led me here." he replied gruffly.

Gavril walked over, took the orb back and activated it.

He held it between the pair of them and explained to her about the proximity alert as they had come closer.

"That's a neat trick!" she said, marvelling at the miniature projection shining from beneath his cupped hand, but Gavril ignored her words and proceeded to the question that he was obviously longing to ask.

"I thought you were dead, Gaia! How are you still alive?"

For a moment, her expression seemed to yo-yo between embarrassment and confusion as the question hung in the air for a few moments.

"I honestly don't know." she said plainly.

Gaia remained silent for a moment as her cheeks flushed red.

"I thought I was dead too, Gavril, but when I awoke, I was

already in this room." she said quietly.

It didn't make sense. Why had the machines taken her so far and kept her alive for this long? It almost felt as if there was a part of the puzzle that was missing; a piece that both he and Gaia could not hope to fill.

Just then, as Gavril crouched down to his backpack to remove one of the canteens from his bag to quench his thirst, another question raced to his lips.

"But how are you alive? It's been nearly a week!" he said, suddenly forgetting his own needs and offering the bottle to her.

Much to his surprise, however, she brushed the offer away.

"Every night when I am sleeping, they place a new container of water by that wall. I have tried to stay awake to try and catch a glimpse of them, but they always seem to know when I am awake! I cannot explain it."

Fear focused on Gavril like the many eyes he imagined were in the walls at this very moment,

Quickly, he began scanning his eyes around the room.

"We have to go!" exclaimed Gavril, grabbing Gaia's hand and hauling her to her feet.

Gavril rounded on the wall with the small trough of water sitting at its base and threw his weight against it. The green energy swelled in his shoulder at the point of the blow as the hidden door began to crumple.

Stepping back, he pounded the wall ferociously with both fists and after several explosive blows, the wall was sent shooting backwards with a loud clash into the gleaming corridor beyond.

Gavril quickly held out a hand and helped Gaia across the jagged metal opening. Gaia, who had seen nothing but her cell for the past week, looked confusedly at the long corridor that spread out either side of them - she was as equally as perplexed as Gavril had been when he entered the city.

Taking out the orb, Gavril sent the map onto the wall and the two of them quickly began to silently calculate which way would be best to go.

At the same time, like a dastardly game of chance, both Gavril and Gaia pointed in opposite directions and shouted aloud: -

"This way!"

They looked at each other in mutual confusion at the other's logic. Then, as if making the decision for them, the pair heard a faint crashing noise coming from the direction that Gaia was suggesting that they go.

"Climb on!" shouted Gavril, removing his backpack and hurriedly fixing it to his front.

Gaia obliged and once more pounced elegantly onto his back.

"Guess we are going your way then!" she said into his ear.

Gavril could sense a hint of humility in her voice but discarded the thought as he carried them away.

He sped them down the corridor at tremendous speed, all the while running his hands along the walls in the hope that some obscured pathway would make itself known. However, just as he was planning to stop and consult a rather windswept Gaia, he unexpectedly saw a dead end fast approaching them.

Gavril slid to halt just in front of the seamless wall and placed a hand upon its surface. With a slight push, the wall retracted just as the others had done and beyond lay a small square room, quite similar to the one he had encountered above.

Thankfully, however, this room seemed to have a floor.

Apprehensively, Gavril poked his head through the doorway and looked up to find that instead of a shaft heading downwards, this room was settled at the base of one.

Unlike the dark shaft that had brought him down, this one was filled with the same white light as the corridors and similarly disappeared into the heavens beyond where his eyes could see.

"Go on then!" Gaia said hastily, after whipping her head back to see if the distant sounds had taken physical form.

He heeded her words and stepped inside.

Instantly, Gavril realised that something was not quite right. He felt like one of their potted plants, bobbing up and down as if the ground was floating atop water. Unsurprisingly, having never felt such a sensation before, Gavril began to flail his arms above his shoulders and shift his weight from side to side in an attempt to stabilise himself.

"Stop Gavril, just stand still!" commanded Gaia.

Somehow, she was right. He calmed his legs and the floor slowly became stationary once more.

"Now what?!" pleaded Gavril.

Frantically, the pair began looking around the small space for something that they might have missed, but there was nothing. The walls were just the same as every other in this place.

"THEY'RE COMING, GAVRIL!" screeched Gaia, who had shifted her gaze back to the corridor.

Frantically, Gavril slammed his palms against what felt like every inch of the rooms walls, but still found nothing.

They were out of options.

Gavril lowered Gaia onto the floor and turned to face the disappearing corridor. He gathered himself up, shielding Gaia all but from view, and readied his fists for a fight - how he wished he hadn't had to leave his sword behind.

Ahead of them, Gavril could see the jagged outline of several of the machines emerging from the vanishing point of the corridor. Their legs were clattering against the solid floor, spinning around so fast that they were almost a blur.

The sound was deafening. It sliced at their ear drums just as it did the polished floor.

Behind him, Gavril felt Gaia slump to the floor and a quick glance back showed that she was cradling her ears and an indistinguishable cry was escaping from her open mouth.

Standing there, his knees slightly bent, and his fists raised, Gavril shot one last hopeful glance up the shaft and suddenly felt the platform beneath their feet begin to rise.

The opening to the corridor and the machines, now just metres from them and drawing their bladed arms up high, quickly disappeared in his peripherals as they shot up the shaft. Half a second later, they heard an almighty crash as their pursuers crashed into the now empty space below them.

Lowering his head, Gavril shot a relieved smile at Gaia. But as he broke eye contact with the towering shaft above them, the platform suddenly ground to a halt.

Panic rippled through the pair as the platform shook beneath their feet and the sound of the bladed arms slashing against the floor panel met their ears.

"What did you do?" screeched Gaia, terror gripping at every feature of her face.

"I... I don't know" he said as his eyes darted round the elevator.

For a moment, his eyes flicked upwards and the platform jumped up several centimetres.

Gaia, who was watching him, spotted the correlation.

"Quick, look up again!" she blurted out frantically.

Gavril did as he was told and angled his head skywards.

Just as she hoped, the platform began to ascend once more, gaining more and more speed until Gavril had to lower his head slightly out of fear that their current course would send them shooting out of the top of the building.

As they continued, Gaia pulled out the orb once more and shone it on the floor. Almost instantly, as Gavril looked down upon it, the elevator began to descend.

"No no no!" she started.

"It seems to be responding to whichever way you look Gavril, so keep your head up!"

"Alright, alright!" he muttered, getting slightly annoyed at her bossy tone, but he accepted her command, nonetheless.

Gaia moved the projection onto the wall so that his head could be kept level whilst the pair studied the map.

After a few moments, she spoke again, as enough time had passed for her to generate the semblance of a plan.

"Okay, so we know that we can't tell from this map what floor the ship will be on. So, I think that we should take this lift as high as it can go, make for the highest point above the ship's location and then work our way down. That way we won't risk missing it?"

After she had finished speaking, she looked into Gavril's eyes, as if searching for confirmation that it was a good plan. But they did not convey an answer, and simply continued to stare down at her.

Gavril had missed her strength.

Missed those beautiful eyes.

Missed so much about her that he thought was lost forever.

A surge of emotion rushed through him and he felt his stomach lurch like the elevator had dropped out beneath him.

Gavril moved forward and pressed his lips against Gaia's.

He almost couldn't believe that it had taken six months and her presumed death for him to act on these feelings towards her. However, in what felt like milliseconds later, Gaia was pushing her arms against his shoulders and prising him off of her.

As they disconnected, Gavril could see from her shocked and somewhat hurt expression that he was the only one reaping any sense of joy from this.

Gaia shot him a look of apprehension, as if willing him to forget what had just happened, then took a few steps back from him and gently raised her fingers to her lips.

Gavril's face was now one of disbelief and sadness.

How could he have been so wrong?

CHAPTER 15 - The Escape

It didn't take long for the platform to reach the top of the building. It came gently to a halt with a small whoosh and a clunk as it locked itself firmly in place.

Both Gavril and Gaia, who had not spoken on the rest of the ride up, were shifting uncomfortably and clearly looking forward to being out of this confined space together. Luckily, the panel behind them hissed and slid aside, bathing both the lift and them in an intense red glow.

As they turned, the pair could not restrain gasps of wonder at the sight that lay before them.

Framed by the opening of the lift was a thin metal outcrop that overlooked the vast cityscape below. They had to be at least a mile above the ground, looking over the complicated arrangement of towers and rooftops that made up the machine's complex skyline.

A few hundred metres ahead of them stood one of the larger spires, shooting a thick red laser upwards through the clouds and into the night sky. At this distance, the deafening noise and searing heat of the beam seemed to penetrate deep into their skin and rattle their bones.

Through outstretched fingertips and metallic columns, they could just see the cracked moon peeking above the horizon, casting it's light upon the basin of the crater and reflecting off the shining machine city.

They might have taken longer to marvel at the view had the platform beneath their feet not begun to shudder and move steadily downwards.

"JUMP!" shouted Gavril, instinctively.

Gavril sprung forward with ease, but Gaia fell slightly short as the floor dropped out from under her.

Almost in slow motion, Gavril looked back to see her hair

billowing up around her face as she slammed painfully against the lip of the doorway. She let out a pained groan as her legs dangled hopelessly over the ever-increasing drop.

Gavril turned as the doors between them began to hiss shut.

Lightning fast, he dropped onto one knee before taking a firm hold of one of Gaia's thin dainty hands and pulled her high into the air. As the door slid ever closer to his outstretched arm, he heaved himself and Gaia backwards, cradling her close to his chest as they both fell with a loud clash onto the precarious safety of the small outcrop.

Hurriedly, as if frightened this embrace might become something more, Gaia scrambled off of him and awkwardly brushed herself off. Squinting through the bright light, she thanked him with a small nod and flashed her eyes quickly away from his gaze.

Gavril felt like a fool; in a matter of minutes and through one regrettable motion, he had managed to drive a wedge between him and the only person he knew or cared about. It was a motion that was obviously so far off base that he wondered if they could ever find their way back.

Choosing to waste no more time staring at the view or thinking about the dreadful timing of that kiss, Gavril gathered himself up and, without speaking, shuffled past her to take the lead as they continued along the thin path that made its way around the outskirts of the tower.

Every few metres, Gavril peeked his head over the edge to the rooftops below. It was a long way down and he couldn't shake the feeling that they had perhaps made the situation worse for themselves by coming up this high. At this altitude, even on a relatively calm day like this one, the wind still blew against them with the strength of a gale and forced the pair to sidestep slowly along the narrow pathway.

They kept their backs pushed firmly against the outer wall of the tower as Gavril's armour rattled and Gaia's jacket whipped about like a flag in the harsh crosswind.

After several minutes of this, Gavril felt a tap on his shoulder.

"WE NEED TO GET OVER THERE!" Gaia called loudly, as she pulled out one of her arms which had been braced against the wall and pointed out to the building ahead of them.

The spire that she was indicating to, across a couple of hundred metres of chill and bitter nothingness, was even higher than their current position.

Gavril simply nodded to show her that he understood - unsure whether or not he had the courage to speak to her yet.

They continued shuffling round the gradual arch of the wall in silence until finally Gavril looked over the edge and saw a small walkway jutting out from the wall below them. It ran between this tower and the next, acting as a perfect bridge between the pair. The only problem was that there was about a fifty-metre drop of blustery air between them and this crossing below.

Gavril looked across at Gaia as she finally separated her gaze from the drop to look at him and he knew that there was only one thing to do.

Before Gaia had a chance to object, Gavril scooped her up in his arms and bounded to the walkway's edge. Forgetting all awkwardness for a moment, she buried her head in his chest in an attempt to muffle the long drawn out scream that she let out as they plummeted downwards.

They continued to fall through the whistling air like a shrieking bomb until Gavril landed with a loud thud against the solid metal roof and his legs cracked loudly in several places.

"Urgh!" Gavril moaned, as the sparks wove his shattered bones back together.

As soon they had, Gavril lowered Gaia onto the walkway and she paced away angrily, wiping the tears that her screaming and the rush of air had driven from her eyes.

Just as she turned to face Gavril, looking ready to explode at him, he saw her eyes soften and her face fall.

A screeching sound behind him made Gavril's blood freeze and he turned around just in time to see one of the bladed machines leaping from the same outcrop where they just stood - it's sharp limbs drawn high, reflecting the fiery sky like red hot pokers.

It hit the walkway about two metres behind them, but it was thankfully only visible for a fraction of a second as its weight was clearly too much for the structure beneath to bare. The metal bulkheads crumpled and sheared away like paper, sending the robot crashing down into whatever room lay below.

Not even pausing for a second to see if it was incapacitated, Gavril sprinted in the opposite direction and grabbed hold of Gaia with one arm like she was some sort of rag doll.

Somehow however, she seemed ready for it this time and spun around his arm and onto his back in one fluidic motion. Notions of the pair of them not having any physical contact now seemed long forgotten.

Gavril hurled them across the walkway until the taller tower's front face came rushing to meet them. He pushed every ounce of energy he could muster down into his legs and launched them both high into the air.

They soared upwards as their cheeks rippled against the passing wind until Gavril tactfully landed them onto a small angled roof that protruded from the building's middle, but he didn't stop there. He was a man possessed; bounding frantically from surface to surface with almost no plan or idea of where he was going. All he knew was that he had to get them as far away from that machine as possible.

Like a pinball, he bounced across the skyline, madly seeking higher and higher points in the structure to climb. However, a few minutes later, a voice shouting in his ear seemed to wake him from his adrenalin fuelled trance.

He relaxed his legs, which were halfway through powering up for another inhuman jump and moved his head to the side so that Gaia could lean over.

"What was that?" she said, looking almost worried.

It was hard for Gavril to hear her over his hyperventilation, but he could get the gist of her concern from her facial expression alone.

"Sorry, I just had to get us away." he said, puffing loudly as he pushed the de-oxygenated air from his lungs.

"Yeah? Well I think you have done enough; you've taken us halfway across the city!" she said, slightly disgruntled.

But he knew her well enough to know that hidden amongst her words was gratitude for carrying her to safety.

She slid from his back and the pair darted across the rooftop into a darkened corner which escaped both the moonlight's glow and the pulsing of red from the city's several spires.

Gaia activated the orb with a flick, and they saw that Gavril had indeed taken them quite a distance in his frenzied getaway. Luckily though, he had not taken them far from their intended objective as the steadily pulsing beacon signifying the ship's location was very close now.

After a few minutes of cautiously scoping out the area beyond the multitude of spires and walls, Gaia pointed to a tall, flat rooftop in the next grouping of towers.

"There, that has to be it!"

She deactivated the orb and tossed it at Gavril, who fumbled with it awkwardly as he tried to keep his eyes anywhere but on her.

As Gaia approached, Gavril fought with anxiety and ease over whether he should apologise for the kiss. If anything happened to them in this last leg, then this might be the last chance that he had to try and mend what he had broken.

He turned to face her, ready to try and right this wrong, but only the first syllable of her name managed to leave his lips before an ensemble of high-pitched cries began to swell all around them.

Like ink spilled upon a sheet of paper, a dense collection of black clouds slipped their way across the horizon and blotted out the several white fragments of the fractured moon. It stole away all-natural light and transformed the city into a mass of burning pyres, with the colossal red beams illuminating everything within the crater's basin.

The metal floor beneath Gavril's feet began to shudder, growing more intense as the sound crescendoed until he could hear the chatter of Gaia's teeth rattling beside him.

And then, just like that, the fire was put out and the screeching noise of a million machines fell silent. The spires suddenly blinked out one by one across the city, sending their columns of light shrinking back downwards through the clouds and plunging them into an oppressive darkness that consumed their entire vision.

As Gavril stood there, his feet rooted to the floor by the edge of the rooftop, he saw a singular red dot of light twinkle into existence in the darkness below them. Then another, and another, until countless lights littered the ground like a sinister mirrored version of a starry night's sky.

Gavril felt Gaia at his side and was reminded of how their first night together was much the same.

Both surrounded.

Both terrified.

A pin prick of moonlight managed to sneak its way through the clouds, illuminating the path before them.

"Let's go!" whispered Gaia frantically up at him.

Her voice was drenched in fear and he could feel her body shaking as he lifted her onto his back.

Despite knowing how visible he was about to make them, Gavril obliged, launching them forward with an explosion of green energy that trailed behind.

Every darkened surface of the city below was dazzled with the light, but as every machine tracked their lasers across the sky, the blended colour across Gavril's body became a golden yellow.

They streaked across the gap like an arching star, shining for the whole city to see, as Gavril reached out a glowing hand for the fast approaching building. He struck the wall with a thud as he punched his fingers deep into the surface like it was made of earth. He held on tight, as his legs flailed above the sheer drop and their eyes fell down to the city depths below.

The sea of red lights had begun to swirl upwards towards them like an angry swarm of bees as the opening in the clouds began to widen.

Moonlight shone down amongst the city's spires, revealing the mass of machines below. They almost looked like water, a rising tide flowing over one another as their metallic bodies scrambled up the exterior of every building. The chilling noise of their limbs sounded like an army of swords slicing and chopping against one another, gouging their own path angrily and upwards to their enemy.

"Go, Go, Go!" cried Gaia as her body wrapped tightly around his torso.

Gavril kicked the point of his shoes into the wall and began to climb as fast as his body would allow him.

He could feel his armour relenting as it caught against the ruptures of the plated wall which were sweeping between his hands and feet. Pieces began to fall away until his arms were stripped bare. Debris tore at his chest and Gavril instantly felt the armour there begin to loosen.

His heart skipped a beat.

Gaia's weight suddenly dropped, and he felt her fingertips clawing desperately at his armour. They were both screaming - a terrified duet as they slipped in opposite directions away from one another.

But just in the nick of time, Gavril felt Gaia manage to grab hold of one of his boots and he ground them to a stop.

"Hold on!" Gavril called down to her.

He twisted his body to the side and slowly raised his leg to meet his free hand.

Beyond the sight of her now outstretched hand, Gavril saw the thousands of robots nearing as they climbed ferociously and spider-like up the wall beneath them.

"GAVRIL!" she screeched, flailing her arm at his outstretched hand which was just beyond her reach.

Burying his fear, Gavril focused his eyes back on her and grabbed hold of her hand.

With a surge of green energy that billowed from his newly exposed shoulder blade, he threw Gaia upwards like a javelin. Gavril caught a momentary glimpse of her shocked face and heard her stifled yelp as she rushed past as she was sent screaming up onto the roof above.

Gavril clawed his way up after her, now beginning to feel the shuddering of the million strong army travelling up through the building's structure.

As he pulled his head up over the precipice, Gaia bent down and tried to help him up by tugging at what little bits of his armour remained across his shoulders, but felt Gavril almost immediately pushing her backwards as he scrambled up - unbeknownst to her, clambering onto the rooftop some fifty metres away was one of the bladed machines.

Pushing her aside, Gavril broke out into a sprint and careered towards the robot like a flesh coloured battering ram as splinters of green surged from every inch of his skin.

As they clashed together, Gavril screamed manically into what mostly resembled the creature's face; he felt blades ripping through his thigh and chest.

Sidestepping the pain, he clasped both his hands together like he was in prayer and spearheaded his fingertips into the machine's torso. The robot's arrangement of lasers fell downwards just in time to watch Gavril throwing his arms open and its body split in two.

Sparks, both electrical and green, danced in Gavril's eyes as he fell to the floor along with the two fiery pieces of the machine.

Slightly woozy, Gavril pulled out the bladed arm that hung limply in his leg and tossed it onto the burning pile.

Gaia rushed forwards just in time to take his weight as Gavril slumped slightly to one side.

"Give me a minute" he said breathlessly as his body got to work repairing the two wounds.

"I... I don't think we have a minute" she said bleakly, as the chiming of metal striking metal continued to rise all around them.

With her free arm, Gaia wrestled the orb out of his pocket and shone it on the floor. To their fortune, they could both see that they were standing directly above the ship's beacon.

Frantically, she began scanning her eyes around the large square rooftop for an entrance or any sign of an opening.

"There!" she cried, but Gavril didn't raise his head to look.

He was concentrating on slowing his breathing and allowing the energy to work its magic.

She was suddenly heaving at his underarm with a strength that he didn't know she possessed, and the pair limped forward as the sparks had almost completed their repairs.

Several metres in front of them, towards a corner of the roof, there was a barely visible platform of similar size to the one they had used to rise from Gaia's holding cell.

With Gavril hobbling beside her, she led them over and the pair stood upon its surface. They both simultaneously angled their eyes downward and the platform began to descend.

The city slowly rose out of sight and a plate slid slowly across the opening above them, plunging them into an unwelcome darkness.

They could no longer see one another, but Gavril felt Gaia's fingertips brush against his lower arm and fumble quickly downwards so that her hand was in his. Gavril felt the same rush he had felt in the elevator and the machine army that was hot on their tails felt a world away.

The lift didn't seem to go that far down before it shuddered to a stop beneath their feet and Gaia released her grip.

"Can you see anything?" asked Gaia.

But before even giving him time to answer, she has activated the orb and it's light streamed out into a cavernous, high ceilinged room.

With a sweeping motion, she checked the ground around their feet and after seeing that it was safe, they both stepped off of the platform. As their feet disconnected from it, white lights in the centre of the room began to activate one by one.

Suspended high above, the lights formed a wide circle around a large, slightly battered object that sat slumped upon three thick metal legs.

They stood there, zombie-like, with their mouths hung open in disbelief.

They didn't need to search any deeper into the spire as there standing in front of them, was the ship.

It was more beautiful than Gavril had ever imagined. It's shape exactly as Hadwin had described it; with gleaming polished panelling and sleek lines.

The sight of it made him almost want to cry.

Despite his leg now being fully healed, Gavril almost forgot how to walk and tripped over his feet slightly as he moved closer.

He slowly side-stepped around the craft, shooting gleeful looks over at Gaia, who was moving around the ship in the opposite direction. Her happiness, however, was oddly subdued.

As the pair met, they saw the crumpled wreckage of the left wing and Gavril's face lost most of its elation and quickly mirrored Gaia's.

"What are we going to do?! This thing isn't going anywhere!" she asked, a note of panic beginning to warp her inflections.

"Those, those machines will be here any moment!"

She frantically began pacing and pointing at the busted wing, almost as if she thought Gavril hadn't seen it.

Gavril let out a roar of anger that made Gaia slightly recoil.

His fury, however, was not aimed at her, but at himself…

All he could think about was how had he led them on this fool's errand, halfway across the continent and that any second, those machines would come tearing down from the rooftop and the only exit.

His brain was firing at rate of knots as his eyes darted about the ship, trying hopelessly to find a way in which to get them out of this, but just then, as he shot Gaia a look, he saw her arm and the pale unbroken skin peeking out from between the clean slice in his mother's jacket.

Suddenly, an idea took hold of him, sending a pricking sensation down into his palms.

His mind dug up the vivid images of the green sparks snaking their way down the mechanical arm of the robot that had speared him and Hadwin over six years ago. If the energy inside him had the power to destroy mechanical objects, perhaps the process could work in reverse and repair the damage just as it had done in Gaia's arm.

Gavril approached the ship and reached up, so that his hands were touching the mangled surface of the ship's wing.

He focused his thoughts, as he had with Gaia's arm, and began to shoot the same light from his fingertips into the damaged, cylindrical remains of the engine.

Gavril opened his eyes and watched as the sparkling green conduits seemed to dance their way in large spirals amongst the inner workings of the engine, crackling slightly as they licked against the sharp tears of the broken plating.

Obviously not content with just exploring the damaged engine, the green tendrils suddenly darted down the length of the wing and dived into the slightly crumpled bulkhead where it joined the main body of the ship. The energy grew like luminous thick vines, burying themselves into all the cracks and broken panels upon its hull.

Unlike Gaia's arm, which had quickly begun to stitch itself back together, no healing or repairing seemed to be happening to the ship. Just a dancing light show that filled the space.

Had he been wrong?

Was this too much to ask from the power inside him?

Gavril could feel Gaia closing the gap between them as the sound of hundreds of mechanical feet could now be heard, cascading across the roof above them like a downpour of rain on a thin tin roof.

A loud creaking sound began to echo around the room and for a moment, Gavril feared that it was too late; a torrent of blades were about to pepper them with stab wounds and no amount of healing would save them. But as he stood there, he felt the wing beginning to rise slightly in his hands and he realised the cracking sound was not coming from above, but from the twisted frame of the crippled ship.

It was like watching time play out in reverse. The metal plating seemed to almost turn fluidic, contorting itself back into its original shape before seamlessly sealing itself back together.

Thin, multicoloured wires within the engine began whipping around, connecting themselves into complicated junctions as metal rivets sprung into existence out of the small green sparks that snaked upon its surface and bolted regenerated metal coverings back into place.

This bizarre process continued on for at least a minute before

Gavril finally removed his hands and the now pristine ship dropped an inch or so onto the metallic floor with an almighty clang.

He stumbled backwards, looking up at it in all of its former glory, the word Gavril printed in a bold calligraphic font across the bow.

Gavril looked across at Gaia who smiled and tapped a finger on the same embroidered word on the breast pocket of his mother's jacket.

"W... What do I do now?" he asked looking back at the ship, without even realising what he was doing.

But somehow, the craft seemed to hear him as a thin panel on the side facing them let out a small hiss of air and released. The panel slowly swung downwards until it connected with the floor and revealed the ship's interior.

"Hurry! Let's get inside!" commanded Gaia and the pair frantically sped up the small ramp.

It was incredible to behold, even in the borrowed light from the room beyond.

Gavril didn't know where to look first.

Silhouetted against the darkness of the wall at the front of the ship, his eyes could make out two rounded chairs and hurriedly, the pair grabbed hold of the supple leather seats before spinning them around and sinking into their soft embrace.

Situated in front of them was what looked like a single sheet of perfect, unbroken glass that arched in an almost impossible, yet beautiful curve that swept around the chairs. Barely visible beneath the smooth surface were faded shapes of icons and screens that did not respond as they hammered their fingers impatiently against them. It seemed that despite Gavril's repair of the damage, the ship remained lifeless and the surrounding console was completely devoid of power.

Outside the ship, they heard the soft humming sound of the elevator as it descended.

"Quick! They are coming!" moaned Gaia.

Frantically, Gavril began to feel his hand around the bridge station, checking the edges until his fingers brushed against a small spherical recess just below the console at knee height.

Looking down, a brain wave shot through him as his fingertips felt the familiar indentations cut into its curved surface.

He wrenched the orb that was still in Gaia's hand, quickly inserted it into the recess and watched as the whole ship instantly sprung into life.

Every surface gleamed with white light and projected a stream of inconsequential data into their watering eyes. Small holograms rose from side panels showing different readouts that neither Gavril nor Gaia could understand.

Just as Gavril reached a hand forward to touch the smooth glass surface, there was a whining sound behind them and the pair both spun their heads round expecting the worst. Fortunately, however, the sound was the ramp retracting and the hatch sealing itself shut.

The craft around them began to shudder as the blackened plating situated above the bridge console slowly slid apart in segments over a thick layer of glass, revealing the brightly lit hanger beyond.

They could both now see that the cavernous room was no longer empty.

Situated directly in front of the ship was a robot unlike anything the pair had ever seen. In fact, the longer that Gavril looked upon it's monstrous form, the more of its construction he was able to see, and he found that it wasn't just one robot at all.

Expertly weaved together like some sort of circus balancing act, were hundreds of bladed robots. Their bodies morphing round one another to create a terrifying mechanical human-esc face, stretching thirty feet up into the air.

Gavril sat there, frozen, as the mouth began to stretch open into a sinister looking smile which revealed rows of razor sharp, shark like teeth. It was a smile more terrifying than he had ever seen.

An image flashed to the forefront of his mind.

No, he had seen this face before, six months ago on the night that he had saved Gaia from that towering machine.

The colour drained from both their faces as they began frantically poking at the cockpit's console, hoping and praying that they pressed something that would get them away from the horrifying entity that now stood before them.

"Destination" called a robotic voice throughout the cockpit.

"What?!" cried Gavril.

"Destination" repeated the monotone and expressionless voice again.

Beyond the cockpit screen, the mechanised face, which was still smiling, began to disassemble and fall apart. The building blocks - hundreds of bladed machines that they knew all too well - began to claw over each other like a nest of angry spiders, each fighting to reach the ship first.

Gavril looked around at Gaia, hoping that she would have the answers and she simply looked at him, gave a small shrug and pointed a finger skyward.

"Get us off this planet!" bellowed Gavril.

Immediately, the ship rocketed upwards, but not in time to miss the leader of the mechanised pack jumping forward and scraping one of it's claws against the ship's nose. It's laser beams gleamed wildly through the glass visor before the machine was crushed between the ship and the hanger's ceiling.

The craft groaned and the pair felt the ship's engines rattling through the hull as it burst out the metal roof, scattering the hundreds of machines that had been lying in wait upon its surface. Some were catapulted from the roof and sent flailing down into the depths of the city, however, those who survived stood rigid and statue-esc, shooting red beams helplessly at the rapidly ascending ship as it rose high into grey clouds and disappeared from their view.

CHAPTER 16 - The Search

As the small ship punched triumphantly through the thick clouds, the moisture that had condensed across the cold cockpit window suddenly began to solidify into an opaque frozen veil that obscured their vision.

Around them, they felt the craft rising even higher as the low hum of the engines vibrated through their seats and knocked their brains around their skulls like pinballs.

A few seconds later, the shield of ice that was wrapped around the front of the ship began to melt in places, creating miniature port holes through which Gavril squinted eagerly. The last sections of the ice that were still clinging to one another continued to thin before finally losing their grip and sliding backwards to reveal the dark void of outer space.

They sat there for a moment, looking out upon the calm beauty of the unending expanse that stretched before them; it was awash with thousands of brilliant white dots of light that somehow seemed brighter and larger now that they had escaped the oppressive sky below.

The ship, having obviously felt that it had satisfied Gavril's choice of destination, began to power down the engines, and seconds later, plunged the pair into silence.

It was Gaia, whose face no longer had the same expression of wonder and amazement as Gavril's, that finally broke the silence.

"What was that thing?" she said, with concern.

It took a few seconds for Gavril to even acknowledge her speaking, let alone make the connection to what she was referring to. Her voice felt like a distant whisper to his preoccupied mind. He was transfixed, staring out into the blackness that he had dreamt of one day reaching since he was a little boy.

"What thing?" he replied, in an almost disinterested tone,

obviously not ready or willing to share his attention.

She grabbed the arm of Gavril's chair, spun him around and wrenched his eyes from the spaceship's window so that they were solely focused on her.

"That thing down in the hanger!

A mixture of fear and frustration layered her voice.

"Relax, Gaia." replied Gavril calmly, spinning his chair back to its original position.

"Whatever it is, it can't reach us up here." he said, slightly laughing as his eyes widened once more and a gentle smile pushed sideways across his cheeks.

Now that they had broken free of the clutches of both the robots and that perils of the world below, Gavril felt oddly at ease.

"I guess... you're right" she sighed, falling back into her chair which began to spin round silently.

Once the bearings finally slid to a halt, Gaia pushed herself up out of the chair's squashy embrace and strolled towards the rear of the ship.

Ahead of her stood a rather squat metal panelled door which did not open as she approached. On the wall beside this was a small, brightly lit panel which she began furiously tapping at - obviously in the hope that this was some sort of locking mechanism. When this, too, did not open the door, she began pushing either side in an attempt to prise it open. For all her effort however, the door did not budge and remained sealed.

"A little hand?" she called over her shoulder.

As expected, Gavril did not immediately jump up to help her but a small forced cough from her throat gave him the incentive he needed. Gavril begrudgingly rotated his own chair and crossed the small compartment towards the door.

He was no more than halfway across the space before a small green light flicked on above the door frame and the metal hatch split in two, sending each side sliding simultaneously into its adjoining wall.

"I think it likes you!" said Gaia jealously, scanning her eyes around the ship.

She gave a little bow as Gavril came closer, spinning one of her hands and indicating for him to go first. It was nice to know that the events following the elevator had dashed all awkwardness between the two of them.

Gavril let out a small chortle as he stooped low and passed through the doorway towards the bow of the ship.

Flanking the corridor beyond were two single beds, cut snuggly into small alcoves within the walls. He wandered slowly between them, allowing himself to run a hand across the almost luminous, white linen as he went. Gavril found it hard to believe that they could have stayed so pristine over the years since his mother's crash and surmised that like the wing of the ship, the bedding had also benefited from a little rejuvenation.

Ahead, the corridor opened up into a slightly larger compartment than that of the bridge area. It was dimly lit at first but like the door, it seemed to sense Gavril's presence as his foot connected with the smooth deck plating.

A soft light began to swell from obscured bulbs built into the ceiling. Their intensity grew and shifted from a warmish yellow into a dazzling bright white that gave the space an almost surgical feel.

Deactivated workstations could now be seen in a circle lining the walls. Their glass topped consoles bent the light raining down on them into focused beams that shot like the display lights in a museum to illuminate a strange glass cylinder in the middle of the room.

Stretching from floor to ceiling, with an inch-thick shell, the container almost looked like it was missing something, like a fish tank that had been emptied of water. As he approached, Gavril watched as his reflection became skewed and stretched into a comical version of itself around the convex surface.

He dropped his eyes and saw a glass barrier, much like the bridge console, sat at waist height. It ran around the circumference of the container with what looked like space for five or six people to work - the ship itself only had two chairs on the bridge, so Gavril wondered what could be so important that it needed so many people to operate.

Gavril stepped forward, touched the surface gently and as its smaller counterpart had done on the bridge, the arching console sprang into life and began projecting various symbols and words in front of him. Most, if not all, the information was meaningless to him, composed mostly of complicated scientific equations and data readouts.

But there was one line that he could read.

"PARTICLE STATUS: Unknown"

The text shone brightly at the top of the projection with the word unknown, underlined and pulsing in red.

"I wonder what that could-" Gavril started, before Gaia grabbed him by the back of his shirt and pulled him away.

"It could be anything. This technology seems even more advanced than what we saw down there in that place." issuing a finger towards the planet below them.

Gavril shot a look back at the cylinder, feeling that somehow this device was not something he should so readily dismiss, but had his attention pulled away and back towards the room's entrance.

Gaia had thrown herself rather dramatically onto one of the twin beds which seemed to consume her, billowing up around her body like a silk parachute. After the air had drifted out of the skirted sides, she wrapped the duvet around her body and disappeared amongst its depths.

After a few seconds, she emerged and threw her head back onto the pillow.

"This. Is. Amazing" she said through joyous giggles.

Not one to let her have all the fun, Gavril ran to the opposite bed and jumped face down onto it.

The pair laughed together, rolling around in their respective beds and for a moment felt like much younger children.

Their laughter continued until the beds began to have the effect that they were actually designed for, as both Gavril and Gaia found their eyelids getting heavier. Their fit of giggles grew more sporadic before fading away entirely as the pair lay back and the lights of the room began to dim back to a soft yellow glow.

Gavril smiled at the roof of his small pod, silently thanking the ship's ability to sense exactly what he wanted it to do. However, just as his eyelids fluttered shut, they glowed bright red as the lights were back to full strength and a deafening alarm began to sound loudly throughout the ship.

The pair bolted upright, with Gavril hitting his head slightly on the low-lying ceiling to which he had just shown his gratitude to.

They locked wide, panicked eyes for half a second, before throwing themselves out of the beds and ran through the open doors to the bridge.

The main console in front of the two swivel chairs was flashing and as Gavril settled back into his chair, the computer quickly displayed a rendition of what looked like their ship and the planet's surface arching wide below them.

Travelling perpendicularly between the two icons was a flashing red dot, that made them both draw in a quick intake of breath.

"It would seem they can get us up here after all!" whispered Gaia to his right.

Gavril instinctively laid his hands on the console, exactly how he had imagined himself doing in all his daydreams, but here he felt no ability or understanding rush to his fingertips.

Just as he feared, he had no idea what he was doing.

"Get us out of here!" bellowed Gavril - if the ship knew when to open doors or dim the lights to help him sleep, then maybe it would have the sense to help them escape from whoever or whatever it was that was fast approaching them from the surface.

But the ship did not move. Instead the familiar robotic voice they had heard back in the hanger sounded once more.

"Destination."

However, this time, instead of simply waiting for instruction, a map of the solar system was projected upon the glass in front of them.

The ship had obviously learnt something about its new pilot - they were clearly not up to speed with planetary locations as much as its previous occupant.

Gaia decided to try and help. She began trying to manipulate projection as she did with the orbs back in their cave, but like the door that had led deeper into the ship, nothing happened. The gently spiralling representation of the planets remained fixed and unhelpful, hanging in the air in front of both of them.

Gavril decided to give it a try and as soon as he raised a hand into its vicinity, the map began to shift and change. He sent Gaia an apologetic glance, for he knew she had always prided herself on her ability to understand this type of technology.

"What do I do, Gaia?" he asked, still needing to rely on her expertise.

"Well, where do you want to go?" she asked plainly, shrugging her shoulders.

She was evidently so disgruntled by her lack of ability to help that she seemingly forgot about the alarm and the fast approaching entity from the surface.

"I don't know, anywhere but here!" he shouted, slightly bewildered, as if he had become the only sane person in the ship.

"Ask your new friend, maybe it can help you" she said dismissively.

She slumped back into her chair and Gavril stared at her bewildered. Surely, she knew that if that red dot was what they believed it to be, and that if they happened to still be around when it arrived, then her life would be in danger, too.

He shook his head, unable to put his frustration into words.

Sometimes, it became blindingly apparent that the pair of them were still children themselves, however much their life experiences begged to differ.

Right now, he didn't have time to try and work out what had gotten into her. Right now, he needed help from the one person who always had the answers.

"Help me Gaia, please!" he panted desperately.

"Maybe ask the ship where it has been?" she suggested, rolling her eyes and crossing her arms in a defiant manner.

The emotionless voice once more "Destination."

"Erm... can you show me where this ship has been?" Gavril asked without much conviction, certain that this ambiguous request would not be carried out.

To his surprise, however, the map zoomed out to show two distinct dots of light positioned across the galaxy. One indicated their location through a flashing aura that surrounded their current location; the other was positioned near the edge of a large sweeping cluster of stars on the outermost rim of the map.

Gavril raised a single finger, before looking across at Gaia.

Their gazes locked for a moment and she nodded her head in approval.

The ship's voice echoed it's question one more time as Gavril tapped the yellow dot in reply.

Immediately, the ship began to rotate and the segmented metal plating that had previously covered the cockpit window began to close over it once more. In the last seconds before the shielding locked shut, Gavril could have sworn that he saw a black and red object dart past the nose of the ship.

"Hurry, hurry, hurry!" he pleaded to the console, gripping tightly to the arm rests of the chair, feeling the leather-like material squeak beneath him.

Almost instantly, a crescendo of noise erupted all around them.

From various speakers around the cockpit, the robotic voice began giving a running commentary as various icons illuminated green.

"Destination... Set. Course plotted with adjustment vectors for planetary bodies... Set. Stardrive ignition in three...two..."

Her annoyance clearly forgotten; Gaia reached out her hand in search of Gavril's.

As the artificial voice's countdown reached one, Gavril flung out his hand and watched as his fingers passed inexplicably through hers. In that moment, her hand had somehow become an opaque version of itself, woven from dancing wisps of green light.

His hand swiped through, falling to his side with a thud as the ship lurched forward and a vacuous sensation seemed to drain the entire ship of all noise. Not even the sound of Gavil's thoughts could materialise within his mind as he stared down at Gaia's shimmering, pearlescent hand.

Then, suddenly, his brain was forced into overdrive as the sound of the engines returned as it frantically tried to deal with the overwhelming number of sensory inputs it was being subjected to.

Gavril tore his confused eyes from Gaia and faced forward determinedly, as every instinct pleaded for him to hide himself away.

He watched through squinted eyes as the bridge and the surrounding bulkheads began to ripple, as an array of multicoloured streams of light burst from the nose of the ship and were carried along a swelling current. The prisming effect sent every colour of the spectrum sparkling into his eyes.

Like Gaia, the hull had become semi-permeable, and Gavril could now see through the shell to the stars careering past the ship as the roar of the engines grew louder still.

Finally, he closed his eyes and surrendered himself to the ship's motion.

Gavril knew that the world and those machines were far behind him.

He was finally going home.

Printed in Great Britain
by Amazon

86630943R00127